the Eagle's VAULT

JANET OPPEDISANO

The Eagle's Vault
ISBN Digital: 978-1-7386998-6-5
ISBN Paperback: 978-1-7386998-7-2

For everyone who's put their plans aside
and let destiny be their guide

Free Novella

To instantly receive the free romantic suspense novella *The Phoenix Heist*, the prequel to the Reynolds Recoveries series, claim your copy at

https://bf.janetoppedisano.com/smbari40im

CHAPTER 1
DECLAN

Jayce and I crouched amidst the blooming roses and an orgy of overpriced marble sculptures. A hulking Roman villa loomed ahead, daring us to breach her walls. Three stories of pale stucco topped with terracotta tiles, surrounded by gardens.

Down here, we had cover. But it was the middle of the afternoon in early May, without a cloud in the sky. Any passerby would see us in an instant once we stood, let alone how many security cameras would catch us. Then there were the cars ambling by on the nearby street.

"This can't be the way in, Jayce. It's too exposed."

"Camera four." She pointed to the eastern corner. "That's our ticket in."

I squinted, following her arm. Sure enough, camera four swept from northeast to east, leaving a generous blind spot to the southeast. Leaving a segment of the vine-covered wall completely open for us.

"Bloody great. We're scaling another wall?" I grumbled, shaking my head. Our boss was going to force me into climbing lessons if Jayce kept this up.

"The answer is always scale it, Dec." She pulled an elastic from her wrist, tying her shoulder-length black hair into a high ponytail. Half a foot shorter than me, but with an attitude far larger, Jayce never met an obstacle she couldn't get over.

"Ever considered the front door?"

"Where's the fun in that?" She shot me a wry grin, unwrapping an obscenely colored candy and tossing it into her mouth.

I huffed and turned over my wrist to check the time. Just my luck, I'd chosen to wear the Submariner instead of something more appropriate for climbing.

"You in a hurry?"

"Yes, as a matter of fact. There's a lovely lady waiting inside for me."

"Lady?" She rolled her eyes dramatically. "You're going up that wall. But if you're worried, I promise I won't let you fall."

"Fantastic." I was all sarcasm, but we both knew the truth of it. She'd saved my ass more than once on these ridiculous excursions, and I'd trust her with my life.

"Suck on this." She tossed one of her wrapped candies my way. "Gives you super climbing powers."

I caught it and gave her an intentional frown. "Very funny. Now, let's get this over with."

"Soon as you take that off." She inclined her head toward my wrist. "I refuse to listen to you whine and moan about a scratch for the next year."

I unwrapped her candy and popped it in my mouth, the mint clearing my nostrils. I hauled off my small pack and tucked the watch into a secure pocket. It had been a passive-aggressive gift from my mother when I took my job with Reynolds Recoveries. A not-so-subtle reminder I was supposed to be a marine engineer.

But cracking safes was far more satisfying. So, I wore that damn watch every chance I could. *That's why you took the Reynolds job, Dec. Because you're doing what you love.*

"Race you," Jayce called, darting toward the villa.

I groaned, tossing my pack on and trailing after her. This was *not* the part I loved.

She scaled the wall like she was born for it. I grunted as I missed a hold, my foot slipping on a vine. Jayce reached down, her hand a steady anchor.

"Don't be scared of the plants," she teased, a grin spreading across her face.

I found a higher hold, pausing long enough to glance around the narrow street that ran next to the villa. How many people were watching us climb this wall? How soon until the polizia came? Or were we making the attempt at precisely the right moment, when no one in the other homes, apartments, or the store below us would notice? "Not scared. Just allergic to falling."

Jayce had a knack for the recovery business. She always knew exactly the right time to sneak down a hallway or burst through a window. No one ever caught her. At least, not since the Reynolds team went after her.

We climbed, her agile figure disappearing over the rooftop as I stubbornly clung to the vine-covered wall. A few loose rocks clattered down, sending my heart into double-time.

"What's the matter now? Wall not being flirty enough for you?" she called down, her voice loud enough to attract attention from anyone who wasn't already watching us. "Focus on the 'lovely lady' inside, and I'm sure you'll find your second wind."

"You trying to get me caught?" I growled back, pushing myself up with renewed determination. With one last push, I rolled up onto the terracotta tiles of the rooftop, sucking in the sweet, horizontal air.

"Welcome to the top." Jayce offered a hand, pulling me to stand. "I had a nap while I was waiting."

I took a moment to steady my legs, ignoring her smug smile. "The house in London was easier than this one."

"The house in London was begging for someone to climb it."

She was right. Instead of a three-story vertical, the bottom floor of that house had sported multiple turrets, giving me a respite every twelve feet.

From the third-floor roof, we eased down to a second-floor balcony, skirting the sight lines of the cameras dotting the villa. The balcony was a forest unto itself, the scent of flowers and damp soil filling my senses. We pushed through the fragrant chaos, and Jayce popped the lock on the glass doors without a thought.

For all my complaining, it had taken less than fifteen minutes from the ground to the inside, with no one the wiser. Jayce knew how to infiltrate any building, but it usually took more preparation than this one had.

Inside, the library was an aristocrat's dream: coffered ceiling, massive bookcases, plush chairs begging to be lounged upon. A second-story balcony housed more bookshelves, their tomes silently judging our intrusion.

My parents would have loved it.

The main attraction, though, was a swung-out bookcase, which normally concealed a six-foot-tall safe.

"Hey there, beautiful," I cooed, running my fingers over her cool metal door. "Sorry I left you hanging, but I had to figure out how they got to you. Jayce insisted on her version of a 'scenic route.'"

Behind me, Jayce snorted in amusement, rummaging through her bag. The rustling of plastic filled the room. She was hunting for snacks, no doubt.

The safe was no ordinary one. She was built to withstand brute force, power tools, and an explosion. Constructed of steel, she weighed over seven hundred pounds. Bolts ran into the brick frame on five of her sides, so there was no removing her from the wall, unless someone backed a truck into the library or blew up the bottom floor. And the bottom floor? Reinforced with concrete and enough galvanized steel rebars to hold up a ten-story building.

This was *my* safe. Built specially by my hands for Edoardo Caetani, an old friend of my boss. And after spending so much time with him when I designed and installed the safe last year, he was now an old friend of mine, too.

One or more thieves had assaulted her, and I was here to get my lady back into fighting shape.

The thought of someone using a drill to mar this masterpiece made my stomach roil.

I set my pack onto the table near the safe and withdrew a borescope. Inserting it into the hole the thieves had drilled, I was able to inspect the inner workings of my lady through the screen on the end of the scope. The light sparkled off millions of pieces of tempered glass, which the amateurs had shattered with their drill. Once the glass relocker had been triggered, the locking bolts were engaged, and it was anyone's guess how to access the contents. Anyone other than me. "They did a number on you, didn't they, baby?"

From my bag, I retrieved my tablet. Its screen came alive, displaying the safe's intricate blueprints. A surge of warmth rippled through me. The glass relocker, the heat-activated door seal, and the ball-bearing hardplate.

Safe design was a unique science. It wasn't about keeping things locked away. It was about challenging the intruder. It was a mind game.

But safe *cracking* was an art. The feeling of the pins setting, the sound of a click no louder than a hummingbird's breath, the sensation on my fingers as I rocked a pick inside a lock.

Jayce, her mouth full of what smelled like beef jerky, mumbled, "Anything interesting?"

"Just admiring the view." I traced a finger over the blueprint and sighed for Jayce's benefit. I grinned at her, her head shaking in response before she headed for the door.

She tossed me a quick, "I'm gonna find something more filling," and then she was gone, the library's double doors closing quietly behind her.

Absorbed in the intricate specifications, time slowed. A small drill hole in just the right spot would allow me to open her up. The repair would be relatively simple, but I could upgrade the security while I had her door open.

Movement at the edge of the room caught my attention. Definitely not Jayce—I wouldn't have noticed her until she was already next to me.

"No, I'm not done yet." I looked up with a smirk as Edoardo, the villa's owner, strolled in.

Edoardo wore his success around his middle. Dressed in a tailored suit which might have fit the last time I saw him over a year ago, he laughed, the crinkles at the corners of his eyes also far deeper than before. "I came to let you know the glass plate arrived."

"Perfect." I straightened and gestured to the tablet in front of me. "Want to see her secrets?"

He held up a hand as he crossed the room toward the safe. Despite his polished exterior, the pungent scent of body odor clung to him, as though he'd forgotten to shower after finishing a marathon. "The only secret I need to know is that your design kept them at bay, my friend."

"No thanks required." My attention fell back to the blueprints. "She's a tough one. I made sure of that."

"Did the rest of the team come with you?"

I tapped the tablet, making a few measurements to the precise location where I'd have to drill into her to release the spring holding the locking bars in place. "They're still in—"

The library's double doors swung open, and Jayce sauntered back in, a massive sandwich in her hand. Her casual gait never wavered, even when her eyes locked onto Edoardo. She said around a bite of food, "Nice house, Ed. Security's got a blind spot, though."

"Not possible." Edoardo's mouth tightened. "I maintain the thieves hacked into the security system."

The safe I'd built sat behind a bookcase to the left of a large-screen television in the library. A similar bookcase to the right hid another. Edoardo had told us about the other safe when we arrived, but she wasn't mine, so it was hands off. Maybe?

Either way, if the thieves had the technology to hack in, they wouldn't have left two damaged and yet unopened safes behind. Maybe one, but not two failures.

"Nope," Jayce said, popping the 'P.' "The camera overlooking the east wall's pointed too far north."

"That's how we got back in," I added, my gaze shifting between them. "Jayce found it."

"I'll have it fixed." Edoardo's words were curt, even though he'd invited us to evaluate his security. "Did you find anything else?"

"No, that was it. You should be good once that's handled." Jayce took another bite, showing little concern for the trail of crumbs she was leaving. "Otherwise, your precious home might get more unwanted visitors."

"That's the last thing I want." Despite not being interested in the schematics, Edoardo lingered in front of the safe. "The designer for the second safe will be here in a few hours with his assistant. Hopefully, they'll have as much success as you."

"Are they locals?" I asked.

"No, no." Edoardo waved a hand absently. "Specialists from the States. I'm not sure about them. The designer was here for the install, but he insisted on bringing someone with him I've never met."

The break-in obviously rattled Edoardo. It was understandable that he wouldn't want anyone new in his home, seeing the inner workings of his security system.

Edoardo's shoulders heaved and he forced a smile in place. "He swears she's the best, so I suppose that will have to be enough for me."

"She?" The implication was thick in Jayce's voice. She cocked an eyebrow at me. "Another 'lovely lady?'"

"No setting me up, troublemaker." I snagged a tape measure and grease pencil from my pack to prep for the drill. This was my world. This was what I lived for.

"Trust me, if I ever saw you ogle a woman half as intently as you ogle those schematics, I'd pull out all the stops."

Edoardo laughed.

Jayce was a skilled gymnast, acrobat, and one of the best thieves I'd had the pleasure of working with. We'd tangled on a couple of recoveries years ago, before we caught her and flipped her. Now she was a productive member of society, recovering stolen objects for their true owners. Or like today, testing their security systems.

"I'll take a safe over a woman any day." A safe was a challenge. She was intrigue and the thrill of the unknown. My opponent, my partner, my muse. She'd always open for me. And if someone hurt her—I stopped next to Edoardo and began measuring—I could repair her.

Not like the women I foolishly dated. Not like Daphne, who never opened up, because if she did, I would have realized she wasn't the woman she pretended to be. Some safes were stubborn, but they never lied and they never criticized you.

Edoardo's tone dropped into mock-seriousness. "Those words are a sin spoken in this country."

"You said the other safe held as well?"

Edoardo looked at the bookcase to the right of the huge television. "It's a very different design than yours, but it did."

I followed his gaze, considering the other safe. My fingers itched. Maybe I could peek at the damage and find some commonalities in the attack. Had they tried drilling it, too? Who was this American designer? "When was it built?"

Jayce shook her head. "Already plotting your next conquest, Declan?"

I returned her grin. "Just thinking about possibilities."

Edoardo lifted his eyebrow, a question in his eyes. "What possibilities?"

I shrugged, concealing the whirring in my brain about the other designer's work. I needed to unravel the puzzle. See what was so different from my design.

And maybe best it?

But first, I had to get my own vault open.

CHAPTER 2

LEIGH

My excitement grew with each step across the rough cobble-stones under my feet. I craned my neck, peering up at the sun-bleached stucco exterior of Edoardo Caetani's villa. Roses hugged the side of the building, their fragrance vying for control over my brother's cologne. An ivy-encrusted balcony garden hung off the second floor, lush and inviting.

Isaac, with his perpetual focus on business, hardly noticed. His fingers flew over his phone, brow furrowed.

"Everything okay?"

"Just a schedule change." He didn't even look up, as though the Eternal City was nothing more than another back alley in Boston. "My meetings start in two days, not tomorrow."

Free time? "That means we could visit the Forum, right? It's only a half-hour walk from here."

He shrugged. "Depends on how quickly we can fix Edoardo's safe."

A rush of annoyance washed over me. We? If he could've done this repair, I'd still be at home.

Safe-designing wasn't about speed, it was about precision, perfection. I made art, not sloppy patch work. I glanced at the imposing door of the villa. Inside, my masterpiece awaited. I hadn't even seen it, other than in the photos Isaac sent after he and Ben installed it.

"I don't rush jobs." I squared my shoulders, while his focus remained on the phone. *But maybe this one time, I would. Then I could see Rome.*

Isaac stuffed his phone into his messenger bag and knocked on the heavy wooden doors. "That's why you're here, sis. Quality work."

A staff woman, prim and efficient, let us in and guided us through hallways crammed with books and huge paintings. Old furniture lined the walls, and several tapestries dotted the various rooms we passed.

I slowed at each open doorway, peering around the old world charm. It was like a house out of a movie, with soaring ceilings and fireplaces in every room. Tall windows without screens were open, letting in the scent of the garden below. How was I going to work in here? All I wanted to do was stare.

When we arrived at the library, my head spun. The room was straight out of a dream. A towering, two-story collection of shelves, stacked with volumes of every size and color. What would the topics be? Were they old encyclopedias? Treatises on the history of Italy? Maybe storybooks with ancient legends and myths?

Dark wood paneling reached up to a coffered ceiling, and an indoor balcony stretched around the second level, offering a dizzying view and hundreds more tomes.

"Don't get too distracted, Leigh." Isaac nudged me, snapping my attention back to the job. "Remember, we're here to fix a safe, not geek out on ancient literature."

Another flush of irritation.

Isaac never understood my love for art, history, or even reading. When I was little, he called me bug—his short-form for bookworm. I let his words slide off me like usual. It was part of our routine.

"Ah, Isaac Barton! Buongiorno!" A man—Edoardo Caetani, based on the pictures Isaac showed me from the Caetani company's website—stood from a desk and approached us. He had a broad smile, a thick Italian accent, and a layer of stress that undercut his tone. The break-in must have rattled him.

"Good to see you again." Isaac extended a hand to shake.

"And you." Edoardo clapped Isaac on the shoulder, then turned to face me. "And this is your new assistant?"

We worked for a family company that specialized in locks, safes, and vaults. Not just any locksmiths, but artists. None of us could be called assistants, unless Dad was the one we were working with.

"This is my sister, Leigh." Isaac gestured to me. "She's filling in for Ben today."

Filling in? For my little brother? *I* was the designer. The brain behind the brilliant safe hidden in this beautiful room.

A knot twisted in my stomach. This wasn't my usual job. I engineered safes, vaults, and other protective housings for special items. But site visits? This was unfamiliar territory. Isaac and one of our brothers, Ben, usually handled installs and conferences. Now, standing in this room, surrounded by opulence and history?

Maybe I'd made the wrong decision when I asked to stay in my workshop in the past. Part of me wanted to skulk back home, but I'd fantasized about coming to Rome since I was a kid, and I wasn't about to skip out on this opportunity. Plus, I had bigger plans for this trip.

"Mr. Caetani," I said, extending a hand. "My name's Leigh Barton. It's a pleasure to meet you. I'm sure we'll have your safe repaired in no time."

"I'm fortunate you were both able to come so quickly." Edoardo took me by the shoulders and kissed the air at each of my cheeks.

As he escorted us deeper into the room, a figure—a gorgeous figure—unfolded from behind a table cluttered with tools.

All the air rushed out of my lungs.

He had a trim, athletic build, like a swimmer or a runner. His hair was thick, dark, and he had tanned, olive-hued skin suggesting part of his family came from Italy. His rugged features, a sharp contrast to the elegant surroundings, framed a pair of deeply intense hazel eyes. Eyes that seemed to trace every curve, every line hidden by my oversized work shirt, before they met mine.

A wave of heat flooded through me.

Finn's critical words and orders of what to wear flashed through my brain, and I tugged at the hem of my shirt. *Focus, Finn's your past.*

Isaac cleared his throat, stepping forward to break the charged silence. He introduced himself to the man.

"Declan Ramsay," he said in a deep voice that skittered up and down my spine. Invaded private parts of me where a stranger's voice shouldn't be able to reach.

My gaze strayed past Declan, to the swung-open bookcase which had hidden a six-foot-tall safe, looming behind him. It didn't look like mine. Considering it was open, it wouldn't have been.

"I'm repairing a safe I built for Edoardo." Declan's gaze lingered on me, the uncomfortable heat continuing to zip through my body.

Isaac gestured toward me. "We work for Barton Safes and Locks out of Boston."

Something flickered across Declan's face. Surprise? Recognition? Had he heard of our company?

I moved closer and shook his hand. Firm, but gentle, his big hands and long fingers completely enveloping my own. Long fingers, long— *Shit, Leigh, down, girl.*

"Is Barton a family business?" Declan asked.

"Siblings," I blurted out, my cheeks heating at my hasty response. It wasn't what he'd asked, but it answered the question I'd wanted him to ask. Isaac and I weren't married. I was a Barton by birth, not marriage.

"The Barton team didn't need to come all this way." Declan's lips curled into a sly smile, amusement dancing in his eyes. "I could have handled both repairs."

"So, Declan." Isaac sauntered toward the open safe, his easy charm on full display. "Who's your employer?"

Declan shrugged. "A small company from the East Coast of Canada. You wouldn't have heard of us."

"Try me." Isaac smiled. "I like to do the circuits at all the trade shows."

There it was. The effortless small talk, the casual ease of conversation. Isaac, the born people-person.

And me? Not so much.

I tore my focus away from the men, from my discomfort every time Declan looked at me, and scanned the books covering the room. Dusty tomes sat piled on tables, their leather-bound covers whispering stories of the past.

The rolling ladder on the balcony would be the perfect spot to reenact a moment from *Beauty and the Beast.*

Which bookcase hid my safe? The faster I could finish the repairs, the faster I'd be wandering the streets of Rome. If I was lucky, we could hit the major points before Isaac's meetings started.

While my brother continued chatting with Declan, the two talking about everything and yet nothing, I turned to Edoardo. "Mr. Caetani, I'd like to look at the damage, so I can come up with a plan."

"Sì, of course." Edoardo waved me toward a bookcase only six feet from Declan's and swung it wide, revealing my safe.

The knot which had been progressively tightening in my stomach twisted harder and lifted into my throat. It was open. Just a crack, but open. Isaac said we were here so I could open it and then repair it. How was it open and the library wasn't in shambles? "Did... did the thieves do this?"

"I told you I could've taken care of it." Declan's tone was irritatingly casual.

I swiveled to face him.

He'd opened it!

How dare he invade my turf? Names and insults and anger pelted my brain. Jerk. Asshole. Cocky prick. He was too hot to be capable of opening my safe without destroying a wall or two in the process.

Isaac, looking equally surprised, turned to Declan. "Wait, you opened Leigh's safe?"

When Declan nodded, Isaac turned to me with a grin.

My annoyance flared. It wasn't enough Declan had broken into my safe, but Isaac had to rub it in, didn't he?

Every safe I designed was a work of beauty and grace, crafted with precision and near-impenetrable without heavy artillery. I could have slapped that look off Isaac's face. Instead, I turned my hot anger on Declan. "You should've kept your grubby little fingers to yourself."

Isaac stepped closer to me, running his hands over my arms. "Leigh, it's fine. You're overreacting."

Overreacting? I took a slow breath, looking at my poor baby, who'd been manhandled not only by the thieves, but now by this—technician? I wasn't overreacting. Overreacting meant a higher blood pressure, which meant danger for me. And everyone in my family worked overtime to ensure I never got too excited.

The quiet, boring life was the one for me. The provincial one! Today was no different, despite Isaac finally bringing me on a site visit outside of the US.

Keep your eyes off Declan and calm down.

Before I could gather my thoughts, another woman sauntered into the room. Shorter than me by a few inches, with shoulder-length black hair and broad shoulders. Confidence oozed from her as she took casual sips from a bottle of brown liquid.

"Jayce," she introduced herself breezily, a grin spreading across her face. "How's the safe ogling going, Declan?"

Declan shot me a quick glance before returning his attention to Jayce. "Do something useful, would you? Fetch my crowbar."

"Why would you need a crowbar at this point?" she shot back, amusement dancing in her eyes. She had a point. Declan was trying to get rid of her.

And I had to get rid of him, too. Or at least stop staring at him, if I was going to get my job done.

Isaac moved into a comfortable conversation with the others in the room, chatting about Declan's safe and how long they'd be in Rome. Isaac told them everything—except that I was the designer—while Declan and Jayce evaded most questions.

I traced the safe's surface, my fingers running over a drill hole near the digital pad, and another two which had been patched up next to the hinges. The latter two seemed out of place, certainly not where an intruder would drill. The Barton plaque, which hid the key backup if the digital number pad didn't work, was untouched. How had Declan opened it? Had he made those holes?

Declan and Isaac laughed over something, the sound churning in my gut.

Enough was enough. "I need a privacy curtain."

I had work to do. And a city to see.

And I wasn't going to let long-fingers Declan snoop around my safe again. He wasn't getting any of my secrets.

Chapter 3

Declan

Leigh's blowtorch clicked off and on again. What was she doing behind the hastily erected privacy screen? Was her slick black hair still pulled into that ponytail high on her head? Or had she wrapped it up like a bun to ensure she didn't burn it?

She hadn't worn a stitch of makeup that I could tell, letting her natural beauty shine through. Nice and simple. Just what I wanted in a woman.

But with a fire hiding underneath those oversized clothes.

Not that I was interested in another relationship anytime soon. The thought of taking anyone through my mother's gauntlet of tests and interviews was more than enough to kill my libido most days. *Fuck, Dec. Safes are better than women, and you have a stunner in front of you.* I clicked the glass plate into position behind the steel door and secured it in place, then wiped the sweat from my brow with the back of my gloved hand.

As the day had worn on, the temperature had dipped, but the humidity was high. And sadly, there was no air conditioning. Like my Nonna always said, switching from hot to cold too fast was bad for you—air conditioning only made people sick.

I paused, listening, parsing the hisses and clicks of the blowtorch for clues.

Nothing definitive. Was she soldering? Melting?

Playing with me? Maybe flirting.

A roll in the hay didn't require interviews.

"So, you're from Boston?" I stood still, waiting for a response, but none came. "Your brother mentioned he had some meetings here this week. Family business, I assume?"

The blowtorch cut off. "That's right."

No, she definitely hadn't been flirting. Of course, if she'd opened my lovely lady, I probably would have been angry, too.

Maybe compliments would fix it. "I've heard of Barton Safes. Excellent reputation. The curved keyway on the Model T-3? Brilliant."

Come on, Leigh, give me something to work with here.

Silence. At least she hadn't told me to piss off. Again.

"I heard there's a new T-4 that adds a paracentric keyway coming out soon."

"How would you know that?" Her accusation sliced through the thick canvas, hitting too close to truths she couldn't know.

Like how I'd broken into Barton Safes and Locks three weeks ago with my crew. We'd been in there prepping for a job and spotted some specs made for The Fenix Group—the mysterious group who kidnapped one of my team members and brought us to Europe.

She wouldn't be involved with them, would she? Our analysts had already researched the Barton staff and said everyone appeared clear—no sudden windfalls, no suspicious travel. So maybe not.

Still, I chose my words carefully. "Just rumors I've heard. I like to test out the latest designs companies put out."

"Is that why you drilled into my safe? Three times?" Her questions came rapid-fire. "Then patched two of them up, hoping I wouldn't notice how inept you are?"

"Whoa, hold on. I didn't drill into your safe." And I certainly wasn't inept. I hadn't needed a drill when I had my Reynolds tech. And even if I had, any patches I did would have been seamless.

The blowtorch reignited, signaling an end to our conversation. I was being dismissed.

"No comment?" I tapped the wall of the tent. "I said I didn't drill into your safe."

"Considering Edoardo didn't mention any other attempts on the safe, it was obviously—"

"Show me." I strode around the entrance of her makeshift tent, ignoring her protests, and slipped inside.

Leigh's ponytail swung as she turned—that answered that question—flaming blowtorch in hand. Her dark eyes flashed behind safety goggles. "Get out!"

The scent of heated metal, burned oil, and something vaguely sweet hit me as I got closer. "Where?"

Her shoulders fell and she switched off the blowtorch. "By the hinges." Lips tight, she gestured toward the safe. "Drilling over there's little more than vandalism."

I closed in on the spot she pointed to. Definite signs of tampering, other than the hole they'd drilled near the mechanical override. The metal around the hinges was smooth. But not smooth enough. I pulled off a glove and ran my fingers over the area, searching for anything out of place. "Looks like someone did a hasty job."

She placed the blowtorch on her worktable. "So, not you or your—what do you call her? Co-worker?"

I crouched, glowering at the safe, rather than turning my gaze on Leigh. Cute, but a pain in the ass already. "Considering we work together, yes, she's my co-worker."

Leigh made a noise in her throat. "So why isn't she up here working with you?"

"Because she gets bored easily," I said aloud, more to myself than to her. "Whoever did this wasn't very skilled. They left clear marks of their work."

"Maybe that's the point. To make it seem like a less-skilled job than it actually is."

I frowned, considering her words. It was possible. But why would someone want to do that? Was it a ploy to throw us off their tracks? Or was there something else at play?

Surely not. The sabotaged camera had to be involved, and no matter what Jayce said about it being easy to get into the library, normal humans would have found it a challenge without climbing gear.

I pulled my company phone from a pocket and swiped to an analytics program.

Leigh's presence neared me, and I caught a whiff of pears. Shampoo, probably. If she didn't wear makeup, no way she was wearing perfume. She peered over my shoulder.

"Now you're curious?" I shot her a grin and marched out of her tent to riffle through my bag for one of the custom phone cases.

"What are you doing?" She pushed the wall of canvas aside and stood at the entryway like a guard dog.

"I want to try something." Something that would impress her. I made quick work of snapping the magnetic case onto my phone so I could mount it next to the Barton safe's processing unit. I'd show her how easy it was to get into her little baby.

Leigh barred my path, holding the open sides of the canvas wall with each hand. "And what exactly are you trying to do?"

"It's killing you, isn't it?"

Her eyes narrowed. "What?"

"You want to know how I got into your safe, don't you?"

The muscles in her jaw ticked, and I could almost imagine the war going on inside her head. Was she as drawn to the puzzle as I was? Or was she simply angry I was better than her? Her gaze fell to the floor, and she sighed as she moved out of the way.

That was too easy.

For all her fire, she apparently lacked a backbone.

"I'll show you how simple it is to bypass." I wasn't just a professional; I was an expert. Of course, I could get into her safe. There was no reason to feel bad about it. All the same, a twinge of guilt slithered up my spine. Unpleasant emotion.

"Your design was good." Now I was trying to make her feel better? What was coming over me? "I simply have tools so amazing they'd make you cry."

Probably not the right words to make things better.

I held up my phone to show her. The damn thing was a technical marvel, created by the Reynolds gadget guru, Will, and programmed by our hacker genius, Brie. It had busted through

her so-called smart lock in five minutes. It hadn't done its wonders in London last week, but no need to share it was fallible.

With the phone app's analysis mode, I'd be able to down-
load data about any false entries and access history. Maybe that
would provide a clue about what had happened. As I moved it
closer to the lock, I said, "Let's see if the thieves—"

"No!" Leigh shouted, almost drowning out the soft click as
it connected with the metal.

Before I could stop or even turn around—

My world was blue.

The safe spat out a cloud of dye, covering my face and shirt.
Filling the air. And a stench worse than rotten eggs. I stumbled
back, gagging.

Behind me, the sound of stifled laughter.

Goddammit. Not only had I not impressed her, I was now
the laughingstock.

More laughter filled the library, and I waved a hand in front
of my face to clear the air. Jayce sounded like a braying donkey,
and I recognized it immediately. Great. First, I'd barely been able
to scale the wall after her. Now she saw this. There would be no
living today down. I was an expert safe cracker, not the court
jester.

I glanced at Leigh, who held a hand over her nose, the other
pressed against her stomach. The disgusting smell and cloud of
rapidly dissipating gas had changed her. Gone was the grumpy
woman avoiding my eyes. Instead, she was still laughing, eyes
bright, tears streaming down her face.

Aw hell.

Leigh Barton, free of pretense and no longer trying to prove herself? She wasn't just naturally pretty.

She was fucking gorgeous.

CHAPTER 4

LEIGH

It took a day and a half to finish my repairs. After Declan messed with my safe and triggered the dye, I'd had to start from scratch, building the security measures back up. Isaac's meetings would begin in the morning—despite it being Saturday—and he'd confine me to the hotel.

'It's too dangerous for you to roam the city on your own,' he'd said to me.

Bullshit.

But what did I do about it? Nothing more than cross my fingers that we'd go out between his scheduled meetings. Sure, being on my own in a foreign country was a risk, but I'd seen the doctor a month ago and everything was fine. No need to worry, he'd told me. Still, my overprotective big brother insisted I keep to the books unless he was with me.

"To Declan and Leigh!" Edoardo's toast pulled my attention to the fantastic meal we'd just finished. He lifted his glass high from the head of the table, his face illuminated in the flickering candlelight. "To their meticulous craftsmanship and two fast repairs."

We all sat around Edoardo's huge wooden dining table, the centerpiece of another room in the villa. A dozen candles dotted the table, while the giant stone hearth opposite me lay quiet. The scents of rosemary and garlic hung in the air from the third course, despite the panna cotta with cherries having just been served for dessert.

I forced a smile, my wineglass strangely warm against my fingertips. I glanced down at the scarlet liquid. Not my first choice. I preferred the crisp, tart notes of a chilled white. But Edoardo offered this local variety generically called *red*, so when in Rome... I held back a chuckle. *When in Rome, Leigh.*

Across the table, Declan raised a footed goblet, filled with a craft beer from north of the city, which Edoardo brought in specially for him. A glimmer of pride flashed behind Declan's deep-set hazel eyes. Despite his cocky exterior, it was clear he was proud of the work he did.

Edoardo continued. "And to Jayce, for unveiling the security breach."

"And to Declan, again, for the unforgettable stink bomb incident." Jayce took a forkful of her panna cotta, covering her mouth to hide the laughter.

The pride faded from Declan's eyes, and they landed on mine. This was not a man who enjoyed losing. "How long until the dye comes out of my shirt?"

I swallowed hard, pushing the bitter red wine down my throat. "Soak it in oxygen bleach for an hour or so. That should do it."

Isaac nudged me, his mouth tight. Another man who didn't like losing, he was probably irritated he hadn't received a toast. "Where'd you come up with that idea? One of your history books?"

When I was little, my mother told me stories about ancient vaults with intricate locks that required a special touch to break into. She regaled me with tales of dye bombs and secret compartments filled with precious items. Mysteries and keys that had to be searched for and assembled from pieces. Dad always said that was part of what made him fall in love with her.

I shrugged, heat climbing up my cheeks. "I thought about it when I got a pair of jeans that rubbed off on my T-shirt."

"You're revenge for a dirty shirt." Jayce swatted Declan's shoulder.

Declan's clenched jaw eased, slowly, until he was laughing with her. "I'm never living this down, am I?"

"Not as long as I'm around," she said.

I chuckled, my insides twisting. I missed that camaraderie—once the norm in our family. After my mother died, my father and brothers rallied, trying to fill in the gap she left. Things started downhill ten years ago. I was working part time while finishing my degree when he re-married, bringing my stepmother into the business. Dad was happier, but he was the only one.

Isaac fiddled with the stem of his wineglass. "How did you get into the locksmithing trade, Declan?"

Declan's eyes cut to me for the barest second. "My father was a structural engineer. He taught me everything he knew about mechanics and security systems. I guess you could say it runs in my family, like yours."

That wasn't the whole truth. Something else lingered underneath Declan's casual response. Had his father passed away? Were they not close anymore?

And what hid behind Declan and Jayce's easygoing manners? Between the co-workers who opened safes with ridiculous technology and tracked down security flaws? High-priced security experts? Or were there darker secrets concealed behind his intelligent eyes?

My thoughts drifted to Finn and how all of my relationships had crumbled under his jealousy. I'd let him control and isolate me, gradually separating me from my friends over our two years together. By the end, I was nothing more than home-Leigh or work-Leigh.

I wasn't even school-Leigh anymore, despite my dissertation being half-finished.

The man who didn't want me in school anymore wasn't the same man Isaac had introduced me to. Finn had hidden a lot at the start. *That's your past, Leigh. You're stronger now.*

No more men who hid things away.

Including me.

Edoardo cleared his throat and leaned back in his chair, the happiness vanishing from his eyes. "I must be honest. The break-in still sits heavily on my heart."

"But they didn't get anything precious," said Declan. "And we'll run through your security again before we leave."

"I know." Edoardo took a deep breath. "But if someone can break into my house, what about my business?"

His business had been a curiosity. He owned a prominent safe deposit box company in the city, yet still maintained at least two large safes inside his house. If his company was so good, why not keep his most precious belongings there?

"I want to be certain..." His eyes slid closed for a moment, and he took a ragged breath. "I want to be certain it's secure."

Jayce snorted. "Surely, you've got twenty-four-hour surveillance there? Biometrics? On-premise guards?"

Edoardo nodded. "Sì, all of these things. Even so, I have a proposal. I need a penetration test done, and I don't know who I trust more than Reynolds Recoveries."

Declan straightened, his cocky smirk nearly masking professional interest. "Obviously no one."

"Is that a service you offer?" Isaac leaned forward, his curiosity outweighing any earlier slight. Why was he so excited? From his wide eyes and enthusiastic smile, he reminded me more of an eager intern than the experienced safe designer he was.

Declan's words slipped out with practiced ease. "We've done jobs from Swiss banks to Hollywood vaults. I think my favorite was the—"

Jayce smacked a hand on the table, practically spitting out her wine. "Chihuahua?"

"I almost lost a finger." A sexy grin spread across Declan's face. He returned his goblet to the table, and the two of them described a job they did testing a Spanish soccer star's home. Fits of laughter and moments of calm interspersed the story, laced with vague details and evasive turns.

Edoardo joined in the tale, weaving a colorful narrative about the soccer star himself. With a pained laugh, he said, "I am truly sorry I recommended that job to you."

My questions about Declan, Jayce, and the whole Reynolds team gnawed at me. As did the way they used words like *com-*

pletely legal and *recovery*, which must have hidden some other truth.

Declan was more than just a locksmith or a safe designer or builder. Definitely more than a technician.

A rogue turned white hat? A thief working for the very people he used to steal from? The thought sent an unexpected wave of heat through me, and I took another deep swallow of the wine, which I barely tasted this time. A blush from the wine, I could explain.

But from the thoughts swirling around my brain?

What would a man like him want with bookworm-Leigh? Why was I imagining what else he could do with those fingers? Or how that facial scruff would feel against my bare skin?

I took a larger gulp from the glass.

Edoardo tipped his wineglass toward Declan. "I'm sure any good thief would start with building blueprints and finding an inside man. I can provide both to save you time. And I can arrange a tour for you."

Without missing a beat, Declan said, "No decisions until we've seen the location. You know we aren't cheap, so I don't want to waste your time or money if we can give you a list of weak points with a cursory glance. Scarlett and the rest of our core team are in Venice. If she's onboard, we can do a full assessment."

"An entire crew with toys like your magnetic phone, Declan?" I mused, the words tumbling out before I could reel them in. Tossing back the wine had been a silly idea. "Maybe Edoardo should hire Isaac and me for the job instead. At least the place won't stink when we're done."

Isaac chuckled, barely even throwing me a condescending glance. "Leigh, you don't have that sort of thing in you."

Thanks, Isaac. I was too quiet. Too bookish. Too high-risk. Too whiny about wanting to explore the city instead of being cooped up in my hotel room while Isaac did whatever the hell he pleased. "I could—"

"But if I joined you," Isaac kept going, right over top of me, "it could be a great learning opportunity for Barton Safes."

I closed my eyes, trying to ignore the rising tide of frustration. *Who flew all the way to fix Edoardo's safe, Isaac?*

"Leigh?" Declan's voice pierced my thoughts.

"What?" My word came out snappier than I'd intended. Too much stupid red wine.

"You're welcome to join us." He was talking to me. Only me. "The more talent we have, the better."

Was that a shot? Or was he being honest?

Rome was a treasure trove of history and art, and I wanted to explore it. Instead, I was stuck in a cycle of work and more work and too stubborn to decline. I forced a smile, my brain too fuzzy. "How do you two know Edoardo?"

Jayce looked at Declan, who looked at Edoardo. Based on the soccer story, they were old friends, but the furtive glances said something different. If we were going to work together, I wanted more information.

"My boss," said Declan, "has been friends with Edoardo for... a long time?"

Edoardo nodded, gaze falling to his wineglass. "She introduced me to my wife twenty years ago."

"Boss?" Isaac asked. "Scarlett? The one you said needs to approve the penetration test?"

"No." Edoardo grimaced, pushing the glass away. "Her mother, Evelyn. We go quite far back. After Evelyn started her company, I've done business with them a great deal."

"Business?" Another word that sounded vaguer than it should have.

"Recoveries." The same look crossed Declan's face as when Edoardo brought up the test of his safe deposit box company. Evasive? "Tracking down looted antiquities, recovering stolen art, finding a person or two."

"Speaking of finding people..." Jayce used her fork to pull Declan's panna cotta closer to her. "How'd you know we were in Venice?"

"I know many people." Edoardo gave a rueful laugh. "You can't work in security for this long and not hear rumors."

Rumors? Like Declan had heard rumors about my new design for the paracentric T-4. "I work in security and don't hear rumors like that."

"I do." Isaac's words hit me out of nowhere. What was he talking about?

The air grew thick around the table, as though there were secrets absorbing all the oxygen. It was quiet for a beat, and I returned to sipping the wine, everyone else doing much the same.

Declan asked, "Where is Martina, by the way? Evelyn asked me to say hello."

"In Florence with her sister." Edoardo leaned forward and gripped Declan's hand. "The break-in scared her and she left right away. I can't thank you enough for coming so quickly. With your assurances, I'm sure she'll come home soon."

"We're friends, Ed." Declan laid a hand over Edoardo's. The men were at least thirty years apart in age, but his words felt genuine. "Don't mention it."

"And you'll do the penetration test?"

Declan pulled his hands back and grabbed his beer. "I told you. Let me see it first."

CHAPTER 5
DECLAN

Edoardo ushered us through the thick glass doors of Cassaforte Caetani the next morning. Like much of the old city, it was attached to other buildings, all the same ochre stucco as his villa. We followed, leaving the view of the Tiber and the treed street outside. "We have a ballistic security facade, including the outer windows and doors."

Soft furnishings and expensive art decorated the lobby. A veneer of comfort draped over the small room, despite its fortress-like purpose. He patted the reception desk and smiled at the women sitting behind thick glass partitions. "Also ballistic grade, with reinforced panels below and emergency buzzers at the ready. We take pride in our security measures."

A guard, stiff and eagle-eyed, watched our every move from a corner.

Edoardo seemed stronger today, full of the confidence he normally exuded. Last night's melancholy had likely been a combination of the wine and his wife's absence.

Isaac wedged himself between Jayce and me, all smiles and superficial questions. "Declan, I've been looking up Reynolds Recoveries, but can't seem to find much detail online. Your website is pretty, but vague. What exactly do you—"

"Isaac." My voice sounded sharper than I intended, even to my own ears. "Let's focus here."

A polite nod and a curt smile. Isaac was professional, but his eyes held a challenge. Was it for Cassaforte or for me? Was he going to be a problem on this job? He'd been sucking up to me from the moment we met. It wouldn't have been an issue if he weren't occasionally putting Leigh down in order to do it.

That part pissed me off enough it came out in my words.

I needed Scarlett here. She could read anyone. She could have talked to Isaac for two minutes and told me his life story.

My gaze shifted to Leigh. She was easier to read. Her eyes lingered on the expansive windows, her mind no doubt stuck on the vibrant city. I'd noticed it outside, how she quietly spoke to Isaac about when his meetings started, when they ended, and how much time that gave them to explore.

"Leigh," I said, too loud in the peaceful room, "you okay?"

She was here, but not here. Like a rare masterpiece trapped inside a safe, waiting to be discovered. She was more interesting than Cassaforte Caetani. She was the real safe I wanted to crack. "All good."

Was she, though?

Jayce, all muscle and coiled energy, was in her element. Her eyes flickered over every detail, internalizing a laundry list of ways to get into the building. No need to take notes. She'd be able to play out at least five options by the time we left. "The lobby's pretty, Ed."

Edoardo placed his thumb against a fingerprint reader by a door at the back. It hummed and the door slid open with a whisper of well-oiled efficiency. I catalogued everything—the sensor placements, the cameras' blind spots, the way Edoardo's thumbprint glowed blue on the scanner after he lifted his hand.

"At the vault, we use facial recognition with a 99.99% rate of accuracy instead of thumb, plus a dual-key system," Edoardo said, pride lacing his words. "Standard security, but the keys are a marvel."

"How so?" I asked.

Edoardo winked at me over his shoulder. "Not yet."

He already had my professional curiosity—that just made it personal. He pushed open the door, revealing a long, well-lit hallway, devoid of any decoration. The air tasted different here, sterile and cold. The second layer of defense contrasted dramatically with the cushy entryway.

I glanced at Jayce, my fingers twitching subtly. A coded language we'd been speaking for years. She nodded, her eyes darting to a ventilation grate near the ceiling. *Potential point of entry?*

"Too small," she signed back.

Facial recognition could be a bitch to get past. I tapped my thumb against my leg twice, then raised my eyebrows at Jayce. *Manipulate the biometrics?*

Her hand twitched. *Maybe.*

I gave her two near-identical twists of my fingers. *Brie and Will?* Our hacker and gadget guy would get through the system if we couldn't. No doubt after their failure last week, they'd have enhanced their analysis programs.

Jayce wrinkled her nose and nodded. A reluctant *Yes.*

Turning back to Edoardo, I asked, "What happens if the scanner can't identify someone?"

The confident Italian paused, his smile turning wolfish. "Then, my friend, they don't get in."

He continued his marketing spiel, but I barely listened. My brain was running through scenarios, playing out different ways to conquer his precious Cassaforte.

Next came the interview area. It was again plush, with a thick Oriental rug and a heavy mahogany desk, walls adorned with high-end art. The kind of place that put clients at ease, but not a room I cared about. It was off the hallway from our way to the vault, had no ingress points, and no access to the ventilation system, even to run a camera.

Leigh strayed from the group, drawn to a painting on the wall of a man in a black hat and suit. Early Renaissance Italian. She looked more at home here among the art than she did amidst the coldness of the hallway, despite the memory of her with the goggles and blowtorch.

"Interested in the painting?" Edoardo asked, following her gaze.

Leigh turned, a faint blush coloring her cheeks. "Just admiring the brushwork."

Fuck, she was beautiful. The way her dark hair fell over her shoulders, not up in the ponytail for once, the openness in her eyes as she admired the painting. Her baggy jeans hid what I was certain were some very fine curves, while her backpack screamed tourist.

"Declan?" Jayce snapped me to reality.

"Right." I pushed away the distraction. I was here for a job, not to daydream about a woman. Especially not one I irritated so much. Although if she got to know me—

A sharp elbow jabbed into my side. Jayce whispered, "Edoardo's still talking, ogler."

"Shut up," I signed to her.

Edoardo led us to the private viewing rooms next. It was an intimate space, more suited for savoring a fine whiskey than inspecting safe deposit boxes. There was a gentle glow from the dimmed lights, and each had a locking door. Everything breathed luxury.

"Owners can purchase a secure video feed," Edoardo said, holding up his phone to show what I assumed was a live feed of one of his safe deposit boxes. "Complete control, complete privacy."

Leigh's eyebrows shot up, and for the first time, she expressed interest. She scanned the room as if she'd finally joined us. "Interesting."

"Where's the vault?" Isaac, who'd faded into the background since I'd shut down his earlier small talk, pointed out of the viewing room and in the direction we'd been heading.

"This way." Edoardo backed out of the room and gestured toward the end of the hallway. The closer we got, the more charged the air felt. The vault door was a behemoth, a testament to human engineering and paranoia.

I drank in the details. She was a beauty, all polished steel and burnished brass for decoration. That was her surface, though. What was in between the layers? There'd be concrete surrounding her, but the door was my target. "What's she made of?"

"That part you'll need to discover on your own." Edoardo leaned toward the facial recognition scanner, entered silent numbers on a near-hidden keypad, and spun the five-spoke handle to disengage the locks.

Leigh inched closer to me, the pear scent invading my nostrils again. "It's an Eisenhart VIII."

I peered down at her, my eyes locking with hers. "Built to withstand ballistic and drilling attacks."

Jayce huffed. "No explosions, then?"

Leigh's eyes went wide as she pivoted to face Jayce, who was behind us. "You're not serious?"

"No, Jayce," I said. "No explosions."

But did she have a time delay at night? If we bypassed the facial recognition, cracked the keypad, would we have to wait an hour? Maybe an overnight duress code that would automatically notify the police?

As Edoardo pulled the door open, a wave of cool air hit me. Security feature or ensuring nothing stored inside was damaged?

"Temperature sensors?" Leigh asked my unasked question.

Edoardo smiled at her. "I'll only say the same thing I would say to clients. We do not leave it open during the day, so we can maintain a steady twelve degrees Celsius temperature and thirty-five percent humidity. It's ideal for document and microfilm storage."

"That's fifty-four Fahrenheit," I whispered to Leigh.

Her brow furrowed and lips tightened—she didn't need the translation and apparently didn't want it, either. So much for our shared moment over the vault door.

Once we were inside, Edoardo presented a set of keys. Not just any keys—chain keys. They resembled the links of a chain link watch encased within a slim tube. Instead of inserting the entire thing into the lock, the user would only insert the very tip. Then they'd push the bow forward, effectively injecting the chain into the keyway.

Leigh's interest ignited, and she snatched a key from Edoardo. Her gaze focused, lips parting slightly. She held it up to the light, studying it like it was the secret of the universe.

"A snake key," she murmured, her tone thick with respect and admiration. "I've never seen one of these in person."

Isaac blinked, his face mirroring his confusion. He had no idea what we were dealing with.

But Jayce smirked, a subtle nod of approval.

"So how would one go about cracking this?" Leigh handed the key to Edoardo. Her eyes were on him, but her question was directed at me.

I rubbed my hands together, the chill seeping into my fingers. The bigger question was how to deal with the cold. My fingers would go numb working in the vault for too long. We'd need our thermal suits, for sure, especially if Edoardo was concealing any additional temperature drop at night.

"This is my box." Edoardo used his two keys—one as a client, one as the owner of Cassaforte—to unlock his safe deposit box, the door easing open under his touch. Inside was a simple chess piece of white wood. "And this is the prize. The proof."

Jayce and I exchanged a glance, silent communication passing between us. We'd faced harder jobs. I ran scenarios in my head for the box itself. Bore out the locks, maybe. It would be messy, but effective. Brute force crowbars would be simple once we were inside the vault. Again, messy.

Unless there was additional security inside the vault? Motion detectors? Vibration monitors?

"Double your usual rate"—a cunning smile curled Edoardo's lips—"if you retrieve the piece without leaving any trace."

Shit. The box doors were full sheets, no separate locks to replace. Crowbars, drills, and metal cutters were out if we were going for no-trace. My mind spun, searching for an option. Could we pick the curved lock? Maybe Leigh's design for the T-4 would have some clue. She'd be an excellent resource for this.

My eyes wandered back to the safe deposit box. Maybe we could replicate the front panel. Destroy the current one, then replace it. That'd be a first, even for us. There'd be proof of the swap, though, unless we could reinstall the existing keyways.

Edoardo was playing hardball, but he didn't really understand who he was dealing with. I wasn't just any safe cracker.

And I didn't play to lose.

Walking the vault's interior, I ticked off strategies. Yet, my focus kept straying to Leigh. Her initial disinterest had faded, replaced with a spark of excitement. It lit up her features, animated her gestures. She was in her element now, the thrill of the challenge sinking its teeth into her.

She ejected the chain key, which fell limp as it extruded out of its housing. Dick jokes flitted through my brain. Totally inappropriate. But from the way Jayce snorted and flicked it, then Leigh laughed with her, I wasn't the only one.

Isaac barely glanced at the special key. "What do you think, Dec?"

Dec? We'd met two days ago, and he thought we were besties?

"Are we going to take the job? Think we can do it? No trace?" Isaac seemed more intent on hanging onto my every move than inspecting the vault. A stark contrast to his sister. It hit me then—Isaac was pretending. He was trying to keep up, hiding behind borrowed knowledge.

"I need to check with Scarlett." Ripping my gaze away from the giggling women and the limp key, I pulled out my phone. "If Jayce and I are running things, we'll be going for quick and easy methods. But if the team's onboard, we'll pull out the stops."

Edoardo's shoulders fell, a broad smile crossing his face. "Perfetto. Tell her I'm asking for no stops. Make it triple your price if you can do it without any trace and before we open Friday."

It was Saturday morning. That gave me one week. Now he was toying with my ego.

Fine.

If Scar said no, I'd call Evelyn. She'd okay the job for Edoardo. Scar wouldn't talk to me for a year, though. Maybe I should just ask nicely.

CHAPTER 6

LEIGH

Sunday evening, Isaac and I made our way along a small pedestrian street by our hotel. It was clogged with people and we had to weave our way between them, dodging the occasional restaurant tables spilling onto the sidewalk. The whole way, he droned on about Edoardo's vault, his all-day client meetings, and technical details he barely understood. I nodded in the right places, knowing my role.

I tuned in and out of his monologue. Cassaforte Caetani's chain keys were all I could think about. A simple and yet complex design—they had Declan written all over them. Annoying. But they consumed every spare moment of thought since we visited Edoardo's company yesterday morning.

"Hey, you listening?" Isaac nudged me, a playful grin tugging at his mouth. "Once I'm done with these meetings, we should take a tour of the catacombs. If you're up for it?"

If I'm up for it? I swallowed a biting retort, settling for a sigh. All this fuss because we were in Rome and not Boston? Ridiculous. If I collapsed, someone in a city this size would call an ambulance.

"I think I can handle it," I muttered, fighting against the urge to roll my eyes.

His chuckle grated. "You say that now, Leigh. But Dad's right. If something happens, any delay could be... you know."

I bit my tongue, mentally drafting a resume for every locksmith in New York City. *Let's see you try to dictate my life then.*

Rounding a corner, strands of twinkling lights draped over a restaurant canopy welcomed us. It was the kind of restaurant I wanted to go to, but not with Isaac.

I wanted a man. One who looked at me with lust in his eyes and intentions on his mind. It was my primary plan for this trip—after I finished Edoardo's safe repair—a grand adventure and a great Roman love affair.

It would be a way to slam the door shut on my past with Finn and launch into a new life. A new Leigh. It hadn't even been a full week since we'd broken up. This trip had finally given me the courage to do it.

When Isaac was originally scheduled to come for the meetings, I'd confessed I wanted to go—Finn said no. Then Edoardo called and they needed me—and Finn insisted he join us. He'd said it was so he could see Rome, but I knew the truth. He wanted to keep an eye on me. When he'd brought it up and I paused, he'd raised his hand as though he was going to hit me.

He didn't. But I got out that night.

Isaac's lecture snapped me back. "Brain aneurysms can be—"

"Enough." I folded my arms to hide the clenching fists. "It's been twenty years."

"But it increases your risk for the rest of your life."

"I know." I held up my arm, showing him the medical ID bracelet I'd worn every day since I'd woken after the car accident. Wasn't staying in a hotel room by myself more of a risk than strolling through the streets? Of course, that wasn't really the issue. They were all scared if I did anything other than read and work, that another one would magically appear. "Just promise me we can see everything I want to see before we have to leave?"

He wrapped an arm around my shoulders. "I promise, bug."

Warmth spread through me at the old nickname. I had to appreciate the things I *did* have and not focus on what I didn't. I needed patience.

As we got closer to the restaurant, my heart skipped a beat. Declan and Jayce sat at one of the outdoor tables with four others.

"Did you know they'd be here?" I asked.

"I didn't." Isaac's eyes lit up. "Think that's the rest of their team Declan was talking about?"

"Probably." My stomach tightened when Declan's eyes found mine. With a mock salute, he acknowledged me, the quirk of his lips stirring something deep in my core. I swallowed hard, heat spreading up my cheeks and down into my belly.

Isaac waved in Declan's direction, catching the attention of more than one other man at the table. "Let's go say hello."

Think about the chain keys, Leigh. Not that panty-melting smirk. He was a business contact, nothing more. Although that stubble... I clenched my thighs. So wrong.

As we neared, a server asked, "Table for two?" Did we really look so American she didn't ask in Italian?

I shook my head and pointed to Declan's group, but Isaac was engrossed in conversation with the server, arranging for a bottle of wine to be sent over.

Red.

Again.

Alone, I approached the table. I caught a few words from a large, muscular man with a gruff voice laced with a French accent. "We tracked Fenix to—"

Jayce nudged him and he stopped mid-sentence. When his gaze rose to meet mine, a shiver of fear shot up my spine. His eyes were deep brown and so intense I couldn't look away. His abrupt silence spread around the table, all attention turning on me.

I clenched my jaw, resisting the urge to squirm or run.

"Hey, Leigh," Jayce said, already on the move, scraping an unoccupied metal chair across the cobblestones. "Have a seat."

Isaac arrived at my side before I could sit, his expression suddenly business-like. He nodded to Declan and Jayce. "This your team?"

Declan stood, radiating confidence and that devilish charm of his. His lips pulled into a broad grin as he gestured to each person, turning the introductions into an informal roast session.

"First, the boss lady herself, Scarlett." Declan swept his hand in her direction, and I studied the woman. Glamor oozed from her every pore, from her expertly tailored dress to her sky-high stilettos. Confidence clung to her, an invisible, magnetic aura.

"Emmett," Declan continued, pointing to a man nursing a drink. He winced slightly, a mosaic of healing bruises spread across his face, and he favored one arm. His grin matched Declan's in its intensity. "Scarlett's brother and resident pain in the ass."

Most of the group laughed, while Emmett stuck out his tongue at Declan. Co-workers and friends, maybe?

"Malcolm here." Declan pointed to a man who finally looked away from Scarlett.

His arm rested around Scarlett's shoulders, posture casual yet fiercely protective. His brilliant-blue eyes radiated charm mixed with something more sinister—much like the rest of the group.

Declan continued his impromptu performance as Malcolm smiled at me. "He's our resident eyelash flutterer and lone wolf. Can't seem to leave us alone, though."

Declan motioned to the burly man I'd overheard talking earlier. The scary one. "And last, our human shield, Rav."

Rav nodded at me, courteous, but practically looking through me. What exactly did a human shield do? Other than terrify anyone who got too close to his team?

"And, of course, you've met the ball of energy," Declan finished, giving Jayce a cheeky grin, which was returned with a playful shove.

I smiled at each of them in turn. "I'm Leigh Barton and this"—I gestured to Isaac—"is my brother Isaac. We work for a safe company in Boston."

"If you're all in Rome," Isaac began, barging his way into the conversation, "does it mean you're going to do the full test of Cassaforte?"

"Sharp, isn't he?" Declan responded, grinning at me. "We are. Edoardo all but said we couldn't do it, which means we have to. There are a couple of team members working remotely, too."

"Excellent!" Isaac's eyes sparkled with excitement. "I'd like to discuss some training opportunities with you. Barton Safes is considering branching into this service at home, and it's a perfect opportunity to learn."

My stomach twisted at Isaac's words. I didn't know we were considering that.

Declan was quick to dampen it. "We're good, bud. Don't need the help."

Jayce gave him a pointed nudge, her brows knitting together. "Oh, come on, Dec. Don't be a spoilsport."

Emmett nodded to Jayce. "You said yourself the vault's going to be tough. Having an extra safe expert on the job would help."

Declan's smirk slid into a glower at Emmett.

"We can discuss it over our meal." Scarlett flicked her eyes toward Jayce, who hopped up to grab another chair. "Our training contracts are more stringent than you may expect, but if you're agreeable to the conditions, we can set something up."

Isaac was practically buzzing, nodding so fast I thought his head might roll off. "Yes, yes, of course."

Where was he going to find the time? "But, Isaac, your schedule's already jam-packed."

He dismissed my concerns with a wave of his hand. "I'll figure it out, Leigh. This is too good an opportunity to miss."

I bit my lip, glancing around the table. Something about this whole deal didn't sit right with me. His free time was supposed to be for our tour of the city. Not for even more work. Although, maybe it would be useful for the business. It might make Dad happy, and that was never a bad thing.

"The first step," Declan started, as he took his seat and gestured for us to do the same, "is to go in on our own. Sign up for a safe deposit box. Feel out the process without Edoardo guiding us and see if we can get more information from the tour guide or the paperwork."

"I can accompany you." Isaac acted like a lovestruck puppy around Declan. "Like Jayce said, another locksmith getting a closer look would be helpful."

Before Declan could respond, Scarlett held up a hand. "I'll go with Declan. Lesson one: A husband and wife duo always draw less attention in these situations."

The table erupted in laughter.

"At least..." Scarlett frowned at Malcolm as a teasing glint lit up her eyes. "When they keep their earpieces in, faux-husbands can be useful."

Malcolm leaned close to her, an intimate moment that seemed to make her as uncomfortable as it made me to witness it. His lips brushed her ear as he whispered, "You say the most romantic things, Eloise."

Eloise? That was a strange nickname.

The dynamic of this team was as confusing as it was fascinating. They worked together, taunted each other, and still managed to focus on the task at hand. My eyes drifted to Declan. This was more than a group of co-workers.

My heart clenched as a fleeting thought crossed my mind—maybe, just maybe, I could fit into a crew like this, too. That was, if I could ever muster the courage to step out of the Barton shadow.

Back to that resume, Leigh.

"How about the best of both worlds?" Declan said, breaking the momentary silence. "Leigh can join me. She's another safe expert, gives the experience to the Barton team, and we have our husband-wife cover."

Isaac opened his mouth, no doubt to protest.

Declan cut him off. "No offense, Isaac, but I want Leigh's opinion."

A warm flush spread through me at his words and the odd spark in his eyes when he looked at me. There was no way he felt the same attraction as I did. No way he was thinking all the better-suppressed thoughts I was.

I nodded, meeting Declan's gaze with an attempt at the confidence I practiced when I was alone. "I'll go."

Scarlett turned her attention to Isaac. "I'll handle the contract details with Edoardo. One of you can put me in contact with the right person at Barton." She looked me up and down thoughtfully. "Do you have any designer handbags, Leigh?"

The question threw me off. "Designer handbags?"

Scarlett simply waved my confusion aside,. "Nevermind. I have an outfit that should fit you perfectly."

CHAPTER 7

LEIGH

My heart pounded as I walked along the narrow cobblestone street early Monday afternoon. Directly ahead, the café where the Reynolds team had set up base for the initial Cassaforte reconnaissance. My heels caught in every second stone, threatening to pitch me over. Beyond the restaurant, there was a paved sidewalk, my salvation.

"You're going to break an ankle." Isaac snaked an arm under my elbow, helping me balance. "I should be the one going in with Declan."

I tugged at the hem of my suit, a pale-blue Italian wool dress and jacket Scarlett loaned me, which molded to every curve of my body. It screamed money, professional, and *I know my business.* It also screamed *look at me* in a way that would have made Finn throw a tarp over me. A thousand bucks, easy. And the tiny handbag? Five times that, at least.

"You will. I'm just doing this one thing." I rolled my shoulders, trying to find some level of comfort in the rich fabric. When I'd first put it on, I'd sank into the luxury, but now it was hard to forget how tight the pencil skirt was across my butt, or how the push-up bra Scarlett had bought for me—bought for me!—made my breasts at least two cup sizes larger.

Yeah, I definitely needed a tarp.

As we got closer, I spotted the woman herself, deep in conversation with Jayce and Declan. Tall, lean Declan, with the impossible-to-read hazel eyes and sexy scruff.

I withdrew my death-grip from Isaac, tucked the handbag under my arm, and rubbed my hands together. Would sweat stain the jacket? Or the clutch's leather?

Declan leaned back from where Jayce's head blocked his view and nodded at us. He leaned farther back, blatantly scanning the length of me, a wave of heat following those eyes. He sat forward and whispered something to Scarlett.

"I brought the distraction," said Isaac as we reached their table.

At the table next to them, Rav, Emmett, and Malcolm looked up from their tablets.

"I'm not a distraction, Isaac." I lowered slowly into the chair beside Jayce and pulled off one of the borrowed Louboutins, rubbing my toes.

"Too small?" asked Scarlett.

We were practically the same size and measurements, other than the required bra. "I'm not used to wearing narrow-toed shoes."

Jayce chuckled. "She tried to get me into a pair of those torture devices once. Never again."

Declan stood and switched to the men's table. He wore a sleek charcoal suit that highlighted his broad shoulders and tapered form. *God, he's hot.* There was something unsettling about how attractive this entire team was. How much confidence of different flavors dominated the space between these two tables.

I didn't belong here. I ran a hand through my hair, shaking off the thought. This was about my talent and knowledge that could help with the vault. This wasn't a heist, it was a penetration test. A safety check. Nothing more.

Scarlett pulled a tiny something out of her purse. An earpiece so small it might get lost in my ear. "Pop this in. We'll be in contact the whole time."

I nestled it into my ear—far more comfortable than the shoes. Voices assaulted me and I closed my eyes, trying to latch onto one. The men at the table next to us, a female not at the restaurant with me, maybe more, I couldn't tell. Each time I grabbed one, it slipped away, replaced by at least two others.

"It gets disorienting with everyone chattering. You'll get used to it." Scarlett touched my hand, and I opened my eyes. Her voice coming at me from the real world and the earpiece shot a wave of nausea through my stomach. "Whatever you do, don't take it out."

Isaac took Declan's vacated seat. "Do I get one?"

Scarlett shook her head. "We only have one spare right now. We'll keep you in the loop."

A female voice piped up through my earpiece. "Hi, Leigh, I'm Brie. I'll be running tech ops at HQ."

"And I'm Will," came a male voice with a slight British accent. "I designed the earpiece and I'd love your feedback once you're done. New users always have the best input."

"Thanks, and uh... hi?" My words sounded odd in the bustling café.

Declan sauntered over, radiating confidence that was nearly infectious and definitely inspiring.

Scarlett held up a hand, cutting off whatever remark he was about to make. "We went over everything this morning. Your cover story is simple: You two are Frederick and Georgia Stirling, a married couple. Declan may touch your hand, waist, or shoulder in a professional manner. No PDAs beyond that."

My stomach clenched—as well as a few other places—at the thought of his hands on me.

Scarlett seemed to sense my doubts. "You don't have to do this, Leigh. I can still go in with him."

No. I had to do this. I was the best equipped to evaluate the vault, to deliver accurate feedback to Isaac. But the idea of playing dress-up with Declan still had my heart racing. I pushed my discomfort aside, nodding at Scarlett. "I've got this."

She handed me a sleek smartphone, its surface reflecting the midday sunlight. "Don't try to unlock it. If you see anything interesting, point the phone's camera at it. Brie and Will are receiving a constant stream from it, so we'll have the intel."

High-tech eyes and ears, an undercover husband, and a mission to penetrate a fortress. This was getting real, real fast.

"Comms check," said Rav, just as gravelly through the earpiece. One by one, the team confirmed, adding to the chaotic chorus in my ear. I tried to keep a normal conversation going with Isaac, telling him what was going on, but the unending chatter made it near-impossible.

"Time to go." Declan offered his elbow to me. "Darling."

I glanced past him to Cassaforte Caetani, two blocks away. The enormity of the challenge ahead settled over me. This was the big leagues. It wasn't little-Leigh sketching designs in her room, teenage-Leigh sweeping up filings to help around the family shop, or nearly-an-adult-Leigh still working on her degree while working part time. This was woman-Leigh, capable and strong, able to step out in a pair of Louboutins and search for security weaknesses.

"Don't worry." Declan's whisper was so smooth I could almost imagine there weren't seven other people listening in. "I've done this plenty of times. I've got you."

The assurance, the words hanging in the tiny space between us, was surprisingly comforting. I managed a nod, snaking my arm through his offered elbow.

Arm in arm, we left the safety of the café and headed toward our target. *Don't let him feel you falter in the damn shoes.* The cobblestone street gave way to a wide paved sidewalk leading underneath thick trees and past a small park.

Cassaforte sat beside the Tiber River, three stories of yellow stucco with green shutters that looked more like a large residence than a safe deposit box company. From the clothes hanging on lines along the side of the building, it was a mix of uses.

Declan pulled open the heavy glass door, its imposing entrance opening to a world of luxury, gleaming steel, and calculated professional indifference. I slipped my arm through his again, holding my breath as we stepped across the threshold.

A representative—name tag proclaiming he was Ignazio—greeted us with a warm yet practiced smile. His gaze traveled from me to Declan and back, a silent judgment of our characters, a calculation of our worthiness to enter this citadel of wealth. The expensive suit and bag Scarlett had loaned me transformed into an all-access pass.

"Frederick and Georgia Stirling." In character, Declan felt taller, more commanding than the laid-back guy who'd messed with my safe. "We have an appointment for a new safe deposit box?"

Ignazio's smile grew and he spoke with a thin Italian accent. "Of course. If you'll follow me?"

He led us to the interview room with the Raphael painting I'd admired during Edoardo's tour. Declan answered a series of questions about the Stirling family, reviewed aspects of the safe deposit boxes, and finally settled on the medium size with the additional livestream option.

Ignazio slid a digital tablet across the table, which Declan picked up and filled out. Was Frederick Stirling a standard cover for him? When he pulled a credit card out of a black leather card holder as though it actually belonged to him, that sealed the deal. Fake name, fake card, fake identity.

Declan Ramsay, and likely the entire Reynolds Recoveries team, were more than they said they were. Had I gotten myself roped into an actual theft?

While Ignazio took care of the payment, Scarlett's cool voice came through my earpiece. "Leigh, he'll ask you to sign the contract. Remember, your name is Georgia Stirling, and the signature won't matter."

Declan handed the tablet and stylus to me, pointing to the X where I had to sign. I skimmed the legal jargon before adding my digital signature and passed the device back to Ignazio.

We were in. It was that simple. We were officially clients of Cassaforte Caetani. At least, Frederick and Georgia were.

Ignazio handed Declan a brochure, then stood and led us deeper into the fortress, toward the vault. The door, the sentinel of metal and security, was as breathtaking as it had been two days ago.

What am I even doing here? A woman who wore baggy jeans and backpacks, who always had her nose in a book—how did I belong in this high-end world as anything but a technician? I was designed to service jaw-droppingly expensive safe deposit boxes in a beautiful Italian city. I wasn't someone who'd rent one, let alone who'd prod at the edges of their security.

I gripped my small handbag, the smooth leather a reminder of who I was. I wasn't just vault-designer-Leigh. I was Georgia—a woman who belonged wherever she damn well pleased.

Declan slid his arm around my back. Maybe he'd noticed my hesitation, maybe not, but the sudden presence of him, so close and warm, grounded me.

The vault door was closed, a guard standing next to it. The same guard as Saturday. Was he the inside man Edoardo promised? As Ignazio neared the facial scanner, I tore the phone out of my bag to capture his steps. This would be interesting to the team, right?

"Got it," said one of the women over my earpiece, probably Brie. "Let me unlock the phone. It will show an inbox with some lorem ipsum text, so pretend you're scrolling through emails. I'll pull up the program while I record."

"Something interesting, darling?" Declan leaned closer, peering at my screen. "Any news from the party planners?"

"Party—" I cut off my question based on a throat being cleared. *Go with the flow, Leigh. Georgia. Give a reason to keep the phone up until the door is open.* "Yes, but I want to read through the details."

"Good job," said Brie. "Dec, we need your phone attached to the door so Will can scan it."

"Sounds good." Declan's response could have been for both of us.

"I warn you," said Ignazio as he turned the handle, glancing at my bare legs, "it's cool inside. The inspection rooms are more comfortable, if you'd like to wait in there?"

"I'll stay." When the gush of air hit me, I squealed quietly, moving my arms and the phone around. Hopefully, I was successful in capturing the single camera trained directly on the vault door, rather than just a blur of movement.

Declan used his arm at my waist to urge me forward, into the chilly vault.

"I should have worn pants," I said.

"We'll be quick." Declan leaned closer, his cologne washing over me. He smelled amazing, like oranges and exotic spices. "Plus, your legs look fantastic in that skirt."

My stomach flip-flopped at the compliment.

It was an act. A job. *Nothing more, Leigh, remember that.*

His hand skimmed down my side as we stepped into the vault. Scarlett had said no PDAs, but his hand was getting awfully close to creeping outside the boundaries she'd set. A near-imperceptible click sounded behind us. Right. I was holding up the phone to record everything and my body was a cover for Declan's magnetic case. The one which had tripped my safe's dye pack.

He was getting handsy with the vault door, not with me.

"We've got contact," said Will.

"Better than the contact you made Thursday," I whispered.

He squeezed my waist, ramping up the velocity of the energy pinging around inside me. "Behave yourself, Georgia."

I swallowed hard at the deep rumble in his voice.

Focus on the job, Leigh.

The phone was close to the hinge, invisible to the guard and the camera. The case melded with the door's color, a chameleon hidden in plain sight. It had been black on Thursday, hadn't it? Declan must have an assortment of these cases.

In my ear, Will continued. "Getting data from the phone. Perfect placement, Dec. Leigh, can you sweep your phone around the vault?"

Relief surged through me as I slipped out of Declan's grip to do as asked. "Are the four cameras in here exclusively for the livestreams? Do they sweep back and forth or—"

"Since you purchased that option, one of the cameras will move when you request access."

"And..." I spun slowly, holding the phone against my chest like I was hiding its screen from the cameras, trying to look inconspicuous. "What about sprinklers? Fire suppression? Do you drop the temperature at night?"

"All the answers are in the papers." Ignazio gestured to the brochure Declan held, deflecting my curiosity with a well-rehearsed finesse. Was it avoidance, or did he genuinely not know the specifics? His smile remained, painted in place, big enough to make us comfortable, small enough to appear professional.

"Of course," said Declan, who tucked the brochure under his arm.

"You're doing great, Leigh," said Scarlett, her slow words no doubt designed to keep me calm. "Try to capture the warding on Edoardo's safe deposit box."

"Here are your keys," Ignazio said, presenting two of the mysterious chain keys.

With a quick demonstration, Ignazio and Declan inserted their keys into the deposit box's lock, while I strolled a few feet away to film the details of Edoardo's box, including the entrance to the keyway. A gentle push and a turn of the keys, and Ignazio withdrew the box, an empty cavern waiting to be filled.

From his jacket, Declan produced an envelope, sliding it inside the box without revealing its contents. He offered a quick smile. "That's all for now."

Ignazio pushed the box back into place with a satisfying *thunk*, the lock clicking shut with a turn of their dual keys. Under Ignazio's nose and the invisible eyes of Cassaforte Caetani, we'd planted our first seed. Everything seemed too easy with the Reynolds team.

As we made to leave, a small motion from Declan caught my eye, a subtle signal. *Distract him*, it said.

"Excuse me, Ignazio." I let my nerves play into my tone, making the touch of concern I wanted to portray more authentic. "I know you said everything was in the brochure, but I'm worried about those sprinklers up there. Won't they damage the documents we store here?"

Ignazio's eyes followed my pointing finger, taking in the sprinkler system. He shook his head. "No, signora, we don't use water as a first step. We have suppression gases instead. They are highly effective, so the water is a last resort we will never need."

From the corner of my eye, I watched as Declan retrieved his phone from the vault door. The magnetic case and phone now concealed, I forced a smile, nodding at Ignazio.

"Got it all," said Will. "Brie, we've got lots to analyze."

"Good job, you two," said Scarlett. "We'll see you at the hotel in thirty and discuss next steps."

Chapter 8

Declan

The wide sidewalk running along the Tiber River didn't hold the same character as the tiny street where the team sat. But with Leigh on my arm, the river walk was a fantastic exit plan. "We're out."

"We're packing up," said Scarlett. "See you soon."

Each step away from Cassaforte Caetani was one step closer to the prep work. My brain whirred, the weight of the chain key in my pocket calling to me. I needed to dissemble it. Find its weak points. Figure out how to bypass the security.

Leigh's arm looped around mine, her excitement almost a tangible entity radiating from her. "I didn't notice it the first time, but the facial recognition? It was the Sperry Vision, state-of-the-art. There's no way you can get past that."

"You'd be surprised," I muttered, letting my gaze slide over her profile. She was lit up like the day we'd met, when she noticed I'd opened her safe. Not angry like Thursday, but vibrant. All fiery enthusiasm and an almost magnetic sense of wonder. Scarlett's makeup job highlighted her brown eyes, as did the borrowed suit. She was classier than her usual formless clothes, but no more attractive—just attractive in a different way.

"And the motion detectors in the vault?" Leigh continued, her thumb brushing back and forth against my forearm.

I grinned, allowing myself a moment to appreciate her passion. It had been a long time since anyone had shared so much interest for this part of the job with me. "We've got a solid start."

"A solid start?" Leigh chuckled, a sound that seemed to bounce around the bustling street, mingling with the voices of people all around us. "I guess that's one way to put it. You'll do all your prep work at the hotel?"

"I've booked a temporary office," said Scarlett, reminding me I wasn't alone with Leigh. "We'll move everything in tomorrow morning and dig in."

Rav, in his usual growl, added, "I'll review the security first."

When we'd headed into Cassaforte, Leigh had been uncomfortable in the shoes and the skirt. Now? She flung one hand in the air, despite the overpriced bag she was carrying, punctuating her words as though she weren't speaking to seven people over an earpiece. "An Eisenhart vault, Declan! It's like stepping inside Fort Knox!"

"Fort Knox doesn't use Eisenharts."

She smacked my chest with the clutch. "You know what I mean."

I laughed, tightening my arm around hers. "Yeah, I remember my first few penetration tests. I was a green twenty-one-year-old, fresh out of university. Thought I was James Bond or something."

She rolled her eyes at me, a playful smile on her lips. "I'm sure you did. How long have you been working for Reynolds?"

"Since I graduated." A flood of memories washed over me. The adrenaline, the challenges, the thrill of outwitting a system designed to be unbreachable. And back then, doing it with one of my best friends and her mother. Evelyn, Scarlett, and I had been an unlikely trio before the rest of the team trickled in.

"And you're always on the move like this?" Leigh asked, her tone softer now, curiosity replacing the excitement. "Traveling the globe, testing safes? You said you do recoveries, too? Jewelry and art?"

"Sometimes." I shrugged, offering her a lopsided grin. "Gets me out and about."

"Well, I hardly ever leave Boston. But this?" She waved her free hand at the old-world charm around us, her eyes wide with genuine awe. "It's like living inside a postcard."

A laugh bubbled up in my chest. "Glad you're enjoying the scenery."

Her gaze flickered back to me, a shy grin shifting across her face. "The scenery's not half bad."

One fake name and a single recon mission, and the woman was flirting with me. Or did she mean the vault was the scenery? Or the river?

"An Eisenhart VIII, eh?" Brie cut off any chance of me testing out the flirting theory. "The Eisenhart VII was a tough nut to crack. The triple cylinder locks took us hours."

"Hours well spent, Brie." Will's slight British accent peppered a word here and there, growing stronger with every month he spent in London. "It should give us a leg up on this one."

"I'm not so sure about that." I was still irritated about that long night, waiting for the two-hour time delay to finish. If Cassaforte had the same, I'd have to bring a deck of cards for entertainment. "She's the new beauty on the block. They won't have just improved things, they'll have changed them up."

Brie remained calm and steady. "I'll hit the dark web, see if there's anything about the VIII. We've had good luck with that in the past, so you never know."

"Good call, Brie," I said. "And, Will, you and I need to cross-reference the data my phone grabbed from the door. It might help us figure out what Eisenhart changed with the new model."

"Got it, Dec."

Leigh turned slightly in our walk, holding the clutch against my arm. "What does the phone actually do? Other than trigger stink gas and indigo dye, of course?"

Jayce's snort reverberated through the earpiece. "Oh, Brie, you've got to hear this story."

"Story time can wait." I tried frowning at Leigh, a not-so-subtle encouragement for her to keep her mouth shut. It was useless, though, since Jayce would spill it all. "The phone's case is more than what it seems. We've got some added testing tools in there. When combined with the phone, it can analyze everything from metal compounds to electronic factors."

"Like a miniature lab?" If Leigh held my arm any tighter, we'd have to stop walking. Her need to understand was visceral, and all I wanted was to sit on the stone half-wall next to us and show her the inner workings.

If Daphne had been a quarter this interested in what I did for a living, I would have held an ounce of regret for our breakup.

"Exactly," said Will. "And after you left Cassaforte, I downloaded a bunch of data from it, including signals from the facial scanner. It's all encrypted, but Brie and I will sort it out."

"Decrypting it as we speak." In Brie's background, the clack of her keyboard ramped up in speed. "That's why the team doesn't move in to the office until tomorrow. We need our processing time first."

Leigh sucked her bottom lip in, head twisting this way and that, absorbing the city around her. "And here I thought you were just a pretty face."

The teasing remark was delivered with such a deadpan, I couldn't help but laugh. "Pretty and talented. What more could you ask for?"

"Oh, I could ask for plenty." She let out a small sigh, a serious expression falling over her. What would Leigh Barton ask for if she could have anything? She lifted her clutch and pointed down the river. "If I didn't think I'd break my ankle, I'd say we should sneak off to the Castel Sant'Angelo. I looked it up before Isaac and I left the hotel and it's only a twenty-minute walk from Cassaforte."

Not what I was hoping she'd ask for. "You really want to see the city, don't you?"

Leigh breathed out, her energy waning. "I've been to virtual conferences, seen presentations about penetration testing and the tools that thieves use. But experiencing it firsthand? It's a whole different ball game."

The way she ping-ponged between subjects threw me. Definitely not as simple as I'd originally assumed.

I cocked an eyebrow at her. "You mean the tools thieves *and* security experts use."

"Right, security experts." From her tone, it was clear she realized there was more going on.

"Leigh," said Scarlett, "Isaac wants to know how you're feeling."

Her body deflated and the woman I'd first met surfaced. "I'm fine. Tell him we're walking slowly."

"And he wants to be sure you're wearing your bracelet."

"Tell him I never take it off." Leigh let go with her clutch hand and began slipping her other arm out of mine, but I clapped a hand on top of it, keeping her there. Trying to keep some of the joy inside of her, instead of letting it melt all over the sidewalk.

"What bracelet?" I asked.

Happy-Leigh was vanishing before my eyes. "What do you do about the temperature? It's not middle-of-winter cold, but I imagine it would cause problems if you're doing precision work for more than a couple of minutes."

"We've got gear for that," I said. "Special thermal suits that keep our body heat in."

Brie asked, "Do you want me to ship the gear, Dec?"

"Hold off on that. I need to finalize the list of equipment we'll need. Not sure we've got a suit that'll fit Isaac."

"Got mine here in London," Will said. "You think it'd fit him?"

"Possibly." I mentally compared Will's broad shoulders to Isaac's narrow. It wouldn't be perfect, but he'd be a better match than Rav. "Ship it over. Maybe we'll get Emmett's shipped over with mine. We'll find one that fits him."

Leigh grew quiet while the team chatted in the background. We needed direct assault plans and a million contingencies. That was Scarlett's forte, ensuring we went in with twice the planning required. But Isaac would be a wildcard. If he was exaggerating his skill level, as I suspected he was, we might need someone else to step in.

Scarlett or Jayce could handle it. I'd have to make sure they had suits, too.

Just in case.

"The only thing we haven't dealt with before is the chain key." A key was normally the least of my worries, but in this case, it was something my team didn't have experience with. It was a variable we could prep for once we'd figured it out. We had two of their keys, so maybe I could manufacture a lock to test on.

"Drilling the locks out would have been easy enough." Leigh's mood remained flat.

I leaned in close and whispered into her ear without the earpiece, "Want to keep going to Castel Sant'Angelo?"

Her step faltered and she peered up at me.

"You know I'm still listening, right?" said Scarlett. "You need to get a cab and meet us at the hotel so we can review the video."

I grinned at Leigh, searching for the spark she'd exhibited when we'd left Cassaforte. "We have until Thursday night. They can spare us for a couple of hours."

"Declan." Scarlett's boss mode kicked in. I'd known her since we were twelve—she'd developed that at the ripe old age of fourteen. She didn't intimidate me. I simply accepted her as the leader of our pack from the day she moved to town.

"Okay, okay." I straightened, maintaining eye contact with Leigh a little too long, nearly careening into a man coming in the opposite direction. I'd become too used to visiting beautiful cities and rarely played the tourist anymore. Our tour guide. I knew Rome well enough I'd be able to surprise Leigh with a few hidden wonders. Maybe after the vault test. "How do we get past those locks without leaving a trace?"

"You want the extra money?" asked Leigh.

Money? That was never behind what I did. "I want the extra challenge."

"Typical," groaned Jayce. She was one to talk. She'd insisted we scale Edoardo's wall to prove someone could make it up without being caught on camera, instead of simply telling him.

"That means we can't drill," I began, ticking off options on my fingers, now that I didn't have to keep Leigh's hand trapped on my arm. "Too much of a mess. We can't torch it, same reason. And no explosives."

Leigh interrupted me with a raised eyebrow. "Jayce wasn't joking? How often do you use explosives?"

Was she appalled or impressed?

"Not often enough." Rav's tone was dry, but Brie's laughter rang out in response.

"Ask me about the chihuahua in the Spanish story later." I couldn't help but chuckle at the memory of whisking Mr. Bites

A Lot away from our work zone. "Today, we focus on what we can do for this job."

"Do you think you could pick the lock?" Leigh asked. "You'd need a specialized tool... and to do it twice."

The spark in her eyes told me she was excited to take on the challenge. Disengaging her arm from mine, she rummaged through her clutch and produced the chain key. Her fingers moved over it with an artist's touch.

There was an unexpected pang of loss at the lack of contact.

Get a grip, Dec. We weren't a couple. We were just pretending for the recon.

"I have a few contacts who might know more about this design." Leigh's gaze remained on the key. "I could..." She paused, correcting herself with a sheepish smile. "Isaac could consult with them."

The reminder brought my mood down as quickly as Leigh's mood had fallen. I didn't want to work side-by-side with him Thursday night. Didn't want to spend hours practicing with him and refining our plans.

What I wanted was to figure out a way for her to replace him. I wanted to see her eyes light up the way they had on our way out of Cassaforte.

"Last chance for Vatican City?" I whispered to Leigh.

"Dec," snapped Scarlett.

Leigh bit her lip, holding back a smile.

"I know, I know." I pulled out my phone to find a rideshare. "See you in twenty, Scar."

CHAPTER 9

LEIGH

Tuesday, the day after my excursion with Declan into the Cassaforte vault, Isaac and I joined the Reynolds team at their office. Isaac had initially suggested I spend all day at the hotel, since he'd have to leave for his meetings after a couple of hours, but I'd insisted I was safer with them than alone.

It was manipulative to use my safety as an excuse, but it worked.

"Focus, Leigh." Jayce's light-brown eyes drilled into mine as she held a delicate white feather in front of me. The wrapper of a granola bar crinkled between her nimble fingers. "You're a statue. Breathe without making that feather move."

I locked my gaze onto the feather, my pulse drumming in my ears. My breath, a whisper against the feather, failed to disturb its barbs, despite the activity all around us in the makeshift office.

"You're getting the hang of it." Jayce grinned, popping a morsel into her mouth. "I'm glad Isaac let you outside to play."

Her words lingered, the weight of them pushing against my lungs. I exhaled, too quickly, too sharp. The feather dipped.

"Easy," Jayce crooned. "You don't want to disappoint your teacher, do you?"

My heart beat high in my chest, and I sucked in my lower lip. It was a silly training exercise that had no practical use, but some centering time might help clear my thoughts. I straightened my back, met her gaze head-on, and inhaled, careful not to disturb the feather.

Isaac sat twenty feet away, in front of a lock mounted in a vise. He was a ball of nerves and agitation. Rav stood watch over him, arms folded so they looked like tree trunks. The air pulsed with the incessant pinging of a blood pressure monitor attached to Isaac, his heart racing too fast for the sensor's liking.

I slid one hand up to my wrist, outlining the medical bracelet.

Isaac's struggle to handle the lock stressed me out as much as he was obviously stressing. In my head, I was feeling for the pins over the rake, willing them to snap into place for him. He didn't have enough pressure on the tensioner, either. How was he so bad at this all of a sudden?

On the other side of the room, Scarlett, Malcolm, and Declan were engrossed in a pile of blueprints spread out on a massive table. I'd skimmed them when Isaac and I arrived. Their focus was on the Cassaforte floor plan and the design of an Eisenhart VII—the older, less advanced version of the vault they'd penetrate Thursday night.

From the corner of my eye, I caught Declan's hand skimming over the blueprint, his knuckles brushing against the large sheets. A flutter jostled in my stomach. I'd said such stupid things after we left Cassaforte yesterday. Calling him a pretty face? I was so lame.

And then I'd said I could ask for more than pretty and talented.

Push it down, Leigh. There was a chasm between his world and mine. I couldn't afford to blur the lines or think there was a way to bridge the distance.

Jayce's uncomplicated demeanor was a breath of fresh air in the whirlwind that was my current life. It was easier, simpler, to be around her. "You're turning red. Calm down and just breathe."

At least, it was simpler when she didn't call me out like that.

Leaning toward her, I lowered my voice, ensuring the others couldn't overhear. "I'm a little stir crazy."

"You and me both."

"I've been in Rome for five days and haven't seen anything."

Jayce blinked at me, pausing with a piece of her granola bar halfway to her lips. "Nothing?"

"All I've seen is Edoardo's, a few dinners near the hotel, and whatever Isaac and I have done with your team. Everything else has been from the window of a car."

"Seriously?"

"Isaac promised we'd do some sightseeing once his meetings wrap up."

She made an exaggerated show of rolling her eyes. "I couldn't help but notice he's a touch overprotective. We're literally a forty-minute walk from the Roman Forum. Hell, we could go over there right now. Tell him we're going to the hotel for something."

My response stuck in my throat as a shadow of the past washed over me. Images of Finn skittered through my mind. He also would've insisted I stay far away from the world's perceived harms. "No, you need to prepare for the penetration test."

Jayce leaned forward. "I'm killing time right now. You need me more than they do."

What was it about her? Jayce was loud and brash, cracking jokes and taunts at every turn. But there was something quieter about her. The more time I spent with the Reynolds team, the more it seemed they all had secrets lurking underneath the polished veneer. As if they'd all gone through tough times like I had.

I glanced at Isaac, my heart heavy with a sudden urge to share, to unload the burden I'd kept buried for so long. It was as though Jayce was inviting me to.

What did it matter if my mom passed away when I was ten? Or that I'd grown up as the only girl in the family, sheltered from the time bomb they all feared was ticking inside my head?

Jayce's eyes softened as she studied me, her snack momentarily ignored. She touched my arm. "Never fear the leap. Fear standing still."

The leap? I had so many directions to leap. Which one did she mean?

"Something one of my coaches said to me once." She waved the thought aside, as though she was falling into her own memories. "He was always talking woo woo stuff like that."

"Come on, everyone," Declan called to the room. "We need all brains on deck."

Rav shook his head, his attention stuck on Isaac. "We're good here. Isaac needs more reps."

Jayce and I exchanged a glance before joining the trio huddled over the blueprint-littered table.

As we approached them, Declan dove in, his finger dancing over the blueprints as he outlined the planned approach. "Cassaforte is one node in a sprawling set of interconnected buildings, shaped like the loops of a figure eight. We've got bullet cameras on the front and back doors. All of them are aimed squarely at the company's entrances."

He paused, looking up at us, his eyes holding an assured spark. "Our ace in the hole is our inside man—Edoardo's security guard. He'll give Brie the clearance she needs to neutralize the cameras from the outside. She'll blind them remotely."

I nodded along, processing the plan I wouldn't be part of.

Declan traced a line on the blueprint toward a busy road and a nearby park. "Main door's a no-go. Too exposed. And thanks to the street and building lights, it's lit up like a Christmas tree."

His fingers danced across the paper, stopping at a side door that was subtly marked. "Jayce, Isaac, and I are going in through here." His tone carried an air of finality, as though he could simply manifest success. "It's on a less busy street and leads to a courtyard, then straight to the rear door."

His gaze flicked up to meet ours, determination set in his eyes. "Our inside guy will get us in there. After that, he's out of the picture. He doesn't have access to the vault, so he won't be any help there."

"I'm still searching for vault specs," said Brie from one of the tablets.

"We'll put that aside for a sec." Declan pulled his chain key from a pocket and placed it on the table.

Will, also on the call, said, "I could manufacture some steel blanks, but I don't think I can have them to you in time."

"What about 3D printing with filament?" asked Scarlett.

Declan nodded slowly. "That might work, and we could practice filing them, but without a lock to test them in, I'm not sure how helpful that would be."

"Filament would be too weak and could break off inside if you use them in the vault." I pulled the key closer and pushed the bow all the way through. "If you try that, you'll need several blanks, plus some way to fish the pieces out if they snap off."

"What about your contacts?" asked Declan.

"Isaac's contacts."

From Scarlett's raised eyebrow, I was pretty sure no one believed me when I'd said Isaac would be in touch with some people who could help.

The sudden clatter of tools hitting the floor jarred us from our discussion. I spun to see Isaac's frustration boil over.

He tore the sensors off his skin, his face gleaming red. "We're not even going to need lock picking for this stupid penetration test!"

Rav watched from a distance, his brooding presence no doubt adding fuel to Isaac's agitation. The tension was palpable, a dark cloud hanging over the room.

"I've got a meeting," Isaac snapped, his annoyance still vibrating in the air. He shot me a quick, almost pleading look, but I couldn't find the right words to offer. Before I could speak, he brushed past me, leaving the room on his way out of the office. "I'll be back in a couple of hours."

We were left standing, staring at the empty doorway, the silence hanging heavy around us.

Could Rav, or someone else, have tampered with the lock somehow, making it impossible for Isaac to pick? Was it a way out of the training contract Isaac had negotiated? His tools lay scattered across the floor, and I went to clean up his mess.

I picked up a tension wrench and a simple rake, their familiar weight a comforting presence in my hands. The vice sat suctioned to the table, and I inserted the tools, feeling for the tumblers inside.

Everything else fell into the background.

Missing Rome.

My angry brother.

Memories of Finn.

Dreams of Declan.

It was more muscle memory than conscious thought, putting just the right twist on the lock, rocking pins up one at a time, the faint clicks a symphony of my own creation. With little effort, the lock clicked open. Not tampered with. I quickly locked it again, hiding my success.

No need to point it out to anyone or celebrate such a minor victory.

"Why is it," Rav's deep voice startled me, "your brother is the one joining us and not you?"

A flush crawled up my neck, discomfort knotting in my stomach. I rushed to Isaac's defense. "He was probably just too stressed to focus. You're a little intimidating."

Isaac was capable, but my success at lock-picking had stirred a pot of doubts. Even still, it was his place on the mission. He had his part to play, and I had mine.

Breathing at feathers and leveraging my contacts.

"Leigh, could you come back here?" Declan pulled me out of my thoughts. "Brie just secured a copy of the Eisenhart VIII's specs. Downloading them now. We could use your input on the locking mechanism."

I nodded, moving to rejoin them. What would Isaac say if they insisted I go? Maybe tonight I could run through some things with him, like we'd done when we were younger and it was nothing more than a game. I could prep him, so he'd be ready.

My phone buzzed in my pocket, and I pulled it out, scanning an email. "Good news. My contact in Antwerp is sending six blanks and a test lock. They should be here tomorrow."

"That *is* good news." Declan smiled. The memory of his suggestion that we sneak off to Castel Sant'Angelo lodged in my chest—if everyone hadn't been listening in, I would have accepted. "But why only six?"

"That's all he's got on hand. He contacted the manufacturer who's out of stock, too, so I guess we should be happy with what we've got coming?"

Declan drummed his fingers on the table. "I have some feeler gauge at home that might be thin enough to feed through the curves. Brie, you at the office?"

"I am."

"All right. Let's review the vault specs, and we'll put together the equipment list and get it shipped over for the morning."

Who would deliver that quickly? One more mystery on the Reynolds pile.

CHAPTER 10
DECLAN

By late Wednesday afternoon, the team had clocked sixteen hours in our rented office. Leigh was lost in her work, a brilliant blur against the humdrum of our temporary Roman headquarters. She'd tied her hair back in her typical ponytail. It swished rhythmically as she focused, adding a kind of music to the methodical sounds of a hand file meeting brass.

She worked patiently, intently. A key took form underneath her experienced touch, her quiet diligence drawing Jayce in.

Yesterday, Jayce ran her through relaxation and focus exercises. Today, Leigh was the teacher.

It wasn't just the work that caught my attention—it was the *way* she worked. No rough edges, no hurried movements, only grace and understanding. It was art. And the artist was explaining her process with a voice so soft it blended with the soothing scrape of metal on metal, creating something akin to a meditation.

"See this?" Leigh whispered, turning the key in her hand to show Jayce the precise grooves that she'd filed. Her fingers moved, tracing the contours like she was revealing the secrets of a much-loved story.

Jayce, usually as restless as a squirrel, sat still, snacking slowly, absorbed by Leigh's teaching.

It was such a contrast to Isaac's showy demonstrations. I stretched my hand out from the way it had involuntarily curled into a fist, the mental image of Leigh's shoulders dropping each time Isaac spoke chafing.

Isaac was all talk, announcing every success as a testament to his supposed brilliance—when he had them.

But Leigh? Leigh had a different way about her. Her work was quiet, meticulous, more about the craft than the applause. It was the difference between a peacock and a nightingale. And damn, if that didn't make me want her all the more.

There was no way she was the one who'd created the manuscript case we'd found in Boston three weeks ago. She wouldn't be working with a group like Fenix. Maybe Isaac, but it was obvious he wasn't talented enough.

That was a problem for another day.

The chain key blanks had arrived a few hours ago, courtesy of Leigh's friend in Antwerp. I'd planned to get my hands on them, get a feel for the metal, the shape, the possible hidden surprises. Yet Jayce's unquenchable curiosity had pulled Leigh into an impromptu lesson with a standard key, which had turned out more captivating than I'd expected.

Leigh had Jayce insert the key into the lock, wiggle it back and forth a few times, then extract it. "See the marks? That's where the pins require more space and we need to file some more."

"I can totally do that." Jayce took over, and I had to fight against my jaw clenching. Filing wasn't dangerous, but all we needed was for our thief to jab a sharp file into her palm and put her out of commission.

What if Will could whip something up to scan the interior profile of the chain lock so we could create a replica of the keys using our 3D printer? If it worked, we'd be shaving hours off our prep time, and that was time we needed.

Although, hauling the printer into the vault was a no-go. We needed a lighter-weight solution. One more challenge for me to hand over to Will.

I glanced at the table where the chain key blanks lay. Six of them, all shiny and untouched.

The first step would be to add the warding that matched the client keys to half, then the warding for the company key to the other half. One of each for the penetration test. One of each held in reserve for fuck-ups in the vault. That left Isaac and me with a single shot each at hand-filing the keys before the big night as practice.

Across the room, Isaac was practicing on the 3D key models, the confidence on his face not quite reaching his eyes. He'd done a few standard keys in the morning, sure, but this was a bigger challenge. Maybe the filament key and files were too different from what he was used to—I'd had a problem with them, too—but he really sucked.

Scarlett sidled up, her gaze flicking between the other women and me. She asked, in her way that was both question and statement, "She's nothing like Daphne, is she?"

A shiver of discomfort rippled through me.

If Leigh was like Daphne, she wouldn't be working quietly with Jayce. She'd be at the table with me, pointing out every error I made. She'd be reminding me how shitty a job I'd done with the filament keys. Just like with my parents, I was never good enough for her, and the constant striving had left a bitter aftertaste.

Just like every other woman my mother chose as the perfect wife for me. "And your new romance with the eyelash flutterer makes you a relationship expert?"

"Watch yourself, Dec." Scarlett's lips tightened, a show of emotion that was only there because she wanted me to see it. She leaned close enough no one else would hear. "Leigh's a people-pleaser and she's liable to say or do whatever you want, just because you ask, for fear she'll disappoint you."

Her words hit a nerve. The fear of disappointment, of being less than, the urgency to prove one's worth... it was uncomfortably familiar.

Yup. Scarlett could tell your life story within seconds.

"You've been standing there for fifteen minutes watching her. Don't even bother trying to tell me you're evaluating the two Bartons, because it's clear she's got more skill than he does." She touched my arm. "Personal feelings have no place in our job. You need to focus."

She was one to talk.

I was *not* letting my guard down. I wasn't allowing sentiment to cloud my judgment. Running a hand through my hair, I let out a sigh. My gaze shifting back to Leigh, who shared a laugh with Jayce, who'd ruined the key she was practicing on. *Don't let Jayce touch the chain keys.*

"She's—she's too quiet," I blurted out, grasping at obvious straws. "Too introverted. She's too scared of her brother. And don't even get me started on her being from a different country."

Scarlett's eyebrow quirked.

I sounded pathetic but didn't care. Leigh wasn't a good fit for me, and I wasn't for her. There were too many differences, too many potential complications. Getting involved was the last thing I needed.

But fuck, did I ever want a few complications with her.

"What you need, Declan, is to keep your eye on the prize," Scarlett said, firm, but quiet enough to be private. "The penetration test. That's our priority. Not your feelings."

"I'm not—"

"Don't waste your breath. I've never seen you this distracted on a job." Then, almost as an afterthought, she added, "Regardless, I think she's better suited for this than Isaac."

I frowned at her. That was too easy. "You what?"

She shrugged, an infuriatingly nonchalant gesture. "Isaac's stressed. He's taking too long on tasks Leigh could handle more efficiently."

I stole another glance at Leigh, at her focused expression, the clean movement of her hands as she started anew with Jayce.

Scarlett was right. Like always.

"Fine." I tried to sound reluctant, but it was exactly what I'd wanted. Or thought I'd wanted. Would I be able to work next to Leigh and keep my head in the game? "We'll see how it goes."

Scarlett called Isaac over, her tone uncharacteristically gentle. "Declan and I have been talking, and we feel Leigh would be a better fit for the job."

"Not likely." Isaac chuckled, as though he thought we were joking. He pointed toward Leigh, still deep in her tutorial with Jayce. "She doesn't have the nerve for something like this. She's doing great now because there's no real stress. If Rav was breathing down her neck, she'd be a wreck."

The strain in Isaac's voice was palpable. It was clear he cared about his little sister—worried about her—but it was too much. And the way he put her down to do so didn't sit any better with me today than the first day we'd met.

I said, "She popped the test lock yesterday afternoon in under fifteen seconds. *With* Rav standing over her."

"What if she gets caught?" Isaac said, barely above a whisper. "I can't let that happen."

"It's a fully legal penetration test, complete with contracts that would protect us if something went wrong," said Scarlett. "We've done this a hundred times."

"I've seen her in action, Isaac," I said, trying to offer some reassurance. "She's more capable than you give her credit for."

Isaac put up his hands. "I know she is, but you need to understand, she has a medical condition. It's not about capability, it's about keeping her safe."

"She held her own when we went into Cassaforte on Monday." I'd been impressed with her during our initial recon, quickly transitioning from nervous participant to vibrant team member. "She asked all the right questions, distracted the guy who gave us the tour, all while taking in every tiny detail. There were no hints of any sort of medical condition that might hamper her performance. She's got a knack for this. You should be proud."

I wanted her with me in the vault. Scarlett's lecture didn't matter. It wasn't about attraction—at least not entirely. This was business. *It's definitely not attraction. She's all wrong for me. My mother would hate her.*

"The vault's too cold," Isaac continued, like a child making ridiculous arguments once he'd been shot down. "You all have gear for that, but Leigh doesn't have a suit."

Scarlett, quick as always, countered, "We had mine shipped out. It'll fit her perfectly."

"But I signed a contract with Reynolds." Isaac's words took on an edge of desperation. What was it? Was he genuinely that concerned about her, or was it sibling rivalry? Simple jealousy? "The contract states that you'd provide penetration test training to me."

Scarlett raised her hand to stop him, calm but leaving no opening for debate. "The contract was for a Barton representative—"

"That's enough." I swept my hand between them, before Isaac thought to argue further with her and incur Rav's wrath.

Scarlett glanced at me, her eyebrow twitching but staying down. She wasn't used to being cut off.

"The only way Barton is learning anything from this is if we're successful. Isaac, you've been swamped with meetings, which hasn't left you enough practice time." I paused, letting the truth of my words sink in. That wasn't a point he could argue with. "You're stressed, man. We have a better shot if Leigh comes in with me."

Isaac looked like he'd swallowed a lemon, but he was listening. That was a start.

"And here's lesson number one in Barton's penetration test training." I locked eyes with Isaac. "You go in with your best chance of success. You don't take unnecessary risks, even if it's just a test. Even if there's little risk to the team."

There was a pause, then Isaac gave a curt nod. The fight had left him, his shoulders sagging slightly. It wasn't a wholehearted blessing, but it was enough.

"Fine," he grumbled. "She can go in."

A wave of relief washed over me, tinged with something else—a hint of apprehension. What exactly was this medical condition? Was she liable to pass out? Have a seizure? Either way, I'd put my foot down and Leigh was in whether or not she wanted to be.

Jayce was showing Leigh one of the magnetic cases for the phones. A pang of concern hit me. She better not be sharing too much. Will was there too, a digital face on the screen next to them. I could only catch bits of their conversation, but it seemed Leigh was questioning Will, absorbing all his answers.

"Leigh," Isaac called.

She glanced up, and when he waved her over, she joined us. "What's up?"

"We've decided you're going in my place tomorrow."

We, Isaac?

Leigh's eyes just about popped out of her skull. "That's your job. I couldn't possibly..."

"That's what I told them." Isaac folded his arms, looking back at me like he thought this was his winning hand.

Scarlett had called it. Leigh was more concerned about Isaac's feelings than her own. Leigh would throw this opportunity away to make sure her big brother didn't have a little tantrum.

It was all too familiar, making decisions based on other people's impressions. It was a shitty way to live.

Maybe Scarlett was also right about Leigh screwing with my focus. But I couldn't stand watching her wilt under her brother's need to feel important.

"How many pins are in the chain lock?" I asked, raising a hand to silence Leigh before she could answer. "Isaac?"

He turned to look at the vices set up with the practice locks, including the chain lock from Antwerp. "Six?"

I raised my eyebrows at Leigh, at once prompting her for a response and hopefully pointing out silently that she was the right choice. Not only was I confident she'd know the answer, but she also wouldn't phrase it as a question.

"Five." Leigh sucked in her bottom lip, eyes almost darting to Isaac, but remaining mostly locked with mine.

"And how long did it take you to pick it?" My thinnest Gonzo hook had proven to be the right size to get inside the lock.

"Eight minutes."

"And who else here could pick it?"

Her eyes *did* shift to her brother this time, then back to me. "Only you."

I was not saying this out loud. She'd seen it and kept it quiet. But everyone needed to know, so I could take the right Barton in. "And how long did it take me?"

Leigh fidgeted with the hem of her loose T-shirt. "Doesn't matter. Filing is faster, so it's the better option."

All eyes shifted to Leigh, waiting to hear the answer, until Jayce gasped theatrically. "Leigh was faster than Declan?"

Leigh shrugged, looking as though she wanted to sink into the floor. Exactly like I'd told Scarlett, Leigh was too quiet for me.

But the arguments were simple. She was the one.

Leigh finally nodded and said, "Okay. I'll do it."

CHAPTER 11

LEIGH

The porcelain sink was cold under my palms, a chilly counterpoint to the prickling warmth of the thermal insulation suit clinging to me like a second skin. Was that even me staring back from the hotel bathroom mirror?

It was just after midnight on Friday morning, and my two fairy godmothers waited outside the door, so they could inspect every inch of me.

Reynolds Recoveries would be paid well for the penetration test. Double the price for leaving no trace. Triple the price to do it before Cassaforte's opening in nine hours. Barton Safes would receive a percentage, plus a lot more training than I'd expected when I boarded the flight to Rome with Isaac a week and a half ago.

I was about to infiltrate a safe deposit box company. A guard would let me in the back door, I'd bypass all the security on an Eisenhart VIII and steal a chess piece as proof.

In.

Out.

Payday.

The adrenaline in my veins was a reminder it was too much, a marathon after a sleepless night. Or maybe it was the caffeine, the overtired delirium of a madwoman. Isaac had asked me about headaches at least a dozen times since I'd agreed to this crazy plan. A mild one pulsed at the base of my skull, but it wasn't the kind he always worried about.

A knock shattered the stillness, followed by Scarlett's voice. "You're stalling, Leigh. Let's go."

"Maybe Declan should take Isaac," I shot back, trying not to let them hear the shake in my voice.

The response was a burst of laughter, Jayce's signature, slicing through my self-doubt. "The only thing Isaac can crack is an egg. Badly."

I opened the door, even though part of me debated peeing again. Maybe vomiting. I covered my breasts with one arm, the other wanting to cover my crotch. "I'm not sure the suit fits properly."

"Quit worrying," said Scarlett. "That suit might as well be painted on. You're golden."

Painted on? That was the problem. I'd thought the skirt was too tight when I did the recon with Declan, but this was a whole other level. It was like a superhero costume, which I did *not* have the figure to pull off.

"But what..." I paused, unsure why I kept asking the same question over and over. "What about Isaac?"

Scarlett crossed her arms, her gaze steady.

"He's been pretty quiet." Under their scrutiny, I was suddenly uncomfortable covering myself up and tried wringing my hands. Crossing my arms. Behind my back? "He might be pissed off that Declan wants me on the job instead."

"Of course he's pissed." Jayce blew a raspberry and pulled a candy from a pocket to hand to me. "Even Declan was pissed you picked that twisty lock faster than him."

I winced, guilt gnawing at me. "Still, maybe Isaac's better suited for this."

Scarlett raised an eyebrow, her cool demeanor unbroken. "Really?"

"Yeah. Maybe?" I held out my hands, showing them the tremors that ran through my fingers. "See? I'm shaking already."

Scarlett grabbed one of my hands by the wrist and held it up in front of herself. Then in front of Jayce. "What do you think?"

Jayce plopped down on the bed next to us. "Looks like me before a big job."

Really? She got nervous?

"How about a compromise?" Scarlett released my wrist. "Isaac can join you and Declan for the test."

My heart eased at her words, the knot in my stomach uncoiling. That would work out perfectly.

"Well, would you look at that?" Scarlett pointed at my hands.

I held them up. Steady.

Was it really that simple?

"You're more capable than you think, Leigh. Believe in yourself more."

"Yeah." Jayce unwrapped a candy I hadn't seen her take out of her pocket and tossed it into her mouth. "And don't let Isaac's little tantrums mess with your head. It's your job, Leigh. You earned it."

Maybe I did. Maybe Isaac was silently proud of me. Maybe after this, he'd stop telling me to stay in my hotel room.

Scarlett opened the handbag she'd brought, another expensive-looking red leather piece, and pulled out a phone like the one she'd loaned me on Monday.

"You'll have an earpiece in, which transmits through this phone, which is a portable monitoring unit." Scarlett's gaze held mine. She was so calm. Ridiculously calm. How often did she do this sort of thing? "It's proprietary tech, so if you lose it, we can destroy it remotely. But try not to. Will loves fiddling with his gadgets, but complains a lot when he has to replace things for us."

I nodded, accepting the phone from her. It didn't look any different from what I could buy at a mall kiosk, but that was true of everyone and everything on this team. One thing on the surface, something else below.

"I'll show you how to unlock it and use the basic features during the drive to Cassaforte," said Scarlett. "You'll wear it on your forearm, so it's readily available."

My fingers traced the sleek lines of the phone. "Will I get one of those magnetic cases like Declan has?"

Jayce exploded into laughter, which was cut off by a cough. "I wish I'd seen his face when the dye pack hit him!"

Scarlett's eyebrow arched. "Okay, I need to hear this story."

"The magnet triggered some security thing in the vault Leigh built for Edoardo." Jayce wiped at her eyes. "It filled the whole place with stink gas and indigo dye. Took us hours to scrub it off of him."

Scarlett laughed, clapping a hand over her mouth. "Seriously?"

"I like to be creative with my designs." Either the thermal suit was doing too good a job, or I was heating under their attention. "Art and history, they're part of it. There's experimental work, like metal foams and new alloys. The best vaults—at least, the best ones I design—they're not just about brute force. They have a story."

Scarlett tilted her head, curiosity twinkling in her eyes. "Metal foams?"

"For the inside, to better disperse heat from a drill, while allowing more space for—" *Shut up, Leigh. No one cares.* I pressed into my wrist, moving the medical ID bracelet underneath my suit.

"You're passionate about this." Scarlett smiled. "Is that why you were so interested in the Eisenhart? I couldn't help but notice how animated you were after the recon."

I shrugged, thinking about the beautiful steel, hiding its secrets from us. "Assembly line vaults are predictable. It's all gears and levers and timers. Once we get past this one tonight, you'll be able to bypass any other like it. They're easy once you crack the code. Edoardo should have installed a custom piece."

"Easy for you, maybe," Jayce said. "I can't open something like that. Even with help from Brie and Will."

"I didn't say tonight will be easy. But after tonight..."

Scarlett's smile spread slow and knowing across her face. "That's why you're perfect for tonight. You see things differently. You're not just cracking a safe, you're interpreting a piece of art. Not one as unique as what you work with, from the sounds of it, but it's still artistry."

The pride swelling in my chest was a surprise. To hear some-one else echo my thoughts, my passions, was a validation no one had ever given me before.

"Let's go through the plan again." Scarlett pulled out a chair from the desk. "Start from the top, Leigh."

"We park the van on the side street, next to Cassaforte." I sank onto the end of the bed beside Jayce, grabbing a convenient pillow to hide what felt like the nakedness of the suit. "Then we enter through the side door of the building complex."

"And if there's a car parked there already?" Scarlett asked.

I swallowed, steadying my voice. "We park next to it. The van should still block off sight of us going in."

Jayce said, "What if the door's locked?"

"We pick it."

"And if we can't?" Jayce would be our third, monitoring the rest of the building while Declan and I dealt with the vault.

"We let the team know." I took a deep breath, thinking through the steps in my mind. "They'll contact our inside man, the security guard, who'll open it for us."

Each step, each contingency plan, all lined up. The test wasn't some nebulous, insurmountable feat. It was a puzzle, and I was good at puzzles. Maybe I was more ready for this than I thought.

"From the side door, we slip into the courtyard, staying in the shadows near the base of the wall," I continued, rehearsing the steps from the video feeds and satellite photos the Reynolds team had provided. "Once we reach the Cassaforte back door, the security guard lets us in and leads us to the vault."

Scarlett pulled a wad of black fabric from her bag and tossed it to me. "Go on."

I pulled the head covering over my hair and face as I spoke. The snug fit was surprisingly comforting, a fabric shield for all but my eyes and mouth. "Jayce is our lookout."

Jayce saluted in acknowledgment, her eyes twinkling as I finally unwrapped the candy she'd given me.

The plan was etched into my mind, each step a small enough piece of the bigger plan that could be mixed and matched when things went wrong. The anxiety that had gripped me earlier was slowly being replaced with a sense of control, of preparation. I was ready for the job. And for the first time since I'd arrived in Rome, the butterflies in my stomach didn't feel like panic or nerves. They felt like anticipation. I was ready for the night, ready for the unknown, ready for the vault and whatever it had in store for us.

"Time for me to suit up." Jayce bounced off the bed. On her way out, she called over her shoulder, "Don't forget your go bag."

The butterflies switched direction, considering panic again. "Why would I need a go bag?"

"Habit." Scarlett waved it off. "In case you hadn't noticed, I'm big on risk management. Edoardo may be paying us for tonight's job, but it's a test for my team, too. We have a timeline we adhere to, as though we're concerned about police. We have go bags in the van, the same as if we're about to go on the run."

I tugged the hood from my head and placed it carefully in my backpack next to me. "Do you have to run often?"

"Often enough."

Recovery agents. Based on what they'd said before and what Isaac and I could find on the internet, their jobs involved a lot of coordinating with international police forces, finding and negotiating the return of stolen goods, and sometimes just escorting things around the world. "What would you have to run from?"

Scarlett gestured to the backpack, my question flying right past her. "Remember to review your tools. Know where everything is. You won't have the luxury of rummaging when you're inside."

I nodded, checking the contents of my bag. Jayce had helped me place everything strategically, from the smallest lock pick to the larger, complex tools of my trade, including the mini drill, in case our tests with filing the keys or picking the locks failed.

"What's in the bag?" Scarlett asked, her gaze never leaving my face.

"A part of the processing unit to bypass the biometrics," I said, touching each item inside the bag as I mentioned it. "The clear box for filing my keys so we don't leave metal shavings. The imprint dust to speed up the filing process..."

Scarlett nodded in approval as I continued. "And your key blanks?"

I pulled them from a zippered pocket on my thigh. Those, my file, one lock pick and a tensioner, stayed on my person.

She stood, smoothing out her ivory blouse. "You and Declan each have one key to file. Remember—he'll handle the master key and you'll do the client key. You've both got one backup in case something goes wrong."

I looked up at her, uncertainty coiling in my gut. "You sure I'm ready for this?"

Scarlett's expression softened. "Leigh, it's a perfectly legal test. Nothing is going to go wrong. You've got Declan and Jayce with you. They've done this so many times, they could do it blindfolded."

Taking a deep breath, I nodded. *Perfectly legal* was exactly what I needed to hear. "Okay. I need to get my plainclothes disguise on over the thermal suit."

"And pack a go bag." With a wink, she headed for the door. "You're part of my team tonight. You play by my rules."

CHAPTER 12

LEIGH

The minivan sat inconspicuously next to Cassaforte Caetani, our sleeping target in the center of Rome. Inside the blacked-out van, our only illumination came from a trio of computer screens shared between Scarlett and Rav in the front seats. One screen displayed Brie and Will, who would monitor our progress remotely. Another screen fed us a live tour of Cassaforte's interior, every gleaming corner of the vault exposed. The last, all squiggles and valleys, dominated Rav's attention.

"Sixty minutes, tops." Rav pointed to the array of graphs. "That's how long the suit batteries keep you warm against the chill. If you're cutting it too close, call a pull out, or deal with the cold."

Rav's clipped commands contrasted with the joking the team did most of the time. Maybe it was their way of dealing with the stress, or maybe they were so used to these activities that the stress rolled off them.

Jayce, one of her gloves resting on her lap, dug into a bag of chips. She smirked at Declan, pointing a potato chip at him. "Try not to rip it this time, big man."

He peeled off his long-sleeve T-shirt and cargo pants to reveal a thermal suit clinging to every muscle. Every. Single. Muscle.

"Try not to leave too small a hole in the chain-link fence next time."

Heat simmered under my skin, pooling low in my belly. The rational part of me wrestled it back. We were here for a job, not romance.

But wow, his suit left nothing to the imagination.

My own thermal suit suddenly felt too tight again. Too revealing. As he knelt to pack his clothes in his go bag, I ordered my gaze away from his ass.

Baggy sweaters and worn jeans, that was my style. But here I was, poured into a skin-tight suit, something Finn would've sworn I was incapable of. His words played on their continual loop in my mind. *"You're not one of those girls, Leigh. Not like you've got anything to show off, anyway."*

I shoved the memory down, attempting to squash it. Tonight, I wasn't Finn's Leigh. I wasn't Isaac's little sister. No. Tonight, I was part of Reynolds Recoveries, like Scarlett had said.

And it was showtime.

Pulling off the layers of my plainclothes disguise, I squirmed in my seat, my movements a far cry from Jayce and Declan's fluid efficiency.

Isaac shifted, jostling past Jayce to get access to me, the worried crease between his eyes deepening. "You okay? No headaches?"

"I'm fine, Isaac." Irritation flared, but I swallowed it. It was the umpteenth time he'd asked since we arrived in Rome. I should've had *I'm fine* tattooed across my forehead for his benefit.

Isaac leaned over, adjusting my collar with a frown. It was typical Isaac, the overprotective older brother, fussing over the fit of my thermal suit. I swatted his hand away, feigning a smile.

In the front seats, Scarlett spoke in hushed tones with Rav. "Emmett's headaches are getting worse. The fucking clowns... I think it's a concussion."

"That's what I was afraid of." Rav didn't even look at her, but his tone made it clear he cared deeply about the Reynolds siblings. "I was surprised Malcolm left you in my hands again, but that explains it."

"I was so wrong about him."

"Which one?" He glanced at her, an intimate moment that seemed out of place in the van.

"Good point." Scarlett lifted her chin and pivoted, her moment with Rav vanishing faster than it had happened. She handed an earpiece to each of us, her voice raising to business levels. "Comms for the night."

It was the same tiny device as I'd worn for the reconnaissance. But this time, when I slipped it into my ear, the explosion of chatter from Will and Brie was a comfort rather than a distraction. An anchor to latch my confidence onto so it didn't float away.

"Everything's green on my end," Brie's voice came in crisp and clear. "Our inside man's done his part. Security feed's looped. Cameras are blind."

Time to go.

We all pulled on our head coverings, masking our faces, holding in any stray hairs that might try to escape. My fingers moved over the straps of my backpack and over the pouches on my thighs. Key blanks. Files. Filing box. The most important tools were all there. All ready.

Isaac cut through my focus. "Last chance, Leigh. You sure you're okay?"

"I'm good, Isaac."

Scarlett, holding all the charm of steel, gestured to the side door. "Stay safe, everyone. Remember, we're here to test their security, not get fancy."

"Speak for yourself." Jayce popped the door and was gone before Scarlett could respond.

Declan and I filed out behind her, the building already open before my feet hit the ground. The courtyard on the other side was quiet, and we kept to the edges, watching for movement in the windows above. The old Roman architecture stood sentinel, shrouded under the cloud cover. Not a minute later, we were at the rear entrance of Cassaforte, which swung open for us.

The guard—from our tour with Edoardo—glanced around the courtyard and waved us in, muttering something in Italian.

Declan, all business, gave him a curt nod. "Grazie mille."

The rush to the vault was a blur of gleaming steel and rushing adrenaline. Declan unholstered his phone, attached it to the vault's biometric sensor with practiced ease, the gentle clink of the magnet echoing in the quiet building.

Will spoke through the earpiece, "Connection's good. I'm working."

Jayce slipped away, vanishing like a ghost into the labyrinth of Cassaforte, ready to monitor and report, ensuring Declan and I could focus solely on the job. We hovered at the vault entrance.

Will had sworn it would take five minutes, but with every beat of my rapidly escalating heart, I was sure it had already been ten.

"You holding up okay?" Declan's question caught me off guard, his gaze searching.

"No headaches," I blurted out.

Declan shook his head. "I meant, are you ready to file the keys?"

"Of course." Heat crept up my cheeks, my automatic response reflecting Isaac's constant health checks. "Yeah, I'm ready. In fact, I think I might be… excited? Butterflies, but in a good way? Does that sound strange?"

A slow smile spread across Declan's face, warming me to my core. "That's normal. The day you don't feel those butterflies anymore, that's the day you stop cracking safes."

His words hung heavy in my brain. Cracking safes. The phrasing seemed out of place.

I gripped my backpack straps. "You mean testing them, right?"

His smile faltered, a flicker of uncertainty in his eyes.

Just as Declan opened his mouth to reply, Will chimed in. "Facial scanner bypassed. Keypad, too."

My jaw fell open. "That was fast."

"Got my ass kicked by a biometric sensor last week. Had to do some major upgrades to the software," Will said, a hint of pride in his words.

Brie added, "I've got good news, too. No timer set on the lock."

A ripple of cautious excitement spread through me.

"I know we're good, but…" It was hard to make out Declan's expression with the face covering on, but the way his eyes narrowed didn't feel good. "Someone tell me I'm overreacting?"

"You're overreacting," said Jayce. "You always do that when you work with a contractor."

"That must be it." Declan nodded slowly, giving me a weak smile. He inclined his head toward the vault. "Do you want to do the honors?"

I reached out, the door's wheel solid under my nervous hands. Nothing to worry about. The heavy door creaked open with a groan, revealing the dark maw of the vault. A gust of icy air washed over us.

My suit hummed to life, a comforting warmth spreading across my skin. It had held my own body heat in well earlier, but powered up, it was a marvel.

"Temperature's lower than I expected," Will murmured. "Adjusting the suits' regulation, but it'll drain the batteries faster."

I let out a quick laugh, a puff of frozen air billowing in front of me. "Can I get one of these suits for Boston winters?"

"Trust me, I tried that last winter." Declan smirked at me, pointing inside the vault. "Our boss doesn't let anyone play with the tech."

We stepped over the steel plate into the vault and pulled out our first tools—working lights to place on the floor and illuminate our workspace.

"Safe deposit box 2460," said Rav.

A number I'd never forget—the first four digits in Jean Valjean's prisoner number in *Les Misérables*. "Ever had a penetration test where the owner booby-trapped whatever you were testing?"

Declan pulled out a tray from the wall, a sturdy platform normally used for the safe deposit boxes. Our filing boxes landed on it with a soft clink. They were simple rectangular containers made of clear, thick plastic, with enough space for a key and two pairs of hands, designed to contain all the residue from our filing.

"The chihuahua story Jayce and I were telling you earlier." Declan bit back a chuckle.

"Is that where the explosives come in?" I asked.

Jayce's laughter burst through the earpiece. "Oh, that was a wild night!"

"The Spanish footballer, right?" Will added.

"Focus," Scarlett cut in, a sharp reminder of the gravity of our task.

"Race you," Declan said, an easy grin lighting up his face as we prepared our tools.

"It's about getting it right, not just right now." I already had my files inside the box.

Rav practically grumbled, "Both would be preferable."

My nerves had settled, hands steady, unlike the trembling mess back at the hotel. The shakes when we were outside the vault must have been excitement.

We pulled out our blank chain keys, dusted them with imprint dust, and inserted them into the two locks on Edoardo's safe deposit box. My mind spun, thinking of my best time picking the chain lock—after practicing more, I was down to seven minutes. Declan's best time was eight.

I focused on the feel of the lock, the resistance as the blank touched the pins, creating a guide for my work. "Our best filing time was five minutes."

"Aiming for four tonight," Declan shot back.

"I'll do three." I nudged him with my hip, the *You're a pretty face* woman coming out for a moment.

Declan grinned. "Keep that up and you won't stand a chance."

I withdrew the key blank, slipped it into the filing box, pushed out the chain, and inspected the marks the pins had left. Unlike filing a standard key, I had to brace the chain so it didn't flop all over the place as I filed. Declan followed suit on his side.

We repeated the act over and over. Insert, wiggle, file.

There was no way I was doing three minutes. I should have set a timer on the phone.

"No sign of anyone else lurking in here," said Jayce. "Buddy's hanging out in the interview room. Does he have a security display in there or something?"

Insert, wiggle, file.

"Nothing in there," said Brie, the sound of her keyboard clacking in the background. "Maybe Edoardo told him to stay out of the way."

Jayce hummed aloud. "Or he's pretending he got tied up as part of the playact."

Insert, wiggle, click. "Booyah!"

My key turned smoothly in the lock before Declan's and a surge of pride swept over me. "Beat you. How long was that?"

"Three minutes, forty-seven seconds," said Brie.

Declan's reaction was difficult to gauge. Something flickered behind his eyes before he resumed his filing and said, sounding overly professional, "Congratulations."

The playful demeanor he had at the start of our 'race' disappeared, leaving me unsettled. This was like me and Isaac. I'd best him and he'd make me feel guilty for doing so.

Next time, I'd go slower and let Declan win.

"Twenty minutes since you entered the vault," Will announced, interrupting the uneasy silence that had fallen between Declan and me. "Suits will hold for another fifteen or twenty at most. Power drain is more than planned."

Declan's key finally clicked in the lock thirty seconds later, and we carefully retrieved Edoardo's safe deposit box, sliding it onto the tops of our filing boxes. Inside, as expected, lay a beautifully crafted chess piece sitting atop an envelope. Declan picked the piece up, turning it in his fingers. "No booby tra..."

His words trailed off as his gaze landed on the envelope.

"What is it?" I asked. Silly question.

Declan's name was written on the front in elegant, precise handwriting.

"We've got a letter," Declan announced, his shoulders tensing. The room seemed to hold its breath. Even the keyboard clacking stopped.

Isaac muttered, "I knew she shouldn't have gone in there."

"Isaac, you're not helping," Scarlett came through, a note of stern authority underlining her words.

"But—" he started, and his words shifted to little more than a faint noise in the background of Scarlett and Rav's communications.

Someone had muted him.

Declan carefully opened the envelope and removed a note card, along with two photographs. He slipped them into a pocket so fast I couldn't see what was on them.

Not good.

He scanned the note, lips turning down, eyes hardening. He swore under his breath, crumpling the paper in his hand.

My voice shook as much as my hands had been earlier. "What was in the note, Declan?"

Chapter 13
Declan

"Declan?" Leigh said, her words sharper than I would have expected from her, as she plucked the traitorous letter from my grasp. Her smoothed it out, her eyes darting over the crumpled paper.

"It's from Edoardo," I ground out between clenched teeth. "It's a fucking setup."

"What?" Jayce asked over my earpiece.

I was already moving, key filing tools in my hands, scanning the neat rows of cold steel safe deposit boxes lining the walls of the vault. My heavy breaths were too loud in the metallic chamber. My mind raced, heart pounded, the edges of my tools biting into my fingers.

"That conniving little fucking prick!" I could have punched the walls. Pulled out my drill and laid waste to the goddamn place. Test the Eisenhart VIII model, my ass.

"A setup," Leigh whispered, just loud enough for the earpiece to pick up.

"I'm waiting for an explanation." Scarlett's voice was sharp. Scary in a different way from Rav's.

"A setup, Scarlett," I snapped. I hauled out the tray underneath another safe deposit box and did my best not to slam my tools down on it. Breaking the thing off wouldn't solve anything. "Edoardo sent us in here to fall into a trap."

"Why?" Isaac's voice, thick with concern, hit my ear next. How had he gotten his mic turned on again?

I flung my hands in the air, as if some invisible force could answer the question for me. "Guess we're about to find out."

My gaze shifted back to Leigh. The note still hung in front of her, fear burning in her eyes. The door had been too easy. I'd known it. There should have been a timer on the door or some sort of backup.

Blueprints and an inside man, Edoardo?

I should have canceled.

"I... I'll read it out," Leigh stammered. "It's a letter from Edoardo. He... he says he's sorry. He says there's another box. We need to find... a notebook? And he's watching on a closed-circuit stream to be sure we do it."

A notebook. Another fucking box. The icy tendrils of betrayal slithered inside me. My movements became rough, unrefined, a stark contrast to the smooth precision I usually operated with.

"No." Scarlett cut through the tension, her tone unyielding. "We're recovery agents, not thieves. We're not stealing someone else's things just because he asks us to."

"No, not *just* because he asked," I growled, frustration bubbling inside of me. I slammed my fist against a metal box, the clang resounding through the otherwise silent vault. "There were photos with the letter."

"That doesn't matter," Scarlett said.

"They're of you." I inserted the company key into the new box and confirmed it worked. Now I just needed a client. "Brie, turn off Leigh's earpiece for a minute and, Scar, make sure Isaac is offline."

"What's going on?" asked Leigh from behind me.

Scarlett had been one of my best friends most of my life. She'd seen the real me years before even I could. "Done."

I bowed my head toward the wall, putting a hand to signal for Leigh to stay away. "It's two photos from the Albrecht house. Just after the car incident, when you grabbed the ring."

A long, slow breath seeped through my earpiece. That was as close as Scarlett got to rage on a job—other than on the very job I had photo evidence of in my pocket. "The answer's still no. We aren't thieves and we won't be blackmailed."

I clenched my hands around the filing box. "I'm not throwing you to the wolves."

Brie piped up. "I destroyed all the video footage. How are there photos?"

"They look like they were taken from the other side of the pool. One of the guests is involved."

"I'll figure something out. I always do." Scarlett sacrificed so much in her life for the rest of us. Not this time.

"I'm the one inside, so it's my call."

"Dec, no."

"You're not taking the fall, Scar."

"Declan Ramsay—"

"Don't make me take out my comms. I've made my decision. Now turn Leigh's earpiece back on." The safe deposit boxes stared back at me, silently judging, waiting. Waiting for my next move, waiting for me to crack under the pressure. I wouldn't. I couldn't. I had to keep it together for Scarlett. "Leigh, put Edoardo's box back in place and bring me your backup for the client key."

My phone buzzed on my arm. Edoardo's name glared up at me from the illuminated screen.

I yanked it out of its spot on my forearm and swiped the answer button, my words sharp, hot. "What the fuck, Edoardo?"

"I... I didn't want it to be this way, Declan." The bleak edge to Edoardo's voice grated on my nerves. "You're on camera, a closed-circuit stream."

"Yeah, I read that. Who gave you the photos?"

"I can hand copies of the photos to the authorities at any time." His Italian accent grew thicker with each shaky word.

"Where did you get them?"

"But I just need one thing from one box, Declan." Desperation dripped from each syllable. None of that mattered. "Per favore."

He'd betrayed us. And now, we were in a vault, playing a game we didn't sign up for. What would cause him to do that? To turn against a twenty-year friendship with a woman like Evelyn Reynolds?

My mind whirled, connecting the dots.

Of course.

"You lied about Martina visiting Florence after the break-in at your house, didn't you?"

Silence reigned for a beat. The team was no doubt on mute, letting this conversation play out while Brie and Will tried to patch into whatever separate feed Edoardo had running.

"Sì," said Edoardo, barely more than a whisper, more a sob. "They took her and said this was the price. Get you into the vault and get the notebook."

This was about more than a breach of contract, more than a setup. It was about the love of his life.

And whoever was behind it had Scarlett in their cross-hairs.

An icy dread crept into my veins. What the hell had we gotten ourselves into?

"Damn it, Edoardo, we're Reynolds *Recoveries*!" I practically yelled, unable to control myself. "We don't just recover things, we recover people, too. You know that! You should have told us the truth."

Silence. A deafening, uncomfortable quiet. Then, "What would you do, Declan? If it was your woman, and they threatened her life?"

I thought back to London, to Venice. How we'd moved heaven and earth to get Emmett back. We didn't turn to the authorities. Instead, we did what we had to, to avoid losing him. We acted on instinct, on loyalty. I couldn't afford to show that hand. Not now.

Scarlett hissed, "Tell him we aren't thieves."

Leigh was beside me in an instant, her wide, panicked eyes reflected in our work lights' harsh brilliance. I wanted to take her in my arms, tell her everything would be okay.

No time for sentiment, Dec. You're a professional. I'd chosen her for this job, and I needed to get control. And so did she.

I pressed the mute button on my phone and leaned closer. I held my whisper steady and tried to smile. Tried very hard not to spook her. "Listen to me. I need you to make a client key for box 5639. Fast."

Her mouth opened and closed, no words coming out.

"Leigh. Fast."

"But we pre-cut the wardings for Edoardo's box. We've got the master, but our backup won't work on this other box, no matter how fast I file it."

"Then you'll have to pick it."

"The warding is the same." Edoardo's voice grew progressively shakier with each word. "I had mine replaced to match."

My heart gave a lurch. He could hear us—of course he could, we were on camera. And he'd planned everything well in advance, hadn't he? I cupped Leigh's cheek through the face mask, her slight tremor under my fingertips doing nothing to calm my worry. "It matches, Leigh. You can do this. You're the best in the business, remember?"

My words were clear, precise, my tone meant to instill confidence, not fear. I was trying to channel my inner Scarlett, which seemed to work.

Leigh took my place in front of the filing box and started on the key, the determined set of her shoulders a small comfort in the unfolding chaos.

My mind raced, thoughts flitting between what was happening now and the worry of not having any backup keys. She could pick the new box, but the batteries on our suits would run out soon, and it must have been close to freezing in the vault.

Each tick of the clock, each stroke of the file against the key blank, all fed into the silent, gnawing dread growing inside me.

This was a risk, a gamble. But I had no choice. Someone was after Scarlett.

Edoardo's repeated apology came through the phone, but I didn't respond. I wasn't about to ease his conscience.

I scanned the vault, landing on the telltale glint of a hidden camera. I walked straight up to it, unmuted my phone, and spoke directly into the lens. "Who owns box 5639, Edoardo?"

"I can't... can't tell you." Edoardo's response was a feeble, panicked stutter. His inability to answer only fueled my determination.

"Jayce," I said, my gaze still fixed on the camera. "I need you to find out who owns box 5639."

"On it," came her response, brisk and efficient. "Brie, let's go offline so we don't mess with Leigh's concentration."

"Got it," said Brie. "Muting us from Dec and Leigh's feed."

Edoardo's pleas turned desperate, his voice cracking over the line. "I didn't know what else to do."

"Five minutes," said Will, calm and professional, despite the problem his words represented. "That's all the suit power we've got left."

I heard Leigh's sharp intake of breath at the news, her breathing shaky behind me as she worked faster on the key. She'd get it done before we lost the heat. It was far colder than I'd expected, but we'd have at least fifteen minutes before her fingers became too numb to complete the job. She didn't need nearly that much time.

"So what will happen, Edoardo," I asked, my tone dripping with a smug challenge, "if we trigger the alarm and bring the police in right now?"

"Leigh…" Scarlett was a soothing contrast to the spiraling tension. "Stay calm, sweetheart. It'll conserve your suit's power."

"Please, Declan." Edoardo coughed, hopefully choking on his guilt. "For Martina's sake."

A sound from Scarlett's end caught my attention. Isaac. He sounded worried, near panic. "I should've been the one in there. Not Leigh."

Before I could respond, Leigh came closer, cutting through the commotion. "Key's ready. What now?"

I turned to her, to her grim smile and quivering jaw. Thank god she was the one in here with me.

"Fine, we'll help, Edoardo. But on our terms." I took a deep breath, grounding myself before I continued. "We're going to get the notebook. Not because you tricked us, but because of what we once had. But after this, we're done. I don't want to ever see your number on my phone again. Understand?"

Silence hummed through the line as I waited for a response that didn't come.

"We'll arrange a hand-off in the morning, but Evelyn will hear about this. If there's a single whisper about us being blackmailed into thieving," I continued, channeling my best impression of Rav and his threatening growl, "nothing you own will be safe from us. We will blow every vault to pieces, crack every safe, and rip every damn painting off your walls. You hear me?"

I jabbed the End Call button and moved back to Leigh, taking the freshly filed key from her trembling hand. "You did a great job. Now stand in front of this camera for a minute."

She did as I asked, and I brushed her cheek with my thumb. Leigh was putting so much faith in me. And what was I doing? Toying with her freedom to save my friend.

I turned my attention to box 5639. The fresh client key slid into its slot. The keys twisted without effort, like they'd been milled by expert hands, rather than filed under stress. The lock released, and I pulled out the box, allowing Leigh to withdraw a small, worn notebook from the top of a pile of papers. Once the safe deposit box was back in its slot, I took the notebook and tucked it into my thigh pocket.

"Pack up, Leigh," I said. "We need to get out."

CHAPTER 14

LEIGH

Lights flashed in front of my eyes. *Calm down, Leigh. Breathe through it. Unclench your jaw.*

I was a criminal.

I'd snuck into a safe deposit box company, filed a key, and broke in. And stole something. What did it matter if it was just a small leather-bound notebook?

I was now a thief. Not in the I-stole-a-candy-bar way and my mom would be pissed, but in the on-foreign-soil-and-broke-a-ton-of-laws way. How many years would I rot in an Italian prison if Edoardo handed the video of us breaking into the second box to the police?

The video wouldn't show Declan opening the box, but it would show me filing the key.

What kind of lawyer could I afford here? The Reynolds crew seemed to have enough money they'd be out within seconds, but me?

What photos had I just risked my freedom for?

Rav steered the van through tiny streets and pulled onto faster ones, weaving a path away from Cassaforte Caetani and my horrible truth.

Isaac sat quietly beside him, fuming. When we'd made it back to the van without detection, he'd threatened Declan. Scarlett jumped to his defense and, when Isaac turned his threats on her, Rav suggested Isaac might be more comfortable at the bottom of the Tiber. They strapped him into the passenger seat next to Rav and we'd driven away.

I stared at my hands, still wearing the gloves which had helped me jump over the line from law-abiding locksmith to safe cracker.

What would my father say when he heard?

The van rumbled through Rome's sleepy streets, a deceptive calm after the storm. But inside my chest, my heart kept pounding, my stomach kept twisting. I'd walked willingly into the lion's den, and now the lions were baring their teeth. And the one lion I'd trusted—Declan—was sitting right beside me, as unreadable as ever.

Scarlett sat in the middle row ahead of Declan and me, having traded seats with Isaac. She was fury and finesse wrapped into a disturbingly calm package. She spoke in rapid-fire exchanges with Will and Brie, attempting to unravel Edoardo's double-cross.

"Find out who owns that box." Scarlett managed two laptops, a harsh authority underscoring her words. "And go through the videos from the house to find out who took the photos."

"We're on it." The rhythmic click of Brie's keyboard—or maybe it was Will's—sounded through the earpiece I still wore. "The access Jayce got me will hold, unless our inside guy is less inside than we thought. It'll just take time to sift through the layers."

"And the footage, Will?" Scarlett asked. "Any luck?"

"I picked up the wireless feed, but it was encrypted. I don't think Edoardo did this on his own."

Scarlett hissed out a curse, then took a deep breath, regaining her composure. "Can you break the encryption?"

"Does it matter?" asked Will. "I doubt he's only got one copy or that it would be on his physical person."

My attention shifted from Scarlett's tense conversation to Declan, his eyes locked onto the worn, leather-bound journal—the reason we were in this mess. He handed it forward a row to Jayce. "See what you can make of this."

Jayce took the notebook and nodded, leaning toward Scarlett's laptop and the light.

If I'd thought I had knots in my stomach on the way in, they were nothing compared to the fallout. I was neck-deep in a situation I couldn't reverse. Acid burned up my throat and I clenched my fists against my belly to stem the need to vomit.

I'd been so focused on the vault and the thrill of beating Declan at filing the keys, that I hadn't fully registered the reality of what we'd done. I was an accomplice in a theft. A pre-planned heist. This wasn't just a field test gone wrong.

This was a crime.

I stole a glance at Declan, stretching in his seat, watching over Scarlett's shoulder to her video chat with Will and Brie.

What could be in the notebook that was so important?

"It's turning into a pattern." Rav looked at Scarlett in the rear-view mirror. "First, the kidnapping. Now, this double-cross."

Scarlett didn't even look up from the laptop. "You think they're after us, not just using us?"

Rav shrugged one broad shoulder as he turned onto a narrow back street. "It's not a good look. Perhaps we should—"

"No," Scarlett snapped. "My mother stays out of this, Rav. Unless there's no other option."

"Scar," said Brie, "she knows you went in there. She'll be all over me in the morning. All she's been talking about this week is how she wants to call Edoardo and boast that her team beat his."

"Tell her..." Scarlett looked up at the roof of the van. "Tell her I want to give her the news and that I swore you to secrecy. Then I can do the avoiding."

Next to me, Declan shook his head. But there was a finality to Scarlett's words, a resolve that told me she'd go to any lengths to protect those she cared about, even if it was shielding her sister from an upset mother. A familiar prickling started behind my eyes. My nerves were on edge. That's all it was. It wasn't a reminder of how my stepmother would have reacted to this or how Isaac had tried protecting me.

The Reynolds crew had been targeted, and now Isaac and I were caught in the crossfire. I should have said no to joining them. Should have talked Isaac out of signing a contract with them, so we could have had our time to tour Rome.

Declan reached up and touched Scarlett's shoulder. "We can't stay at the hotel. Edoardo arranged it. He'll be expecting us there."

My heart skipped a beat.

Isaac spun in the passenger seat, a worry lining his face I'd never seen before. "He arranged ours, too. Leigh's and mine." His eyes practically bulged out of his head. "Do you think he'd come after us? He already has that fucking video. What are you going to do to protect Leigh?"

What *were* they going to do to protect me? Scarlett said I was on their team. Would they protect me?

I pressed my lips together, kept my face stoic, like I always did when Finn went on one of his rants. I had practice at masking things. "I have my go bag, so I don't need to go back to the hotel."

Declan slung his arm around my shoulders and leaned in, whispering for me alone. "We won't let anything happen to you or Isaac. I promise."

I looked up at him, his face close to mine, and something in his gaze made the panic fade away. He was normally cocky and self-assured, seeming to let every moment slide off him like nothing mattered. But there, huddled in the back of the van together, he was my lifeline.

"We'll sort out another hotel. Fake identities, the whole she-bang," he continued, his tone calm and reassuring.

"Do we need all that?" The question tumbled out of me before I could stop myself from revealing the overwhelming fear beating inside my brain.

He gave me a half-smile, the kind that held more determination than mirth. "It's a precaution. We like to stay proactive, keep one step ahead. It's how we've stayed out of trouble this long."

There it was again. The slip of information. They'd *stayed out of trouble*, like they weren't just security experts. Like he'd mentioned cracking safes instead of testing them.

I wanted details, but at the same time, his proximity offered a comfort that was as soothing as his words were unsettling. Even if he was a thief, he was looking out for me.

Without smothering.

I shifted closer to him, absorbing the calm his strong arm provided. His warm scent. His solid frame. I'd known this man all of a week, but here I was, snuggling up to him.

And then he kissed me.

Chaste, protective, right on my temple—kissed me.

I looked up at him, at his lips, his soft smile. The thought of more flared in my mind, wild and untamed. It was ridiculous. Here we were, in the midst of a crisis, and all I could think of was how his lips might feel against mine, how a kiss might help calm my racing heart.

About ripping the thermal suit off him, to see those muscles it highlighted.

My cheeks warmed at the thought, the blush hopefully hidden by the dim light in the van.

"We did well back there." Declan's tone was casual, but the praise was welcome. "You were amazing in the vault. Not gonna lie, I was a bit ticked you beat me to it. But I needed you to be that good."

"You were... you did really good, too." My words were clunky, inadequate, but they were all I had to offer in the moment, when I was imagining his hand brushing my belly on its way between my thighs.

His lips parted, gaze dropping to my mouth. He felt it, too. It wasn't just me.

As the silence between Declan and me stretched, Jayce cleared her throat, jolting me back to reality. She held the journal open over her shoulder from the middle row, with a photo I couldn't see clearly without more light. "It's full of notes about some ancient vault."

Vault? My heart leaped inside my chest, almost strong enough to tear my eyes from Declan.

Scarlett's attention left the laptop and she snatched the journal. "I know him."

"The guy in the photo?" asked Jayce.

"That's Dr. Daniel Weber."

Who?

Rav said, "The early Roman fresco specialist?"

"Look through it, Dec." Scarlett handed the journal over her shoulder to Declan, breaking the spell between the two of us. She looked down at the laptop again. "Brie, see if you can find anything that links Daniel Weber to that safe deposit box."

"On it," came her quick reply.

Declan unwound his arm from my shoulders slowly, then leafed through the notebook.

"Why would Edoardo want it?" I asked, my gaze lingering on the worn journal that had thrown our lives into chaos. "And why involve your team?"

"I don't know." He pulled out his phone, turning on the flashlight and shining it over the pages.

Dark pen scratches covered the surface, starting in a tight, precise hand, shifting into a hurried scrawl as the pages progressed. Maybe twenty pages had been filled, including images of golden spirals, the Fibonacci sequence, and three-dimensional sketches of Platonic solids.

"The vault's at the back," said Jayce.

Declan handed the phone to me so he could flip to the end. And there it was. The smiling photo of the man Scarlett recognized, surrounded by three others, all in front of a stone wall. Somewhere underground. Declan slid it away to reveal a two-page spread of diagrams. One large rectangular door with notes and arrows, pointing to the hinges, to some sort of cylinder at the top, and a listing of Zodiac signs decorating it.

I moved the photo so Declan's camera light illuminated it. "That's what they're standing in front of. Some sort of stone vault?"

"Take photos," said Scarlett, glancing over her shoulder. "We may need them."

Declan nodded and took the phone back, handing me the notebook so he could capture the contents.

"Why do you need photos?" asked Isaac, who'd been surprisingly quiet. Not so surprising, given Rav's glower whenever Isaac uttered a syllable. "You already know who you have to give it to."

Declan stopped taking images and frowned at him. "We may need them for leverage."

CHAPTER 15

DECLAN

How had things gone so wrong?

Rav pulled up behind the hotel, the early-morning air crackling with energy. Rome slept while we dashed out of the van to the back door.

"A more interesting evening than I was expecting," Jayce muttered, her eyes darting around.

The door creaked open, and Malcolm greeted us, his silhouette a welcome sight. "Emmett saw a car out front. Been there longer than it should."

I didn't like this. The car could be trouble. Could be police. Could be whoever was behind Edoardo's blackmail. Could be a damn coincidence.

Scarlett was first to the door, her arm brushing Malcolm's in a gesture more intimate than the situation called for.

Next came Leigh and Isaac, then me, Jayce, and Rav pulling up the rear.

"Move your ass, Dec," Jayce snapped, nudging me forward.

As I slipped by Malcolm, I took in his hard gaze. A flicker of a nod passed between us. I hadn't seen him on the job in London or Venice—I'd been on the other end of an earpiece from him several times—but finally seeing his work face made me feel better. The more competent people on this team, the safer we all were.

Scarlett hissed over her shoulder before she started up the stairs, "Rav, we still clear?"

Rav pulled the door closed, sealing us all in at the base of the stairs.

My skin prickled with a familiar unease. I glanced at Leigh, her face pale but resolute, the stubborn set to her jaw sending a twinge of admiration through me. This was what I'd signed on to when I joined Scar and her mother in their fool company. But Leigh? She'd been thrown into this mess and was hanging on better than I'd expected.

"Rav, you're with Isaac. Make sure he's quick." Scarlett's order was firm, clear, no room for argument. She started up the stairs first.

"I can help Leigh," Jayce piped up.

"No." Scarlett was half a floor ahead of us already. "Jayce, pack your shit and get outside to watch our exit. We need eyes out there."

A protective surge kicked in my chest. Before I could stop myself, the words flew out of me. "I'll grab Leigh as soon as I'm packed."

Leigh, already detouring onto the second floor, paused. "Room 204." Her jaw had clearly been a disguise because her voice shook slightly.

Isaac scowled. "We don't need a chaperone. I can look after Leigh."

Scarlett halted at the stairwell turn to the third floor and leaned over the railing. "Go solo if you want, Isaac. But I told you from the get-go you do things our way or you do them alone."

Isaac's jaw clenched, a flash of annoyance crossing his face, but he conceded. "Fine."

Leigh and Isaac broke from us to the second floor, while the Reynolds team spread out on the third. As I hurried to my room, I couldn't shake the look in Leigh's eyes.

Let alone the look when I'd kissed her temple.

In my room, I moved with practiced efficiency. Years prepared to bolt at the slightest moment—that was how Scarlett planned things. I'd learned to live out of one bag, essentials only. A few clothes, the tools of my trade, everything packed with purpose.

The worry in Leigh's eyes, the guilt—I'd almost undone her seatbelt and pulled her into my lap. I could have wrapped my arms around her and held her there. Whether it would have been for her or for me wouldn't have mattered. I would have had her warm breath at my neck.

My fingers moved with a mind of their own—go bag was in the van, grabbed the toiletries bag from the bathroom, stuffed errant items into the duffel. I zipped the bag, swung it over my shoulder. Looked around the room one last time. Good to go.

This was supposed to be a simple job. Safe. But I packed most things every morning out of habit. I was glad for it now.

I left my room at a near-dash, the first one out. Down the hall, down the stairs, to Leigh's room. A nagging worry gnawed at my gut. We didn't have time for the delays that came with civilians. But I wouldn't leave her there. She'd come through for me with the keys, and I owed her.

Leigh's door swung open, her eyes wide, breath coming in short, sharp bursts.

Fuck. She must have been in shock in the van, because this was not the same control she'd shown back there.

"Hey," I whispered, grabbing her wrists as we let the door close behind me. Her pulse thudded against my fingers, wild and unsteady. In that moment, with her chest heaving, I thought about pulling her toward me again. Doing something stupid, like hugging her.

This still wasn't the time.

"You were perfect in the vault, Leigh." In my mind's eye, I saw her hand-filing the keys with surgical precision, a stark contrast to my own pathetic attempt. The memory sparked a jolt of embarrassment. She'd been faster, better. Nudging me with her hip as a taunt. "I need you to be perfect a bit longer. Just breathe."

Her eyes searched mine. "You were angry in there."

"We need to focus and pack," I said, tightening my grip on her wrists. "Once we're at the new hotel, then we can fall apart. But we do this now. We get out, we stay safe."

"And then?" she asked, her whole body trembling.

"And then we figure everything out." Hopefully, we'd figure it out. If nothing else, we'd have next steps. "And we'll do it together. You're on this team until we're safe. You got me?"

She nodded and flew into motion, tossing things haphazardly from drawers into a hard-sided suitcase.

"Do you need any help?" I asked, my gaze falling to her cluttered bed, half her clothes missing their mark.

"Just the books." She pointed at a stack on her bedside table, her finger slowly pulling back, as though unsure about something. Then, her tone changed, something sharper creeping in. "You're really giving the notebook to Edoardo?"

As I grabbed the pile of books, the titles caught my eye. *The Fortress Within: A History of Safes and Vaults* by Thomas W. St. John. *Vaults of the World: Noteworthy Safes from History* by Josephine Hartley. "These your idea of light reading?"

She hesitated for a breath, cheeks flushed, and a hint of unease passed over her face. "Sort of."

"Is this where you get your design ideas?" I was supposed to be helping her hurry—the team would be waiting. "Like the stink gas and the dye?"

"They're inspiration." She flipped the lid over on her suitcase and started stuffing loose pieces out of the way of the zipper. "Did you know the Svalbard Seed Vault is designed to withstand a nuclear missile strike? And Leonardo da Vinci had some sketches related to vault doors in his Vitruvian Man—" She stopped abruptly, her cheeks turning a deeper shade of red. "Sorry, I ramble when I'm nervous."

Puzzle pieces. Clicking into place. She shut down around Isaac. She hid her talent so it wouldn't make anyone feel bad. Was this part of it? Her passion, buried under layers of fear and self-doubt? Finally revealed in this ultra-shitty moment?

"We better go," I said, tucking her books into my bag, the question lingering in the back of my mind. A puzzle for later. For now, we had to get out.

She was still in her thermal suit, the plainclothes sitting in her go bag inside the van. Every inch of her was on display, and what a display it was.

Calm, cool, collected, Dec. I was the guy who talked to vaults, who was more at home with schematics and cogs and wheels. Not the Casanova like Emmett. Maybe I should've let Rav or Jayce take care of Leigh. They'd do it without a second thought, without the tangled mess of emotions that threatened to derail my focus. But she needed someone, and I'd stepped up. Because I wanted to. Needed to.

"Ready?" I asked, shouldering her backpack over my duffel and opening her door.

Bag in hand, Leigh paused. "I should check on Isaac—"

"No," I cut her off. "We need to go. You trust me, right?"

She just blinked at me.

I didn't give her a chance to answer, a pang of fear at the response I'd get. "You can trust Rav to get Isaac moving. He knows what he's doing."

She crept into the hallway ahead of me, aiming for the back stairs. "Does this happen a lot?"

I thought about the job a couple of weeks ago in London. The chaos. The close calls. The guy with the gun. She didn't need to know any of that.

"We're professionals, Leigh." I channeled my inner Scarlett. "We've got this under control. Let's just get out safely, okay?"

She nodded, and we made a turn down the too-bright hallway to the stairs. The sudden ding of the elevator shot through the silence like a gunshot. It was four in the morning. Who'd be in the elevator?

Adrenaline spiked in my veins, instincts kicking into overdrive.

"Shit," I muttered, yanking Leigh to the side, pressing us both against the wall. If it was danger, I'd protect her. If it was someone with questions, we'd be a couple making out in the wee hours.

A man stepped out of the elevator, his face obscured by a sweatshirt hood. He didn't spare a glance our way, walked past us, fumbling with a keycard. I studied him, my senses on high alert. A guest, nothing more. From the smell of him, he'd been out drinking all night.

Once he'd disappeared into his room, I turned back to Leigh. "Just a guest. He's not a danger to us."

Leigh was pale, her breath coming in shallow gasps. "I've never been... this... before." She pressed a palm to her forehead.

Panic splintered through me. The headaches Isaac was always asking about. We didn't have time for this. "Are you okay?"

"Fine." She looked up at me, her pinched cheeks a mix of fear and embarrassment. "I'm not usually like this."

"Oh, you mean, being brave and facing danger head-on?" I quipped, feigning ignorance, hoping that teasing her might help break some of whatever was going on in her brain. "Yeah, I can totally see that."

Her eyes widened a fraction, but I saw the hint of a smile. We held each other's gaze for a beat, my body still pressed against her, unspoken words hanging heavy in the silence. It was just us, and the world outside had ceased to exist.

The logical part of my brain said run for the stairs, but every other part said *Kiss the fear out of her.*

Rav's voice came from down the hall. "Thanks for waiting, lovebirds, but we're good now." He headed in our direction with Isaac in tow.

I stiffened. "We weren't—"

But Rav had already brushed past us, the hint of a smirk on his face.

"Come on," I said, another moment lost. "Let's get to the van."

Chapter 16
Declan

St. Peter's Square looked like an oil painting under the dawn's light. Scarlett, Rav, and I lingered behind the massive pillars at its periphery, their shadows long in the early morning. A sweeper here, a trash collector there, their shifts over as the blush of sunrise arrived. A handful of tourists—too few for comfort, their wide-eyed gazes pinballing between the square's marvels and us.

The world was still half-asleep, and all I wanted was a pillow. The night had been too long and we hadn't slept since running from the hotel.

I strained to pick out movement in the shadows at the edges of the square. Anyone could hide there, from Edoardo's goons to the morning breeze playing tricks on my mind.

Scarlett's sigh was soft, blending in with the distant sound of traffic. "Never thought I'd get homesick in the middle of a job."

Malcolm, on the other side of the square, said over our earpiece, "Soon enough, honey lips. We'll be out of here once this is over."

A chuckle caught in my throat. Scarlett and Malcolm were the last people I needed reminding me of their couple status. Every knowing glance, every time Malcolm's hand found the small of her back. His plan was to move in with Emmett when we got home, but I had a feeling Emmett's spare bedroom would remain just as empty as it was right now.

"Just a few more hours and we're out of here." Rav, his gaze as sharp as his words, scanned the scene with binoculars. "I'll be happier when you're home, and we can deal with these photos."

"Don't worry about me. The photos aren't an issue. They only show my hand near the ring and don't provide evidence I took it. Besides, it didn't belong to the Albrechts, so what legal ground do they have to stand on?"

I checked Scarlett's shoes, watching for the telltale sign she was scrunching her toes, releasing her emotions in the way her mother had taught her. There it was. She was evading the truth. She was at least as worried as we were.

"When I get my hands on whoever thought they could black-mail you..." Rav trailed off.

"Get in line, Rav," said Malcolm.

"Focus, guys," said Scarlett.

I checked the square's edge again, the sneaky shadows playing hide-and-seek.

God, how had I let things go so far to shit?

Leigh.

Damn, she'd been on my mind since we stashed her in a room at the hotel, safe with Jayce. I'd looked into her eyes, saw the spark of fear tempered with trust, and it made me feel more protective than I'd been in forever. I would've stayed with her myself, watched over her as she finally slept after the long night.

That would've been crossing a line I wasn't sure I was ready to step over. Or maybe it was stepping close to a line I wanted to cross.

Jayce was more than capable.

It was ridiculous. There she was, the woman who'd literally designed safes and vaults to keep men like me out. She shared a passion with me, one I'd never found in anyone else. But she was the other side of my coin; the builder versus the cracker.

I'd spent a decade perfecting the art of getting into places I shouldn't be able to, and she'd spent hers perfecting the art of preventing it. But I wasn't a thief. I didn't take what didn't deserve taking. I returned what was wrongfully taken.

Sometimes, we blurred right and wrong, but the ends always justified the means.

Bloody hell, why couldn't I have met a nice private eye like Scarlett had? Someone who walked the line like our team did. Jayce and I worked together so much we could have watched each other's backs. Except I'd never been attracted to the diminutive ball of energy.

No, instead I dated women like Daphne, who had a love affair with the dollar figures my family and profession brought. Until it wasn't enough. Until we got the jet and my frequent flyer miles vanished. Until the way I cleaned the kitchen became a personal affront.

Daphne. Not just hand-selected by my mother, but a mirror of my parents. It was never perfect enough. I was never perfect enough.

Leigh was a different kind of perfect. A genius at the workbench. The way she handled her tools reminded me of an artist in their studio. I couldn't match her speed, her precision. Another failure to chalk up.

Like trusting Edoardo, and walking the entire team into this mess.

"Thanks for grabbing the notebook." Scarlett had seen every scraped knee and stolen kiss since I was twelve. She knew I was beating myself up. Was she trying to make me feel better, or did she genuinely appreciate it? Did that make things better or worse?

"Any word from Brie yet?" I asked, clumsily changing the topic.

Scarlett nodded, scanning the square. "Talked to her earlier. She's almost cracked the encryption on the client database. We should know later today."

Malcolm said, "Got eyes on Edoardo. He's coming through the middle, heading for the obelisk."

The obelisk, an exposed meeting place smack in the center of the grandeur of St. Peter's Square. At dawn, with the first tourists and the departing cleaners, the square was wide open, an escape route at every turn.

Scarlett said, "See anyone else suspicious?"

"He seems to be alone," said Malcolm.

"Same from our side of the square," said Rav. "You two go meet him. We'll keep an eye out."

I stayed beside Scarlett, matching her long stride. I wore my easy grin, the casual mask that gave away nothing, learned from years of watching Scarlett. She could blend into the world around her like one of the city's stone-cold statues.

Seeing Edoardo's hunched figure, I couldn't help but bark out, "Look who it is, Judas himself."

St. Peter, strike me down.

Edoardo looked up at my words, his face pale in the dawn light, lines of worry etched deep into his features. His eyes were shadowed, body language screaming fatigue and desperation. The sight of him, of my friend, twisted my gut.

How the hell hadn't I noticed earlier? The strained smiles when I'd been tinkering with his home safes, the worried glances over dinner. Even during the tour of Cassaforte, it had been there all along. I'd been too damn blind to see it.

Cursing myself for lowering my guard and leaving him the opening he stole, I steeled myself for the confrontation.

"Mi dispiace, Declan." Edoardo's apology spilled out as I handed him the notebook. "I'm so sorry."

Just as I was processing his words, Malcolm said, "Got a shadowy figure hanging around the pillars. Rav, he's by the fountain north of the obelisk."

"I'm moving in that direction."

My pulse spiked, but I kept my face impassive. Scarlett's eyes flickered, the only sign she'd heard the message.

Edoardo was still talking, desperation leaking from every pore. "The tape... I've destroyed it. And the guard... he didn't see you, did he?"

"No faces," Scarlett said.

Edoardo's sigh of relief was more visible in his shoulders than audible. It didn't feel like a trap anymore. It felt like he'd been broken.

It dulled the rage simmering inside me more than it should have.

Rav cut in over the earpiece again. "Shadowy figure is no threat. Just a lovesick guy trying to propose at dawn. She said yes, by the way."

The absurd normalcy of it all brought an involuntary smirk to my face.

"You can expect a call from my mother." Scarlett's words were sharp. "She won't take kindly to this, Edoardo. You know that."

A new pallor washed over his face. Even I shivered at the thought of Evelyn's reaction.

"Per favore." Edoardo clutched his hands together, as if in prayer. "Let me make the call. I want to do it myself. It's better to seek forgiveness than to hide."

"I'll give you one day. No more."

As Edoardo nodded, the severity of his betrayal sank in deeper. His choice to face Evelyn's wrath was as much a testament to his regret as the desperation in his eyes was.

"We're done here." Scarlett turned and left.

I should have been in lockstep with her. Instead, my foolish words tumbled out. "When are you meeting the kidnappers?"

He waved his hand dismissively, stuffing the notebook into his jacket pocket.

"I said, when, Edoardo?"

His eyes fluttered closed. "Midnight. By the bridge to Isola Tiberina."

"I'm sorry it came to this." I meant it, even if a part of me was still reeling from his betrayal. "I hope Martina's all right."

His tears reflected the sun rising over the columns. "Grazie. So do I."

I caught up to Scarlett, almost back in the shadows at Rav's side already. "Are we going tonight? Find out who's behind the blackmail?"

Rav grunted in agreement. The next step in keeping Scarlett safe was knowing who we were up against.

"Good plan." Scarlett's shoulders raised with a deep breath, her face unreadable. "We return to the hotel, get some rest, and at midnight, we'll be at the exchange."

Chapter 17

Leigh

Not only was I a thief, but I was now sleeping in the same room as another thief.

If I could sleep.

"I can hear you breathing." Jayce was motionless under the blankets of her bed, a sleep mask secured over her eyes. "I thought I showed you how to control that?"

Daylight streamed in around the pale curtains. Their meet had been at dawn. "Do you think everything went okay with Edoardo?"

She snorted a laugh. "Declan's fine."

"I meant all of them." I definitely wasn't worried about Declan. And I wasn't thinking about the way he'd ogled my books. Or how he'd held me with those big, strong hands, and told me to keep it together. Or the way he'd looked at me in the van. The same heat flared between my thighs that did every time I imagined his hazel eyes, twinkling with an unshakable amount of confidence.

The room sank back into silence. But sleep continued to elude me. "What if—"

Jayce bolted upright, sleep mask coming off in one swift motion. She swung her legs over the side of the bed, rubbing her face with a sigh. "Enough talking. Let's get some breakfast."

"Breakfast?" I eased up on my elbows, trying to play it cool. "Is that what you want?"

"Leigh…" Jayce's dark gaze fastened onto me. "Have you ever made a decision for yourself?"

"What?"

Something about Jayce's directness threw me. I was more accustomed to people who said one thing and meant another. Said something nice and meant something… not nice.

Jayce lifted her brows and crossed her arms. "It's a simple question. It seems you always do what others tell you. And if no one gives you a command, you're asking what they want. You deflect. Do you ever make your own choices?"

I swallowed hard. I made decisions.

Didn't I?

Memories of Finn flipped through my brain. He'd constantly overridden my choices, my wants, until everything I did was at his direction. Then there was Isaac, who'd insisted I wait for him to show me Rome, turning my solo sightseeing aspirations into shared expeditions that never came.

"Yeah," I muttered, tracing the pattern on the blanket. "I just have a lot of people who look out for me."

"And that means you should erase everything you want?"

"It would be rude to make them worry. They care about me. I'm lucky to have them." It was easier to go with the flow.

Jayce didn't answer right away. She just watched me, her gaze holding an unreadable expression. She wasn't judging me; it was more like she was trying to understand, trying to see the world through my eyes. "Do you think that's what's happening now, Leigh? You think I'm being forced to look out for you?"

"Scarlett told you to stay with me, even though Isaac said he could—"

"And you think you're making me do something I don't want to do?"

"I'm forcing you to sit here, to talk, when you want to..." I trailed off, unsure. Did she want to sleep? To eat? I found myself back at square one. "What do you want, Jayce?"

She sighed, sliding off the bed. "I want breakfast, Leigh."

Relief flooded me. A decision made. I pushed myself out of bed and grabbed some clothes.

As Jayce dressed, she said, "I want to eat, Leigh. So we're eating. I'd also love some sleep, but you're obviously still a ball of nerves and we have more to discuss. Plus, breakfast is being served downstairs."

My body was exhausted, but she was right. There was no way my brain would calm down anytime soon.

"Let's get one thing clear, though. I'm not being forced to do anything. I like you. And I'd say you're better off spending your time with someone as awesome as me, rather than being cooped up with your brother's misery." She pulled on her shoes and glanced at me with a smirk. "But hey, if you're looking for a different bodyguard, there's always Declan. I bet he'd be more than happy to guard your body."

I had to keep thoughts about Declan firmly planted in the back of my brain—where they belonged. "Do you think Edoardo went to the police? Could we end up in jail?"

Jayce and I walked through the hallway, taking the stairs winding around the central elevator.

Nearing the main floor, I blurted out, "Do you think the notebook's owner will come after me? Would I be safer at home in Boston?"

Jayce paused on the bottom step, turning to look up at me. "If they do, Boston won't be any safer than Rome. You're under Scarlett's protection here. You're as safe as you can be, anywhere."

"But what about..." I bit down on my lip. "What about the kidnapping Rav mentioned? Emmett, I think? If they got to him—"

"You're a sharp one." Jayce resumed her walk to the lobby. "Some bad guys took Emmett a few weeks back, but he was alone when it happened." She waved a dismissive hand. "Well, not exactly alone. He was with Malcolm. But Malcolm wasn't part of the team then, and I probably shouldn't be spilling those details."

Only a few weeks ago? Malcolm seemed to fit in with the crew better than that.

She waggled a finger in my direction as I came into step beside her. "My point is, the team hopped a flight to London and then to Venice at a moment's notice to get Emmett back. That's the kind of crew you're with now. So yes, you're safer here with us."

Reynolds Recoveries was a tight-knit group, tighter even than Barton Safes. We used to have that kind of closeness at work. Over the last few months, my relationship with Isaac had soured. The longer I was with Finn, the more every relationship in my life had collapsed.

Maybe I *was* safer with the Reynolds team. But the question remained. Safer from what? And for how long?

We stepped into the breakfast room, the aroma of freshly baked pastries and brewing coffee wafting toward us. It was a small, cozy space, scattered with little tables and metal chairs under the soft glow of overhead lights. From one end, light spilled in from outside, while a counter lined the opposite wall, a variety of sweets set out waiting for us.

Thoughts of Isaac flickered in my mind. He'd told me he had meetings later in the day, so he'd be sleeping all morning. I wouldn't get to see any of the city. More stress knocked around my chest. Would I even be safe touring the city with *him*?

Jayce and I loaded our plates with food and poured ourselves steaming cups of coffee. We settled at a corner table, Jayce's plate overladen with easily twice the amount I'd taken.

"You eat a lot." I clamped a hand over my mouth. Had I really said that out loud? She was already rubbing off on me.

"Fast metabolism." Jayce shrugged, tearing a pastry in half. "Now tell me—if you could go anywhere in Rome, where would you go first?"

I nearly choked on my apple cake. It was as if she'd read my mind. I chased down my bite with a sip of coffee, its intense bitterness a perfect counterpoint to the sweet cake and its powdered sugar. "That's a tough one. There's so much to see, and I've never been here before."

"Pick something at random, then." Her unspoken challenge was clear: Make a decision.

I took another bite of my apple cake, chewing as I weighed the options. "I think I'd want to go to the Vatican Museum first.

And the Sistine Chapel, of course. Probably the Catacombs after that."

Jayce grinned, leaning in closer. "Scarlett has a few disguises with her. I'm sure she'd let you borrow one. And you could go out with someone from the team. You know, as a safety precaution."

My heart fluttered at the thought. I could actually *see* Rome, not just *be in* Rome. And I could do it with— I pushed the thought away before it could fully form. But it was too late. The idea had taken root, and I smiled at the thought of visiting it all with Declan.

"And if you don't do that, what else are you going to do all day?" Jayce shriveled her nose, a playful glint in her eyes. "Sit around in the room and read?"

I shrugged. "Other than the work I did for Edoardo and with your team, that's mostly what I've been doing."

Jayce rolled her eyes, letting her head fall back dramatically. "Girl, it is time you did something you want to do." She straightened, her gaze boring into me with a fierce determination. "When Scarlett and the others get back, I'm talking to her. You and I are going to see Rome."

Chapter 18

Declan

In the dim light of the overhead bulbs in the Roman Cat-acombs, Leigh's disguise screamed like a neon sign. Scarlett's flaming-red curly wig clung to her head, a stark contrast against the pitted stone and mossy scent of the ancient labyrinth. Thick, black-framed faux glasses perched on her nose, amping the disguise up to costume level.

When Scarlett wore it, it was convincing.

But Leigh? It was almost comical.

Quiet, thoughtful, and as much a puzzle as any safe I'd cracked. She hadn't needed the disguise—I wasn't wearing one—but Jayce had recommended it. Maybe it helped get Leigh out of her shell, pretending to be someone she wasn't. Maybe it helped her stand up to her overbearing brother and wake him before his meetings, announcing her intention.

Although that meant he'd joined us.

Either way, she'd left the hotel for some sightseeing.

Our tour guide, a stick-thin man with spectacles as old as the Catacombs, droned on about the history of the underground crypt. His nasal Italian-accented voice carried, as though he'd been born to the theater. The rest of the group hung on his every word, consumed by the tales of early Christians and papal intrigue. We, however, lingered at the back, keeping our heads down and volume low.

Jayce walked next to Leigh, as though they were now besties. Despite the protective layer of her own disguise—she'd insisted on wearing Scarlett's short blond bob—the former gymnast looked ready to pounce at any second.

I found myself stuck between watching Leigh and the dank confines of our subterranean tour. Even in her loose jeans and nondescript black T-shirt, she had an understated beauty that would give any Roman goddess a run for her money.

Her head whipped back and forth as she absorbed everything, sending the curls bouncing around her. The catacombs, by contrast, were grim, oppressive, their cold stone and shadowy alcoves whispering of death and long-forgotten secrets.

A part of me chuckled. The other part, the part that lived for the thrill of danger, of doing what I did best, felt an uncharacteristic twinge of fear. She deserved better than to be caught in this mess. But as I followed her and Jayce through the humid catacombs, I couldn't deny a selfish spark of joy at being here with her.

"Why the Catacombs?" I asked Jayce as we descended farther into the labyrinthine tunnels.

"The Sistine Chapel was a no-go," Jayce said over her shoulder. "Too many open spaces. Too many people. Scarlett was a real party pooper on this one."

I grunted. Scarlett had been insistent. Low profile. Avoid crowds. It was just our damn luck Leigh wanted to see Rome's most popular tourist sites.

"And Rav?" I asked. "He normally gets the bodyguard duties."

Jayce craned her head around and waggled her eyebrows. "Scarlett needed him for something else."

I snorted, crossing my arms over my chest. "I'm second choice then?"

Jayce's smirk widened into a grin. "Third, actually. But don't worry, pretty boy. You're doing a stellar job."

My eyes shot back to Leigh. She'd said I was more than a pretty face after the original recon job. Jayce had found her new favorite word for me.

Before I could ask who the second choice was, as though it mattered, Isaac cut through my thoughts. "Did you know the Christians used to hide down here from Roman persecution?"

He'd been chatting me up since we left the hotel, asking dozens of questions I couldn't answer about my job. It was tiresome, competing with the tour guide's monotonous drone. The man didn't take any of my hints.

"That's not true, Isaac." Leigh turned around, the vibrancy of her wig catching the dim light, and a spark of energy flared in her eyes. The kind of energy she had after our first visit to Cassaforte. Her gaze met mine for a fleeting moment, setting off a strange excitement within me. "Why wouldn't the Romans search down here if they were looking for someone? They knew the Christians buried their dead here."

Isaac just stared at her as we continued through the tight, damp tunnel, his brow furrowed. Obviously, he wasn't used to being challenged, especially by his sister.

"Where'd you hear that, Leigh?" I asked.

Isaac let out a snort. "She's always got her nose in a book."

Leigh's shoulders stiffened. She didn't reply, but her pace quickened. Annoyance curled within me, directed at Isaac. I had a brief, vivid fantasy of shoving him into one of the catacomb's burial niches and bricking it up. The thought drew an involuntary chuckle out of me.

Since that wasn't really an option, I had a second: Flirt with Leigh. It would have had its benefits. One, I'd get to flirt with a gorgeous, intelligent woman. And two, it'd tick Isaac off. Win-win in my book.

Instead of diving headfirst into that, I picked option three and shot back at Isaac. "You should respect a woman with an inquisitive brain. It's an attractive quality."

Jayce's tone dripped with sarcasm. "As long as they're not too inquisitive, right, Declan?"

I nudged her playfully, giving her a knowing grin. "Says the woman who can't keep her hands off other people's shiny things."

Jayce let out a snort of laughter. "Five years, bud."

Five years sober, she'd say. Sober from stealing for profit or for the thrill alone. Working for us had turned her sad life around.

As we followed the tour guide deeper into the catacombs, I let my gaze wander back to Leigh. She was walking ahead, the faux red curls bobbing with each step. Isaac's petty quip had dampened too much of her spirit.

Leigh glanced over her shoulder, a soft smile gracing her lips as our eyes met. Then she turned away, leaving me with the remnants of that fleeting connection.

Bolstered, I couldn't resist another jab at Isaac. "In fact, Isaac, I'd say your sister's book smarts make your average safe look like a jack-in-the-box."

Isaac glared at me, but before he could retort, Leigh came to his defense.

"My brother's skills are just as impressive as mine. We're a team." Leigh stood up for her brother, as she should, and I'd put her in that position.

That's not how to win a woman over, Declan. Failed again.

We fell into silence, the hushed delivery of the tour guide magnifying his level of theater. "No one," he said in a stage whisper, "has ever fully mapped the Catacombs of Rome. And just recently, an earthquake opened up a new passage."

The guide led us through a narrow tunnel, his flashlight casting long, grotesque shadows against the walls. The air grew denser, colder, as he continued his tale.

"At the end of this new corridor, scientists discovered a door." His voice dropped even lower. "A mysterious door that no one has been able to open. The door is marked with symbols of the zodiac and ancient frescoes of keys and animals surround it."

Murmurs rippled through the group. I felt a thrill rush through me, the allure of the unsolvable, the need to learn the unknown. Leigh seemed to sense it too, her head perking up, walking faster to close the distance with the guide.

What was the door no one could open? And if I stood in front of it, how long before she opened up to reveal her secrets to me?

"Declan," Isaac began, his tone suggesting a forthcoming conversation.

"Isaac, be quiet," Leigh snapped. "I want to hear this."

His head jerked back, his lip curling. I'd only known them for a week, but Isaac's stunned expression confirmed my guess—she never talked to him like that.

The guide paused, shining his flashlight down a narrow side tunnel, the light vanishing into the distance. "They say the markings are reminiscent of Leonardo da Vinci's engineering sketches, including a series of three-dimensional shapes."

At that, Leigh froze. The information jolted through me, so strong I lost track of my movements and bumped into her. I instinctively reached out, gripping her shoulders. A soft scent wafted up from her, a mix of pears from her hidden hair and something spicier, making my pulse quicken. Her body stiffened under my touch.

Had Isaac's words or my unexpected contact unsettled her? I should have let go, but my focus drifted down the corridor, and she was an anchor for my curiosity. The tour group wandered on ahead, their chatter buzzing through the ancient tunnels.

Leigh pivoted so swiftly she remained nestled within my grip. "That sounds like... doesn't it sound like one of the sketches from the notebook?"

Isaac nodded, staring down the corridor with us. "You're right. It does."

"Yeah." I released her and took a step backward.

Leigh stepped forward, maintaining the gap between us. She ignored Isaac's agreement, her attention solely on me. "Do you have the photos you took?"

"I've got a copy." Jayce pulled out her phone and started scrolling through an array of pictures. She handed it to Leigh, who accepted it and held it so I could see.

Leigh swiftly navigated through the images, stopping at one in particular. She zoomed in on the screen, enlarging it before passing the phone to me. As she moved closer, she gripped my forearm. My brain was a mess, sizzling with the energy from her touch and the mystery in front of me.

The image was clear, the sketch detailed. It was the two-page spread from the back of the notebook. I'd barely registered it at four this morning, but now? It depicted a series of concentric screws, several intricate drawings of twelve-sided shapes, and a rectangle that had to be the vault door. We studied it, her breath warming my cheek.

"Could it be the door he was talking about?" Leigh's eyes lit up, excitement washing over her. "The photo of that guy Scarlett and Rav knew—the fresco expert—looked like it could have been taken inside the catacombs."

"Daniel Weber," I said. "We should call him. See if he knows anything about this."

Isaac weaseled his way in, flicking through photos on Jayce's phone before I pulled it away. Undeterred, he pointed at the phone, which showed a sketch of an eagle. "I didn't get to study the notebook last night, but I remember seeing a map? Maybe it leads to the door?"

I scrolled through the pictures, passing by several shots of Jayce's extravagant meals, and found an image displaying a jumble of lines. "Here, look at this," I murmured, holding the image beside the tour brochure that Isaac clutched.

Isaac squinted, studying both images. "They're similar."

"We've fallen behind the group." Jayce huffed out a breath, signaling she was about to make a ridiculous request. "Why don't we go find that door now?"

My eyes fell to Leigh, her own ablaze with sheer wonder. Part of me ached to chase this new lead with her, to dive headfirst into this mystery. But Jayce was the daredevil of our lot, and Scarlett tasked me with keeping Leigh safe.

Isaac was supposed to be on my radar too, but Leigh was my priority.

I shook my head, painting on my casual smile. "We could easily get lost down here without someone monitoring our progress. And who knows if this map is even accurate?"

Jayce didn't buy it. No matter how hard I tried to mask the flutter in my chest, she knew it was there. She knew I was struggling. The thrill of an unsolved puzzle was a siren call. A vault concealed within the catacombs, undisturbed for centuries? What could she be guarding? Was she made fully of stone? Or was there metal at her core? Wood?

As my heart throbbed with unspent curiosity, I handed the phone back to Jayce. "We better catch up with the group. We don't want to miss out on the rest of the tour."

But in my mind, the gears were already turning. As soon as we surfaced, we'd reach out to Daniel Weber and find out what he knew. There was more to this than the blackmail and the notebook, and I was going to uncover exactly what it was.

CHAPTER 19
DECLAN

I leaned against a sun-drenched wall, a swirl of tart lemon gelato on my tongue. Around me, Rome hummed, a symphony of chatter and street musicians. The excitement of the city held little sway.

My brain was still far below.

The catacombs, with their dark, hidden vault, nagged at me. This wasn't just any vault. Inscriptions like da Vinci's? Da Vinci himself? What would he have been hiding that he'd have to go all the way down there for?

We only had one photo of the vault, which was more about the men in front of her than on her quiet beauty. This wasn't about the thrill of cracking her open, it was about understanding her, appreciating her complexities. And the artistry of Leonardo da Vinci.

I savored another spoonful of gelato, letting the icy sweetness cool the churn of my thoughts. Going back wasn't just a matter of curiosity, it was a risk. Doing it right would include Scarlett's buy-in, earpieces, monitoring from the surface, GPS coordinates to ensure we didn't get lost. How cold would it be in the depths? Who were the scientists working on her, other than Daniel Weber? Could we contract with them?

Going after her alone would be a gamble. A danger. But dammit, if she wasn't calling me.

"You've got it bad." Jayce tapped my leg with her foot, cutting into my thoughts. She inclined her head toward Leigh.

Leigh and Isaac stood a few steps away, engaged in their own debate over ice cream versus gelato.

"You've got me wrong for once."

Jayce waggled her eyebrows at me again. "Prefer her as a redhead?"

Before I could shoot back, Isaac sauntered over. "You're brooding," he announced, as if he knew me.

"Just keeping my eyes open." That part was half true. If Scarlett heard we were wandering the streets eating, she'd demand we run back to the hotel. This was hardly the low-profile order she'd given me.

Isaac stopped beside me. "Let me guess, the vault?"

Maybe he *did* understand a little about me. "Among other things."

"I'm curious, too." He pointed his small spoon at me. "The photograph didn't show a dial or locking mechanism."

"Could be a key somewhere." If there was a key that unlocked her, there'd be a way to bypass it. Pick it, imprint it, fly Will out to Rome to create some tool that would scan the inside and reveal all the beauty's mysteries.

"It's like an *Indiana Jones* movie." Isaac widened his eyes and gave me a toothy grin. "Did you ever want to do that sort of work when you were little?"

Stealing ancient relics to hand over to a museum? I held my laugh at bay. That was precisely what we'd done in London.

Leigh drifted closer, her brown eyes glinting behind the over-sized glasses. "Could I see the photos..." She trailed off, hesitation lining her face.

Isaac gave her a look, irritation—at her interruption?—clear from his tight lips.

"Yeah," I said, fishing my phone out.

Her gaze dropped, a pensive furrow between her brows. But I didn't push. Instead, I opened the gallery, the images of the notebook unfolding on the screen. The vault stared back at me. I flipped past a few incidental shots until I reached the ones that mattered.

The gelato in my cup was melting, but the vault door held more interest. It was a harsh contrast to the sleek Eisenhart model we'd bested at Cassaforte. And there wouldn't be any specs on the dark web.

Italian scrawl ran down the margins of one image, a tangle of words that hinted at a story. I zoomed in on the tiny script, my mind scrambling to decipher it. My Italian was passable, but the owner of the notebook had clearly written the notes as reminders to themself, rather than for instruction. They made no sense.

I glanced up, looking at Leigh and Isaac.

They were watching me, their expressions a mix of curiosity and concern. All I could see was the vault, her secrets taunting me, begging me to go back.

I needed to know. I had to find out what lay beyond that stone door.

"Legends say there are treasures buried in those catacombs." Isaac's words held a sense of awe and wonder. Maybe we had something in common, after all.

Leigh nodded, adding softly, "There are stories of Mithraic relics and Templar artifacts hidden down there."

Isaac chuckled at her. "Going full Dan Brown now?"

Leigh fell silent, Isaac's dismissive tone leaving her fiddling with the hem of her shirt instead of eating her gelato. A flush crept up her neck.

What the hell was his problem? She was practically saying the same thing he had.

Jayce nudged him—harder than necessary—and covered it up with a laugh. "I love his books."

"You never know." I handed my phone to Leigh, who skimmed through the photos. "The catacombs have many secrets. Who's to say what we might find down there?"

"True." He gave Leigh a weak smile. "Who knows more about ancient vaults than my sister, right?"

I glanced at Leigh. She was still quiet, fumbling with the phone and her gelato cup. I wanted to say something, but what would make her feel better? If I harassed Isaac, she came to his defense. If I complimented her, he deflected it before she could.

Still, they were right.

Questions nipped at the back of my brain. What if this vault was connected to the Venetian treasure, the Tesoro di San Marco? The one we'd recovered most of in Venice? The thought set my pulse racing.

Abruptly, Isaac's phone chimed, a jaunty tune that sliced through the air. He held up the screen, cursed under his breath, and pocketed the device. "I've got to run. Meeting's in a half hour."

I quirked an eyebrow. "What's with all the meetings, Isaac?"

He sighed, pinching the bridge of his nose. "Dad wants to expand the business here. Wants to supply a couple of companies. But you know how Italians do business—it's all food and drinks and lots of time getting to know each other."

There was an edge of bitterness to his words. As quickly as it surfaced, he covered it up with a thin smile.

"I better get going." He didn't move. The weight of his obligations seemed to anchor him for a moment, his gaze flickering to Leigh, then back to me. A silent exchange passed between us. *Take care of my sister*, it said.

Isaac softened as he addressed her. "Be safe, bug."

"I'm fine." She balanced the phone under her cup and popped a mouthful of light-brown chocolate gelato into her mouth before giving him a dutiful smile.

"Jayce is here." Isaac nodded at Jayce. "She'll keep an eye on you."

Before I could snap at him about me being there, too, he turned on his heel and vanished down the road. The tension in my shoulders eased slightly, but throwing my gelato cup at him would have made me feel far better.

"Isaac's a real jerk, isn't he?" Jayce waved her spoon in the direction he'd gone, then jabbed it in Leigh's direction. "I mean, I've told you that already. You've got to stand up to him, Leigh."

Her tone was brusque, her words direct. Classic Jayce. Beneath her rough exterior was a genuine concern, a budding friendship that only strengthened my respect for her.

I rolled my eyes in Isaac's general direction, when I spotted a broad man farther down the pedestrian street, speaking with someone.

He gave off the same vibe Rav did. Serious. Deadly. Not someone you wanted to meet in a dark alleyway, let alone a sunlit one.

I wrapped my gelato-toting arm around Leigh and took my phone back. I held it up, pretending to take a selfie. "Smile!"

Jayce jumped in front of me to ensure she was in the photo. "Hey, you aren't even—"

"Quiet." I spun with Leigh under my arm and headed in the opposite direction. I'd used the rear camera instead of taking a photo of us. A quick sidestep toward a trash can, and I tossed my gelato out. "Did you see him?"

"Who?" Leigh began to turn around, and I pulled her closer.

Jayce hopped in front of us, walking backward, as though we were having a fantastic time. "Creepy guy, five o'clock?"

"That's the one." With one hand, I forwarded the photo to Scarlett. I glanced at the wide street, choked with people. The gelateria was behind us, a clothing store to the left, a café farther beyond, closed doors, graffiti-covered garage doors. What else was there? "Which door's most likely to get us off this street?"

"Declan?" Leigh shuddered in my grasp.

Fuck's sake, could we not catch a break?

Jayce pointed at a small inset door, almost invisible behind stands full of memorabilia. "That one's my guess. They'll want tourists inside and won't complain too loud if we say we're going to the washroom then just keep going."

Done. I steered Leigh toward the shop and flipped my phone up for another faux-selfie, using it to track the man's progress. "He's following us."

"That he is." Jayce ushered Leigh into the shop first and ripped the red wig off her when we were inside. She grabbed a shopping bag with 'Rome' written all over it and stuffed her own wig on top of the red one. "I'd normally chuck them, but Scarlett loves these wigs."

We kept going, past displays, gaining speed as we progressed deeper into the shop so narrow we had to walk single-file.

My phone rang. I didn't have time for this, but a quick glance showed it was Scarlett, and I answered.

Before it was all the way to my ear, she snapped out, "Get Leigh back to the hotel. Now."

Her words hit like a punch. Scarlett was always measured, her emotions as calculated as the plans she crafted. When she said *hurry*, she damn well meant it.

"Keep your profiles low," she added, her level of urgency sending a chill down my spine. "Fast as possible, Dec."

My heart pounded in my chest, a drumbeat of panic. My mind raced with possibilities, but quickly landed on one. "You recognize the guy, don't you?"

We waved to the shopkeeper as we neared the back and the sign for the bathroom. Her well-painted lips provided a broad smile. Jayce knew her hiding spots.

"What's going on, Dec?" Jayce asked from ahead of me.

"Scarlett," I hissed, keeping myself to a bare whisper. "Who is it?"

Leigh looked over her shoulder at me, almost stumbling as I pushed her forward.

"Keep your head down. Act natural."

Jayce snorted, a sharp sound that broke the tense silence. "Yeah, because nothing screams 'natural' like ducking your head and looking terrified."

Despite her jokes, Jayce was alert, ready for action.

"We'll be fine, Leigh," I said, squeezing her shoulder reassuringly. "Just stick with us."

The words sounded hollow in my own ears, but they were the best I could offer.

Scarlett made a quiet noise, as though expressing her irritation. "We've just figured out who owned the box we took the notebook from."

"And?"

"Giovanni Ferraro."

My blood turned to ice. "The antiquities smuggler?"

"He's retired," Scarlett said. "But still very influential. And the man you snapped a photo of is his head of security."

Fuck me. "How did they figure it out so quickly? Didn't Brie hijack the camera feeds? How do they even know the notebook's gone?"

Jayce hit the rear door, opening into the bright sun on another pedestrian street. She glanced at her phone and pointed to the left. "We can grab a taxi in that direction. Five minutes, quick march."

The goon was nowhere to be seen, no one else giving me the heebie-jeebies. All the same, I said, "Let's make that three."

Scarlett said, "No more excursions. Switch cabs at least two times, and walk some distance between them."

"I know what I'm doing, Scar." But did I? I'd let Jayce talk me into this crazy adventure. If we'd limited it to the catacombs, Ferraro's man wouldn't be on our tail. "The guard didn't see our faces."

"It had to be Edoardo," Scarlett said.

No. There was no way. He wouldn't have set us up and then sold us out.

The truth dawned on me, but I kept it to myself. Leigh didn't need more to worry about. The guard *did* see our faces. He was the one working when Edoardo brought us into Cassaforte the first time.

My stomach churned. Not for myself or for Jayce—we were used to running—but for the innocent woman next to me. I had to keep her safe.

CHAPTER 20

LEIGH

I slumped into a plush hotel chair, staring out the tall window at the building across the street. More ochre stucco. Everywhere. A stack of tourist brochures littered the desk next to me. I was supposed to be on the adventure of a lifetime. Instead, I was a player in some twisted cloak-and-dagger escapade that was scaring the shit out of me.

My phone buzzed from the table, tearing me from my thoughts. It was Ann, my stepmother. Her text message was all sunshine and emojis, followed by, *How's your great Roman adventure going, sweetheart?*

A brittle laugh escaped my lips. If only she knew.

I rubbed at my temples and stretched out my neck. The anti-inflammatories would kick in any second and dull the ache pounding through my skull.

The reality was far from the trip we'd talked about before I left, but I couldn't burden her with the truth. The smiley faces and the cute Italian flag emoji—they didn't need to be smeared with my spiraling anxiety.

I dialed her number and forced a cheerfulness I didn't feel into my voice. "Hey, Ann. Rome is something else."

"Tell me all about it." Her words were smooth, the same positivity as she'd texted me with coloring her tone.

"Well, let's see." How many non-nightmare moments had I had? What could I tell her? *Make it up, Leigh.* "I visited the Catacombs, the Forum, and three different museums." A small chuckle escaped me as I added, "A real whirlwind of art and history."

"Wow, that sounds wonderful! And how are your colleagues treating you? The ones Isaac did the safe deposit box test with?"

"They're great, Ann. Really." Another half-truth. Yes, they were great in the way a pack of wolves was great: fascinating and fearsome in equal measures. *Plus, Isaac didn't do the test. I did. Believe it or not, Ann.*

"That's my girl, always making friends wherever she goes." Her words were like a chisel, chipping away at my facade. I couldn't tell her the truth. It'd worry her, disappoint her. So, I just let out a hollow laugh, pretending to brush off her praise.

"Speaking of new friends, Leigh," Ann said with an obvious connotation, "met any handsome Italian men yet?"

Images of Declan flashed through my mind. Tall, handsome Declan, who wasn't local, but spoke the language and knew the city like he could have been. I also wasn't about to tell her—or anyone—about him. Or his hazel eyes. Or the scruff on his jaw. Or the way he kept wrapping his arm around me.

I'd cooked up a crazy fantasy before leaving the States, one where a passionate Italian man romanced me. He'd whirl me through the narrow streets of Rome on his sleek Vespa, our conversations filled with broken English and sparkling eyes. In my fantasy, we'd make love under a canvas of stars, not a care in the world.

Instead, reality featured a labyrinth of dimly lit tunnels, a notebook worth kidnapping for, and a burgeoning attraction to a guy whose primary conversational topic was vault doors.

"Well, Ann," I said, my tone careful, "I've been working really hard. Mr. Caetani's safe was a simple patch job and the penetration test at his safe deposit box company went well. I think Isaac learned a lot he could use at home."

She worked with the family company, so work talk was relevant. And it deflected her away from my nonexistent love life. "And how *is* Isaac doing? I've been trying to reach him, but he hasn't answered my calls."

I sighed, twirling a strand of hair around my finger. Isaac wasn't answering because he didn't particularly like Ann. He'd never gotten over the loss of our mother. Hell, neither of us had, but while I had a lot of blank spots in my memories, Isaac was older and remembered more. The sting of our father remarrying, of replacing our mother, had never healed for him.

"He's been busy." My gaze wandered to a pigeon who'd landed on my windowsill. The window was open, and they didn't use screens, so the bird could have walked right in. If it did that, I'd have a perfect excuse to get off the phone. "You know, meeting with new clients. They go to a lot of dinners and stuff."

"One client, you mean?"

"One?" The flurry of meetings Isaac had been part of didn't add up to just one. Although that might explain why he complained about them so often. "I didn't realize. He seems busier than that."

"And speaking of busy, I almost forgot why I called." Her tone was light as a feather, as always, even though she was avoiding my question. Or didn't care enough I'd asked. "Your boyfriend, Finn, came by the house looking for you."

"Finn's not—" I began, but Ann talked right over me.

"He's such a handy young man. Did some work for me, even cleaned the gutters."

I gritted my teeth, listening to the stupid praise. The real Finn was far from the rose-tinted version Ann painted. He was anything but nice, a fact only amplified by the disdain in his eyes when I'd brought home those vault history books, an enthusiastic grin plastered on my face. He'd made me feel small, insignificant, deriding my passion for safes as a daddy's girl's obsession.

Better a daddy's girl than an asshole, Finn.

Unlike Finn, Declan had shown genuine interest in those books. He'd been curious, not dismissive. Why couldn't I meet a man like that, who appreciated my passion?

I had. I'd met Declan.

But why couldn't I meet one who didn't turn my life upside down and send me running from smugglers, the law, and god knows who else?

"I'm done with Finn, Ann." My words were more forceful than I'd intended. Where had that come from? "I broke up with him before I left."

"I know, sweetheart." So why did she call him my boyfriend? "That's why I was asking if you've met anyone over there."

What game was she playing?

"Finn wants you back." She practically squealed with girlish delight, as though we were in the middle of a slumber party, gossiping about boys. "You won't find someone as good as him. He's attractive, financially stable, smarter than any other man I know."

Then maybe you should divorce my father and marry him instead.

The fear churning in my gut since we read Edoardo's note in the vault shifted. It rose in my throat and bubbled up, bursting out in a way I hadn't intended. "He never let me be me. He always made me feel"—*Fuck, the same way you make me feel, Ann!*—"like I was useless and ugly and immature. He told me I wasn't allowed to go to Rome without him."

"It's a business trip, sweetheart. Why would he care about that?" Had she listened to a word I'd said?

"I'm done with him." My father, Isaac, and my other two brothers were bad enough. I didn't need to share my life with someone who was more controlling, more overprotective than them. Finn had even convinced me to put school on the back burner for a year. "So please, stop talking about him. I'm never going back."

There was a pause on the other side, and at least three times, I had to stop myself from apologizing or saying I'd give it a shot, just to take the sting out of my harsh words. Instead, I took a long breath and said, "Now, if you'll excuse me, I need to get ready for dinner."

"Isn't it a bit late for—" she began, but I cut her off.

"Italians eat really late, Ann." And with that, I clicked off, severing the connection with a vicious tap.

My breaths came out in ragged gasps, a tidal wave of emotion threatening to break through the dam I'd been holding up for so long. My fists clenched at my sides, knuckles straining around my phone. I hated this. I hated all of this. The lies, the secrets, the pretending—it was all too much.

Fury pulsed through my veins, fueling a desperate need to let go.

So, I did.

The phone in my hand flew like a missile, shattering against the far wall, shards of glass and plastic ricocheting off the pristine walls.

The pigeon flew off with a grunt.

The room fell silent, the sound of the phone smashing into the wall ringing in my ears.

Holy shit. I'd destroyed my phone—the one Dad doled out for work. Guilt gnawed at me, making my stomach twist as I knelt to collect the fragments.

"What did that phone—"

I spun so fast, I nearly fell over. When had Jayce come in?

"—ever do to you?"

Of course, she'd be quiet. Jayce was a thief, after all. Noise was her enemy. How much had she seen?

"It slipped." I focused on a fractured piece of glass that was once my phone's screen.

"Slipped, huh?" Jayce said with a hint of amusement. "I saw the whole thing. Heard about your ex, too."

I swallowed hard, feeling my cheeks burn. "I thought I was having a private conversation."

"Nope, not so much." Jayce shrugged, her indifference less of a surprise today than every other time she brushed things off. She paused, looking out the window. "The guys are setting up for the kidnapper exchange. Couple of hours from now."

I nodded, not trusting my voice.

Jayce glanced back at me, her eyes searching mine. "You really going out for dinner?"

"I don't have any plans." I sank to the floor, staring at the shattered remnants of my phone. And maybe that was the problem. I had dreams, sure, but no concrete plans. My dreams of Rome had given me the strength to call things off with Finn. But if he'd been with me, I would have been touring the city instead of... all of this insanity with Reynolds Recoveries.

"Well then, we should go out for dinner." Jayce crossed the room and returned with a wastebasket. She knelt in front of me and tossed a piece into the basket. "As soon as we clean up your slip."

"But I'm supposed to stay put." That was the only rule Scarlett had given me, and I wasn't about to break it.

"That was last hour's plan." Jayce's casual tone didn't fit my reality. "Scarlett got in touch with Giovanni. They're meeting him tomorrow, so there's no risk of his goon coming after us tonight. And since the kidnapper hand-off is tonight, we're clear from Edoardo and the kidnappers, too."

One of the fifty thousand muscles in my body finally unclenched.

We worked in silence for a few moments.

"Nothing personal, but if you took any pictures or recorded anything about our events over the last week, I'm going to have this destroyed." Jayce held the motherboard gingerly between two fingers.

I nodded. "I don't think I did, but if you think that's best?"

She stood and slipped the blue board into her suitcase. "Let's go find something to eat. I'm starving."

"Just a quiet meal? No adventure? No danger?"

She blew a raspberry. "I'd never promise anything of the sort."

"Maybe I should stay—"

"Dude, I'm hungry. No amount of danger gets between me and a good meal."

Nothing had been quiet since I met these people. Hopefully, dinner would be a first. "Okay, let's go eat."

Chapter 21
Declan

I leaned against the cool stone of the half-wall dividing the sidewalk from the drop to the riverside walk, my senses razor-sharp. I clutched my binoculars, sweeping the area below, with Rav mirrored beside me. The cobblestone path next to the river was empty.

"Got anything?" Rav whispered.

"Nothing yet." I dropped the binoculars for a moment. Moonlight slithered through the leaves above us, shadows chasing each other over the ground. Across the glistening Tiber, Malcolm and Emmett played lookouts from their own hidden station on Tiber Island.

"Same here," Emmett responded with a stifled groan. He wasn't fully recovered from his kidnappings and the beatings he'd received, but he'd insisted on joining us.

Rav's eyes never left the scene. Next to him, our new camera with a telephoto lens stood on a tripod, so he could photograph the man behind Scarlett's blackmail photos. We hadn't traveled with one, but Rav wouldn't let the evening go by without gathering intel. Targeting Scarlett would be the last mistake anyone made.

Over the quiet rush of the river, the buzz of a drone blended with the light breeze. Will was our eye in the sky. "All clear from above. I've got a good view of the entire riverside."

"Stay on it," I muttered, my pulse throbbing in my temples.

Anxiety was a hard ball in my gut. It had been the right choice to monitor the kidnapper's exchange, but it was ten past midnight, and no one was there yet. Had Edoardo lied to me again? About Martina? No. Maybe about the location. Or it had been changed and he wouldn't have any reason to tell us.

In our secluded spot, under the veil of darkness and anticipation, we watched, waited, and prayed. And the night, full of uncertainty and secrets, stretched on.

If something happened—something that required intervention—a long set of wide stairs was a twenty-foot dash away. It would have to be serious for me to help the traitor.

Finally, Edoardo emerged from the shadows of the bridge crossing the river at the western end of the island. His shoulders hunched like they had when we'd handed over the notebook early this morning.

"Got eyes on Edoardo." I kept my volume down—the earpieces Will had built could pick up a breath. The sight of my old friend, forlorn and desperate, ignited a spark of sympathy. Betrayal aside, no man deserved to see his wife in the hands of wolves.

"He doesn't look good." Rav pivoted his body to check the surrounding area. He wasn't a man of many words, but his sentiment was clear.

"Got movement at the other bridge," said Malcolm.

Sure enough, three figures emerged from underneath the bridge leading to the island, their faces hidden in the shadows, trailing a smaller one. A woman. My throat felt as though it were stuffed with cotton.

"That's Martina." I gripped the binoculars tighter, an uneasy knot building in my stomach. My gaze bounced between the approaching group and the surrounding area and back to Edoardo. My instincts screamed at me, telling me to rush down the stairs and help. But there could be more than the three, hidden somewhere.

"I see them," said Emmett. "Watch your backs. We don't know who else is out there."

The exchange began, a horrible dance under Rome's moonlight. Edoardo lunged forward, a gun was pointed, Edoardo's hands flew up. Muted voices. Chatter. A sob from Martina.

I could almost forgive him. Almost. Maybe someday, but not yet.

Martina, roughly sixty and with her hair a bedraggled mess, was shaking, huddled under the grip of one of the kidnappers. Her wrists were bound in front of her, as though she were some threat to these lowlifes. A ripple of anger swept through me, churning my stomach.

"He should have fucking called us for this," I hissed.

Rav made a hard, angry grunt of agreement.

Edoardo eased the notebook out of his jacket pocket.

"Here goes." My heart pounded in my chest as Edoardo extended his arm, the notebook passing from husband to kidnapper.

One of the men pulled out a flashlight, bathing the notebook in a harsh, cold beam of light.

As the glow illuminated his face, I sucked in a breath. "Son of a bitch."

"What?" Rav shot me a glance, lowering his binoculars.

"That's the London guy." Ice splintered down my spine. He'd tried to snatch the Chalcis Ring from us outside of London. "Same scar over his left cheek."

Rav cursed, Emmett groaned in our ears, and Malcolm fell silent. The game had taken an unexpected turn, questions building on top of questions. London guy meant this wasn't a one-off kidnapping. This was the start of a damn vendetta.

"Is that the prick who had a gun to my throat?" Malcolm's voice was rough.

"Yep, that's him," I said.

"Noah's man," Malcolm whispered. "The one with the phoenix tattoo."

Shit.

"So they're with Fenix?" Rav asked, shifting to take photographs.

"That's the asshole who did most of the damage to me," Emmett growled, a harsh edge to his usually light-hearted tone.

In response, Rav let out a grunt, a sound as eloquent as a speech to us.

"They're either with Fenix," I said, my gaze never straying from the unfolding scene below, "or this is the worse fucking coincidence I've ever seen."

The tension in the air was a palpable force, wrapping around us like a noose. Fenix. Noah's man. A London escape with Scarlett bloodied and Malcolm nearly killed.

The only thing I knew for sure—we were far from the end of this mess. "Wait, does this mean Ferraro's in bed with Fenix?"

"Why would he pay these thugs to rob himself?" Rav asked, skepticism lacing his words.

"What if more than one person owned that safe deposit box?" There were too many options. Too many threads to this spider's web.

Rav turned to me again, his eyes narrowed. "I don't like any of this."

"Welcome to the club." The sick knot in my gut constricted. We were dealing with far more than Edoardo's double-cross. "But I'm guessing that means you were right in the van this morning. First, Fenix kidnaps Emmett to get the ring, then they rope us into this to get the notebook."

As we played through theories, the exchange below grew heated. Even from our hidden vantage point, the body language screamed aggression.

"Will, get the drone in closer," I said.

"On it." He dropped the drone until I couldn't hear the soft hum of its rotors anymore. "Can't get too close without them hearing it."

Tattoo Man was gesturing wildly at Edoardo, his volume loud enough to be picked up by the drone's microphone. "We warned you not to tell anyone."

Shit. Edoardo had confessed to us. My mind raced, throwing me back to this morning. Could they have been watching when we'd handed over the notebook?

"Were they in St. Peter's Square this morning?" We'd seen so many people, but which ones could they have been? "Cleaners? The proposal guy? Tourists?"

"No way," Malcolm dismissed immediately. "We had eyes on the entire square."

Rav stayed silent for a beat, then quietly agreed. "It's possible."

But if they were at St. Peter's Square, why not take the notebook then? There were only the four of us this morning, plus Edoardo. They could have dumped Martina anywhere. Maybe they were monitoring him some other way.

The next moments were a blur. The kidnappers shoved Martina. Her scream pierced the night as she plummeted into the river.

I sprang into action, the raw instinct to save her overriding everything else. Her hands were tied. She wouldn't be able to swim. But Rav was faster than me, his hand planted squarely on my chest, stopping me in my tracks.

"Martina!" Edoardo was at the edge, desperately attempting to reach her. The kidnappers were already vanishing into the night. Martina's terrified yells echoed over the water, the sound cutting through me.

"I need to save her!" I pushed against Rav's hand but didn't turn it into a fight I'd lose.

"Not until they're gone." Rav sounded as calm as stone, but I knew him well enough to hear his concern. Our safety came first. I knew that was the cardinal rule. But dammit, she was panicking. Edoardo wouldn't be able to get her out.

"Go!" Rav's hand lifted, releasing me.

I was off. Sprinting toward the stairs, taking them two, three at a time, my mind spinning with worry. How deep was the Tiber? Head first or feet first?

I knew the river saw traffic, but the depth of a boat's keel? I had to go feet first. Safe.

Edoardo glanced up, but his reaction barely registered. If there was any justice in this world, his face had been filled with regret.

I hit the water, the cold jolt almost a relief. I grabbed Martina, who writhed in my arms. Years as a lifeguard told me it could be shock and I should let her go limp so she didn't take me down with her. Instead, I gasped, "Stop fighting me, Martina."

Maybe it was the use of her name, but her panic ebbed enough I got a hand on the edge. With every ounce of strength I had, I shoved her upward, her hands finding purchase in Edoardo's waiting arms.

As I pushed, I lost my grip, and the river swallowed me once again. Rav should have been the one in this river. He was the rescue diver, the man with a plan. But no point in wallowing. I'd done what I had to. Martina was safe.

I surfaced and pushed against the slick stone, hoisting myself up, Edoardo completely ignoring me. No help offered.

"Nice one, Declan!" Emmett's congratulatory cheer over the miraculously still-intact earpiece was a small comfort.

Edoardo and his wife were sobbing, huddled together on the stones.

"Grazie, grazie mille." Edoardo repeated his cries over and over, the Italian words carrying across the night air. He was broken, the devastation clear.

"Yeah, yeah, save it." I shook the water off, the cold clinging to me. My anger surged, and I delivered my news. "For the record, Giovanni Ferraro's man came after us."

Edoardo's eyes widened. Good. "Mi dispiace, Declan."

"That security guard you trusted? You might want to reconsider that." My words were harsh, biting. "Unless, of course, this was your plan all along. Get us to steal the notebook, and then let us take the fall."

"This..." He rocked back and forth with his wife, tears coating his face. "This was not what I wanted."

"Well, it's not exactly what I wanted, either." I shook the water from my hands. The night was hardly cold, but now that I was drenched, all I wanted was a warm shower. "Now tell me, who was it?"

"I don't know," sobbed Martina.

"What do you know about Fenix?"

"Nothing, Declan!" Edoardo reached for my hand, but I flung it away from him. "I swear I don't know who and I don't know why, except for the notebook."

Useless. Edoardo's information, my anger, and coming to watch this spectacle. Not useless. At least I got Martina out, and we knew who took the photos of Scarlett.

That thug had been at the party, so he'd taken them.

With a final glance at my betrayer, I turned my back and headed for the stairs. We'd be meeting with Ferraro himself later in the morning. Would Fenix be there? Had Scarlett signed our death warrants by agreeing to the meet?

And if not, how would we find the man who'd turned her into a pawn?

CHAPTER 22

LEIGH

Saturday morning, a lifetime away from Friday morning's panicked escape from Cassaforte, I was in a whole other world. The car, a glossy luxury sedan, wound its way up a serpentine driveway. Rav, all precision and efficiency, manned the wheel. Scarlett, perched in the passenger seat, was the epitome of calm.

"Stay close to Declan." Scarlett's words broke the quiet hum of the engine. "Follow his lead and everything will be fine."

My throat tightened. Declan, next to me, didn't react. Cool as always. I looked out the window at the whitewashed villa that came into view, perched like an elegant ghost atop the hill. Beyond it, the Mediterranean stretched into the horizon.

Tall cypress pines lined the driveway. Bushes, gardens, and small buildings surrounded the three-story villa southeast of Rome. Giovanni Ferraro must have had an army of gardeners working for him.

"What's going to happen?" The drive had taken less than an hour, just enough time for me to suppress my need to leap out of the car and run for home fifteen times.

Dinner with Jayce last night had been quiet, but I hadn't stopped looking over my shoulder to enjoy it. After escaping from Giovanni Ferraro's security man yesterday, I could have sworn someone was watching me every minute.

"Don't worry, Leigh." Scarlett turned to give me a gentle smile. "We've worked with Giovanni before. We have a good relationship."

Her casual tone was a stark contrast to the tension I felt. I swallowed, trying to calm the rapid flutter in my chest.

"Still," she continued, "you'll see a lot of men with guns. Some of them big ones—both the men and the guns. Just remember, they're not there for you."

"We're the good guys, right?" Declan's fingers drummed a quick rhythm on his knees, betraying something underneath his cool facade.

"That's right," Scarlett said, grinning at him. "So be a good boy and keep an eye on Leigh."

"Guess you're stuck with me." Declan winked at me, causing the flutter to sink deeper in my belly. The engine's hum seemed to fade into the background. "Boss's orders."

I managed little more than a nod, too caught in the pull of his gaze to form a reply.

"We'll be fine." If Scarlett said it enough times, I might believe her.

I sucked in my bottom lip, my heart a chaotic drumbeat. Thoughts ricocheted inside my skull, my desire for the safety of home warring with Jayce's words that I was no safer there.

Glimpses of crumbling ruins at the base of the hill caught my eye, the hint of a once-grand villa, now reduced to a hollow testament of time and decay. I sat up taller in my seat, scanning the ancient floor plan. It ran toward the sea, a natural pool forming between the remnants of a sea break. That was more like what I was hoping to see when I came to Rome.

If only I'd come a day early. If only Edoardo's other safe hadn't required the subtle touch of Declan's skill. A different timeline, a different Leigh. Would I have remained blissfully ignorant of the pandemonium I'd been thrown into?

A voice punctured my thoughts. "Leigh, you hearing me?"

Scarlett's question pulled me into the moment. The leather seat beneath me felt too real, too present.

"Yeah." I eased back into the seat, watching as a tower looming behind the villa stretched over us.

She cocked an eyebrow at me but didn't press further.

Declan's hand wrapped around mine, his grip strong. He was a rock in the raging storm inside me. "Nothing bad is going to happen."

I wanted to believe him. God, how much I wanted to believe him. But the pit in my stomach argued otherwise, churning with uncertainty. I offered him a shaky smile, hoping that the tremor in my grip didn't betray the riot in my head.

Nothing bad is going to happen. I repeated his words like a mantra. Yet, the white-knuckled fear gripping me begged to differ. *Focus on the hot guy holding your hand. Distract yourself.*

Declan wore navy slacks and a white, short-sleeved button-down. A pair of sunglasses hung from where he'd undone a few buttons of the shirt. A steel-banded watch adorned his wrist, the crown emblem on it hinting at wealth. Images of him in the thermal suit flooded me, the hard slope of his pectorals, ripped abs, perfect ass.

Scarlett had loaned me another outfit, ensuring I fit in with the group for this meeting. Skinny pants and light-pink silk blouse with a neckline enhanced by the new bra. Ballet flats instead of heels, and a diamond necklace that likely cost as much as Declan's Rolex. Hiding under a tarp had only entered my thoughts three times—when men I passed on my way to the car had turned and stared.

A small urge to take a selfie and send it to Finn flashed through my brain. I mentally composed the text to go with the photo: *I do have the kind of body for clothes like this, asshole.*

This was about more than clothes and fine appearances, though. Giovanni's conditions for the meeting required the thieves to accompany Scarlett and Rav. Not Jayce. Just Declan and me.

The thieves.

I swallowed hard, still not confident with the plan. "Scarlett, are we sure about this? Apologies are hardly magic erasers. And we're not dealing with an ordinary retiree."

Scarlett twisted in her seat, her face far too calm for the situation. "Giovanni might be out of the game, but respect holds value. Especially for a man like him."

"But his guy came after us." Racing down the street, through the store, changing taxis over and over to be sure we were clear. I wasn't built for this.

"That was before they knew we were involved." There was a certain courage in her, a raw determination that inspired me, almost enough to stop the tremble in my legs.

Declan's hand, wrapped around mine, felt right. A snug fit, like two puzzle pieces, finally finding their place. Yet, there was a familiar tinge of guilt as my thoughts flew back to Isaac. I'd spent more time over the last week with the Reynolds crew than my own brother, a strange shift that unbalanced me.

A quick look at Declan's hand, steady and assuring around mine, and I reconsidered. In this whirlwind of chaos, he was an anchor. I felt a smile, small but genuine, creep up on me. Maybe I was glad to be here with him. He was far from the polished, predictable men my stepmother usually envisioned for me. Like smart and cleaned-her-gutters jackass Finn.

How shocked would she be if I brought Declan home? Her perfectly coiffed hair would go haywire. She'd fumble over her words, staring wide-eyed at the rugged safe cracker who'd stolen her stepdaughter's attention. A delicious bubble of glee expanded within me at the thought.

"Scarlett will take care of negotiations." Declan's deep rumble broke through my daydreams. "We just have to sit back, stay quiet, and nod."

"Is there going to be some sort of deal?" The borrowed clothes weren't decoration for me as a sacrifice, were they?

"What, you think we'd trade you in like some sacrificial lamb?" Declan's tone was light, teasing, but how close it hit to my doubts made my stomach clench.

My hand twitched in his grasp, a jolt of fear reverberating through me. "That's not what I..."

My words faltered as the car eased through an archway, emerging into an open courtyard. Four men, armed with automatic weapons, stood at attention. Two watched our arrival from atop wide marble steps, the other two scanning the sky and the entrance from the pebbled driveway. Their nonchalance with the big guns strapped over their chests sent chills down my spine. My reflex was to retreat, to pull my hand away from Declan, but he held on with a viselike grip.

"The worst-case scenario," he said, his tone even, "is that we have to do a job for Giovanni. Pro bono. Can you trust me with that?"

I looked at him and nodded. "Yes. I trust you."

A soft smile tugged at his lips, a quiet promise underlying his words. "Then you have nothing to worry about."

The car ground to a halt, the hum of the engine replaced by a heavy silence. Thick white columns supported a roof over the stairs. Its underside was painted, and all I could make out were cherubs and the sky. Opposite the stairs, a multi-car garage housed a few black SUVs.

Two men appeared from the double doors at the top of the grand staircase, their figures dwarfed by the enormity of the dark-wood doors. Giovanni Ferraro's home was designed to impress and to intimidate.

A knock on the window startled me. The men who'd been watching our arrival, their faces hard, had approached the car.

My heart took another jump. *You'll be all right.*

"Everyone, keep your mouths shut. You only talk if I say so." Scarlett hardly had to tell me that—I couldn't have spoken if I'd tried.

The terrifying reality of where we were, who we were dealing with, swallowed my words. A weight pressed down on my chest, making it hard to breathe.

Declan leaned closer to whisper in my ear. "You trust me, remember?"

A memory came back to me—his hand, gentle yet firm, cupping my face in the vault. His gaze had softened the steel of the vault we were trapped in. It was a reassurance I yearned for now, more than ever.

I nodded, taking strength from him.

He leaned closer and the fantasy about his hands on my face switched to his lips on mine. I wanted to shut everything else out. Forget the world, the insanity, and give over to something better. He was so close, the spice of his cologne enveloped me.

I gave in to the fantasy and pressed my lips to his cheek.

He paused, neither separating from me nor moving closer. Not even breathing.

Oh god. He was leaning in to whisper. To make me feel better. Not to kiss me. What was I thinking?

"Sorry. I don't know what..." My weak words trailed off. Why did my brain turn to such mush around him? I eased away, but he maintained our intimate proximity.

"I was going to say..." His warm breath hit my ear, his volume so low the duo in the front wouldn't have heard him over their own conversation. "Scarlett's the best at this part of the game."

"Thank you," I whispered back.

"No need to be scared."

"Working on it."

Declan squeezed my hand one last time and, as though accustomed to acting in unison, they all exited the car.

Taking a deep breath, I followed, staying close to Declan as his hand came to rest on my back, the motion soothing. Finn wouldn't have bothered with comforting gestures. He wouldn't have even noticed how I'd felt. Things would've been different if he'd been more like Declan, encouraging me instead of criticizing. Kind instead of cruel.

How was that possible when the Reynolds team barely stayed on my side of the law? How could my law-abiding ex be the tyrant and Declan be the champion?

A tall, broad Italian exited the double doors, his size rivaling Rav's. He was familiar. Too familiar. The same man who'd trailed us the previous day. My knees wobbled, my heart pounding. In a thick accent, he said, "Follow me to Signore Ferraro's meeting room."

You're strong, confident. I repeated the mantra in my mind as we walked, but my body betrayed me, fear seeping into my veins.

"Well, look who's here. Back for more trouble?" The Italian behemoth leered at Scarlett as she joined him at the top of the stairs, a predatory grin on his face. "Always a pleasure, Scarlett."

"Leonardo." She patted his chest, a smirk playing on her lips. "Likewise."

Rav moved closer to her, tension rolling off him in waves. Was there a past between Leonardo and Scarlett? And was it why Scarlett had refused to bring Malcolm, despite his protests? And what about Isaac, who'd made a scene when Rav told him—in no uncertain terms—that I was going and he wasn't?

Inside, the grand hall rose to all three stories, adorned with luxurious details. Pillars, antique furniture, paintings, and gold leaf adorning every surface. A wall of glass offered a breathtaking view of well-tended gardens, which melted into the endless expanse of the sea a couple of hundred feet away.

"God, this place is gorgeous," I gasped, unable to hold it in.

A sudden tug from Declan yanked me closer to his side. His eyes flashed a quick warning. I bit my lip, remembering Scarlett's words. Just nod and be quiet.

Leonardo ushered us into the meeting room, a rectangular sanctuary where sunlight spilled in through arch-topped windows, illuminating a table of aged wood. The room was a testament to balance—nature's raw beauty held at bay by Giovanni's cultivated refinement. The hilltop's native rock jutted into the room, causing an irregular wall at the back. Why hadn't they blasted it away?

At the center of it all, a man in his mid-sixties stood, beaming with an infectious smile. His salt-and-pepper hair was carefully combed away from his face, and his eyes danced with a warm, welcoming light. A younger man, bearing a striking resemblance to him, hovered at his side. Two other men, pistols casually hanging from their belts, lingered at the back of the room.

"Giovanni," purred Scarlett. "I appreciate you seeing us on short notice."

The older man stepped forward, placing tender kisses on both of Scarlett's cheeks. After she finished our introductions, Giovanni clapped his hands twice. The sharp noise made me jump.

"I wish to speak only with the thieves." Giovanni spoke with a strange mix of severity and charm. Fear invaded the edges of my confidence. That didn't sound like *Nothing bad will happen.*

Scarlett smiled softly, her control mesmerizing. "As I said on the phone, they're my employees, and they can't promise or offer you anything without my say so. We're here for apologies and restitution. They can provide the first, but only I can provide the second."

Giovanni maintained his smile, reminding me of a snake biding its time before a strike. To my surprise, he gestured toward the younger man who resembled him. "You remember Cristian, my son?"

"One of our men will take you and your bodyguard for a tour of the gardens. They are lovely this time of year." Cristian stepped forward, gesturing to the men with the guns. "Your thieves have nothing to worry about while we speak with them. Talk only. I promise."

A shiver ran through me, and every cell in my body demanded I run. But Declan's big hand on my back didn't falter.

"Giovanni," drawled Scarlett, not reacting to Cristian. "I reached out to you, out of respect for our past dealings. To hand over the digital copies of the notebook and to answer what questions you have." She shot a quick glance our way, eyes icy with determination. "I did not agree to abandon my team members, even if just for a few minutes."

I inched closer to Declan, waiting for an end to the stalemate. He'd said Scarlett was good, but was she as good as an antiquities smuggler who owned a mansion on the edge of the sea?

After too many minutes of consideration, Giovanni clapped his hands again, a gleam in his eyes. "I've always liked you, Scarlett."

CHAPTER 23
DECLAN

Giovanni, the retired smuggler whose grin hadn't faltered since our entry, waved us toward the imposing dark oak table. Nodding, I steered Leigh toward a chair, my hand a protective presence at the small of her back.

Her lips had found my cheek in the car. A moment. No more. But damned if it didn't keep replaying in my brain. It was just her way of saying thanks. Right? It wasn't as if she'd draped herself over me. It was a peck on the cheek, for Christ's sake. We were in Italy. That's what you did in Italy.

But the way she'd leaned into my touch, like she was absorbing it, soaking it in. The way Scarlett's blouse fell low enough on Leigh to reveal the swell of her breasts, the way she walked with increasing confidence when she wasn't swallowed up by her formless clothes.

Shit.

Once we were all seated, my fingers itched for something more familiar. A lock, a key, a pick. Anything to fiddle with and get my brain off the kiss.

After we got out of this snake pit, I'd ask Leigh out. A real date. No stolen notebooks or retired Italian smugglers looming over us. Maybe it wouldn't go anywhere. Maybe it would be the night I needed to close the door on Daphne for good. Or maybe she'd laugh and call me a joker. But hell, we could have one evening to remember.

"Shall we begin?" Giovanni's rhetorical question sliced through me, his eyes sparkling like they held secrets I was better off not knowing.

A woman sidled in then, a tray of pastries in hand. I eyed the array of sweet treats as she placed them on the table. Jayce was going to be pissed she missed this part of the trip. She would have sold her soul to be in this room right now. But as Scarlett had said, Giovanni knew exactly who was in the vault, and it wasn't Jayce.

With a polite nod, the woman exited the room.

Scarlett slid a thumb drive across the table to Giovanni. But before it reached him, Cristian's hand swooped down, snapping up the device.

"Those are photographs Declan took of the notebook," Scarlett said matter-of-factly. "Before we passed it over."

The dangerous glint in Cristian's eyes was unmistakable. Like father, like son, although Cristian lacked his father's quiet menace.

"I want to apologize, formally." Scarlett nodded at me.

"So do I," I said.

As I braced myself for an argument, Giovanni flicked his wrist dismissively.

"How did you get into my box?" His question was simple, but the weight behind it was immense. What consequences did my reply hold for Edoardo?

Scarlett's lips parted, her brain surely firing up a strategic response.

But a sharp rap from Giovanni's knuckles on the table stopped her short. He pointed at Leigh. "I want to hear from her."

My blood turned to ice. Leigh, out of all of us, was the least prepared to speak up here.

"I was lead on the vault job," I said, trying to deflect his attention.

Giovanni's genial smile warped into something far more predatory.

"Leigh was only there for training." I maintained a steady voice, despite the adrenaline coursing inside.

"That's exactly why I want to hear from her." He was an old lion, hungry for young, weak prey. Was that all it was? Or could Edoardo have given him the surveillance tapes? Did Giovanni Ferraro know Leigh was the one who'd worked the key?

Leigh turned to me, her eyes wide and questioning.

I gave her an encouraging nod, wanting to hold her hand again. Move my chair closer. "Tell him about the chain key, Leigh."

It was the safest ground. Something she could discuss in detail, while it would steer us clear of discussing the state-of-the-art tech we'd used on the vault. The less Giovanni knew about that, the better.

Nodding, Leigh turned to Giovanni, a polite apology spilling from her lips. She explained the existence of the two unique chain keys for each safe deposit box and her technique of hand-filing them. She presented a calm exterior, but I'd spent enough time with her to spot her discomfort.

Desperate to rescue her, I cut in. "Leigh's an innovative safe designer. She's into the historical, the artistic. Her vaults are works of art, literally."

Giovanni pointed at the thumb drive Cristian held. "And the notebook?"

The terrain was growing riskier by the moment. To lie or to tell the truth? We had our theories about the notebook—but didn't have any confirmation.

"The images seem to be of a recently uncovered vault in the catacombs." I held Giovanni's gaze.

Across the table, Scarlett narrowed her eyes at me. *Deflect or say nothing, Dec.*

Giovanni leaned back, his fingers steepling in front of him. "I put the notebook in the safe deposit box because I feared it would fall into the wrong hands. We had a few incidents at the villa after your last visit, Scarlett, so I didn't trust the security in my own home."

"Speaking of that visit..." Scarlett's eyebrows arched. "I saw a photo of Daniel Weber in the back of the notebook."

Giovanni's nod confirmed our suspicions. "Sì, I would've thanked you for introducing me to him in January, but he vanished a month ago."

Scarlett and Rav looked at each other for a beat. Their shared glance spoke volumes—they were as concerned about Weber's disappearance as Giovanni was. I wasn't privy to that job or how they knew Dr. Weber, but it obviously had something to do with Italian antiquities smuggling.

"I worried Daniel might try to recover the notebook, so I had a contact at Cassaforte keep an eye on things," Giovanni said.

It must have been the security guard—our so-called inside man. We'd walked right into a setup on two sides.

Leigh leaned forward, the nervous glint in her eyes replaced with a spark of curiosity. "Are we right about the vault? Is it the one in the catacombs?"

Giovanni pursed his lips, then nodded. "Sì, I funded a study of the vault, and Daniel was my lead researcher. Leonardo suspected something was going on with him, so we put a pause on the project and locked up the notebook."

Rav asked, "Did Daniel have a phoenix tattoo, by any chance?"

Giovanni and Cristian exchanged a glance before looking toward Leonardo, standing sentinel behind them. All three shook their heads.

"We were forced into stealing the notebook by a trio of men," said Scarlett.

Leonardo moved closer, his brow furrowed. "From what I heard, there wasn't any distress from your team during the theft. You didn't seem forced."

Rav pushed back his chair slightly, a protective wolf ready to defend his leader. "We're professionals."

Cristian raised a hand, muttering a low "Leo," and Leonardo backed off.

Scarlett continued. "One of the men behind it all had a phoenix tattoo on his hand. It's a mark of the Fenix Group. Are you familiar with them? Do you have any idea why they'd want your notebook?"

A vein in Giovanni's forehead pulsed like a warning signal. I shifted closer to Leigh. Something about the scene didn't sit right with me. Hell, nothing sat right with me about this.

"I've heard of them." Giovanni's gaze hardened, which he turned on Leigh. "I trust Reynolds. I've worked with them. But you"—another accusatory finger—"are an unknown entity. I will not discuss business in front of you."

To my surprise, Leigh leaned forward, her chin lifted, eyes unflinching. "If you were researching a mysterious vault and someone wanted the notebook stolen, then someone else is after your research."

Giovanni leaned forward and whispered, "That means I'll have to act before they do."

"Research doesn't move fast." Leigh seemed unaffected by the threat hiding in Giovanni's words. She leaned in to mirror him, holding his gaze. "But cracking a safe does. So if that's what they want—to open the vault—maybe they'll do it before you can find a new researcher."

A grin spread across Cristian's face. "I like her. Reynolds Recoveries should hire her."

Giovanni locked his eyes on Scarlett. "All I can say is that Fenix is collecting artifacts. They're not amassing a fortune, but from what I hear, it's a highly targeted set of items."

Scarlett unlocked her phone and showed a picture to Giovanni. It was a shot of the thug who'd tried to nab the ring from us in London—I'd captured his ugly face pretty well. "This man is behind it. I also have some personal reasons for finding him."

Personal reasons. Right. The bastard had held a gun to her new boyfriend's throat, had beaten her brother, and he worked for Scarlett's former fiancé. As if we needed more complications.

Giovanni looked at Cristian and Leonardo.

Leonardo stepped forward. "Send me the photo. We'll ask around. If we find anything, we'll let you know."

I felt a wave of tension leave the room, replaced by an uneasy truce.

Giovanni started again. "There are myths about a Pope."

Leonardo added, "Leo X."

Giovanni nodded. "He received an ancient artifact and commissioned Leonardo da Vinci to build a special vault deep within the catacombs to hide it."

"I was thinking about that," said Leigh. "But the catacombs were only rediscovered in the late sixteenth century. Da Vinci died long before that."

"And you believe every story you hear?" Giovanni pointed at her, and she shook her head. "The Church has been known to keep secrets, and this was one of them."

"Of course," Leigh whispered, her eyes widening. "So what do they think is inside?"

"The eagle standard of the lost Roman legion."

Leigh gasped, her hand flying to her mouth. I turned to her, not understanding the significance. But there was that light again, the one that flickered in her eyes when we faked our way through the Cassaforte vault. It was a snapshot of her passion, her curiosity. It was magnetic.

My mind flipped back to the car, the feeling of her lips against my cheek. It had been horribly chaste, that kiss. And in that moment, I wanted more. So much more.

Like when I'd kissed her temple in the van yesterday morning.

Jesus, these were the stupidest thoughts to be having right now. If Scarlett knew what was going through my head, she'd smack me for it.

Giovanni's eyes landed on Scarlett, a faint smile curving his lips. "I appreciate you coming to me, Ms. Reynolds. It reflects well on the character your family is known for."

Did he know Scarlett's mother? Or her father?

"But we must discuss a repayment for this slight." Giovanni's tone grew business-like. Simple and straightforward, none of the earlier menace present.

Cristian slid the thumb drive back across the table to me, his gaze heavy and cold. "We find ourselves in competition to crack that vault, and our resident expert in ancient frescoes and architecture is missing. So, we expect your assistance."

Inside, I was jumping around like a giddy schoolboy.

From the moment I'd heard about the vault in the catacombs, I'd wanted to get my hands on it. But on the outside, I was cool, offering a casual nod as if he'd asked me to help change a tire. "I'll do whatever Scarlett agrees to, but you don't need Leigh. As I said, she's learning and isn't qualified for this job."

Giovanni nodded, beckoning one goon over. "Escort Mr. Ramsay and Ms. Barton to the gardens, would you? I have some details to negotiate with Ms. Reynolds."

CHAPTER 24

LEIGH

Declan and I strolled down a pebbled garden path, the gentle sea breeze ruffling red and white flowers around us. Our shoes crunched against the gravel, mingling with the breeze, piercing the hush of the sprawling garden. The squared hedges, round bushes, and meticulously edged flowerbeds were like a postcard.

Over the top of the garden wall, the Mediterranean spread out in a vista of sapphire, teal, and turquoise. And at the center of the garden, the most breathtaking sight—a stone angel, ten feet tall, reaching toward the heavens with a lyre clutched in her hand. Water cascaded down from her fingers, each drop shimmering in the warm Italian sunlight.

"Amazing view, isn't it?" Declan's voice cut through my thoughts, his easy grin aimed at the sea.

"Yeah." My gaze was still on the fountain. It was breathtaking, all of it. How could it be so beautiful when the owner was a smuggler? Why did bad people have the corner on such beauty? Why did a man like Giovanni Ferraro effectively own that da Vinci vault hidden deep in the catacombs?

And why did Declan say I wasn't qualified?

Declan came closer, so close I felt the shift in the wind as he blocked it. "Something on your mind?"

His words from earlier bounced around in my head. Not talented enough. Like Isaac saying he didn't need me at a trade show because I was too quiet. Or Finn making fun of my books. Like a blow, each time they crossed my mind. Never enough.

"When you said I wasn't qualified, what did you mean?"

His brows winged up, face a mixture of shock and confusion tinged with something else. Something tender. Regret? He sighed, staring out at the sea again. "I didn't mean it like that."

"But that's exactly what you said." I stepped in front of him, forcing his attention to me. Our eyes locked, flecks of gold dancing in his hazel depths. "Why would you say it if you didn't mean it?"

He ran a hand through his hair. "You've gotten caught up in some bad stuff since you arrived in Rome."

I crossed my arms and took a deep breath. "I know. One little job led to another. Fixing Edoardo's safe, then the Cassaforte test, stealing Giovanni's notebook, and now? Now we're visiting a wealthy smuggler's villa."

"That's the problem." He sounded uncharacteristically tender. "It sounds like Giovanni wants us to crack the vault in the catacombs. But what comes after that? And what if we're not lucky next time? Why would you want to go even further down that rabbit hole?"

No idea.

"What if it's something worse?" Declan's gaze grew distant. "I mean, what if there's something diseased inside? Bodies, maybe. Why would a pope commission a vault down there? Hidden away for centuries?"

I shivered at his words, the breeze suddenly much cooler. "You have a point. They must've wanted to keep something secret. Something dangerous, maybe."

"Exactly. Giovanni thinks it's the eagle standard of this lost legion. But who knows?"

"Plus, Martina's kidnappers wanted the notebook. They're obviously after whatever's inside the vault, too."

His gaze fell on me, a hardness in his eyes. "Which only adds another layer of danger to the whole mess."

A wave of anxiety washed over me, the familiar knotting of my stomach. This wasn't what I had in mind when I dreamed of Rome.

Snapping us away from talk of danger, he asked, "What is the lost legion, anyway?"

"It was a Roman military legion that disappeared, theoretically at least, in northern England in the second or third century."

"I've never heard of that." He stared up toward the angel's hand, a rainbow forming in the mist around the spray. "You're a smart woman."

Flower petals floated around the pool at the base of the statue. The burbling noise, the wind, the scent of the flowers all around us. And a man paying me a compliment. My ex-boyfriends found my curiosity, my love of learning, too nerdy. Especially Finn. Finn, who everyone wanted me to get back together with. Finn, who Ann proclaimed was so smart, but my brain threatened him.

"What do you need a PhD for?" Finn had laughed. "You work for your family."

I wanted more than my quiet little life with everyone suffocating me, for fear I might breathe in the wrong direction and keel over.

I'd wanted a Roman adventure, the type my stepmother teased me about, the kind my overprotective brother Isaac tried to prevent. I wanted to experience the world outside of the vaults and locks at Barton Safes.

And now, here I was, in the middle of a real-life Roman adventure, wrapped up in danger and intrigue. With Declan and the Reynolds team, no less. Ironic, wasn't it? *Be careful what you wish for, Leigh.* Instead of the lust-fueled adventure I'd hoped for, I was left with one that could cost me more than just a broken heart.

"Do you... do you like smart women?" The words were out of my mouth before I could stop them, and I held my breath, suddenly aware that his answer mattered. More than I wanted to admit.

Declan looked down at me and took a step closer, sharing a silence that wasn't awkward. His irises were pale in the brilliant sunlight, reflecting a depth, a mystery. He took my face in his hands, his big hands with the long fingers, and leaned closer. Before his lips met mine, he whispered, "Very much."

His lips were soft, yet insistent against mine. It wasn't like the car when I'd misread his actions. His tongue probed into my mouth, and I opened to him, tasting the pastry he'd eaten from Giovanni's table.

I melted and slid my arms around him, skimming over the hard muscle of his back, each flex with his movements sucking the willpower out of me. I sighed into his mouth. His taste, his fingers moving into my hair, his hungry moan.

This was what I'd wanted from my trip. The villa, the garden, the stunning views. And a man like Declan Ramsay. Strong, daring, complex. A man who kissed like he was claiming every inch of me.

One of his hands lowered to my waist and he pulled me closer, so close his hardness pressed against my belly. Oh god. He wanted me. The realization filled me with a strange power—a power I'd never felt before—that a man could want me so hard and so fast.

I flexed one hand on his back, gripping the muscle along his spine, and his hand dropped lower as he deepened the kiss. His thumb skirted over my hipbone in a teasing circle, and I shivered at the sensation it sent throughout my body. My heartbeat pounded in my ears, a vision of straddling him on the nearby bench overwhelming me.

The moment was wild and exciting; I wanted to take what he offered. I could feel his arousal growing against me, and I ached for more contact with him.

This was real.

Raw, primal, and utterly delicious.

A Vespa. That and the Trevi Fountain are all I need now. What a silly thought. I slid my arms around his neck, raking my nails over the back of his head.

His tongue swept against mine, circling, prodding, learning. It wasn't a battle. It was a dance. *This man can kiss.*

When our mouths finally separated, we remained wrapped in each other's arms. His breath was warm against my lips as he looked at me, a smirk playing on his lips. "Are you going to apologize for that kiss, too?"

"No." I could barely breathe, need pooling deep in my core. "I'm not."

His smile was soft, teasing. "Good. Because I do like smart women. Even ones who cover me in indigo dye."

I would have laughed if my brain weren't halfway to the bench. "It was a good color on you."

"It was fucking brilliant." He kissed me again, even hungrier, his hand trailing to my ass, pulling me against his hard cock.

I pressed myself against him, wanting more of what he had to offer. Our tongues stroked each other in a desperate frenzy, and a thrill rushed through me as his second hand started tracing the line of my back down to the base of my spine. His touch felt like fire against my skin.

When he pulled away again, his eyes searched mine. "I've wanted to do that since the day we met."

"I felt the same." My heart pounded in my chest, the raw honesty sending a burst of heat through me. Not a *What do you think?* or a *Are you okay?* No, just an *I want you.*

Rav cleared his throat, announcing his arrival. I jumped, startled, but Declan barely moved—other than to shift his lower hand up to my waist.

A barely-there smirk lifted the corners of Rav's mouth. "Sorry to interrupt."

"No problem," Declan replied, a casual smile playing on his lips. "You just walked in on a very important discussion about the catacombs vault."

Right. The catacombs vault. Giovanni Ferraro. "What's the decision, Rav?"

"Scarlett's agreed for Declan and Jayce to do reconnaissance. Then we revisit with Giovanni." He strolled over to the stone bench I'd been eying, where a kitten had poked out its head. He knelt to give it a scratch. "There are contingencies and options, but it's a fair deal."

The twinge of disappointment surprised me, but I squashed it quickly, accustomed to hiding things like that. Scarlett was looking out for her team, after all. And I wasn't really part of her team. I'd just fallen in with them and was tagging along while things spiraled out of control.

But now, I wanted to stay with the Reynolds team for a different reason. Declan. Determination flared in my chest. "I'm coming with you."

Rav smiled. "I had a feeling."

Declan frowned. "It's too dangerous, Leigh. I'm not letting you fall any deeper into this crazy disaster."

A bitter laugh escaped my lips. It was all too familiar, the same patronizing concern Isaac had shown me, keeping me holed up in Rome. The same thing Finn used to do, declaring I needed a man to handle whatever was going on. He'd even had the nerve—after convincing me to take a year off school—to suggest I stop working and get pregnant. I'd told him I wanted to wait a few years, but he expected things of me on *his* timeline.

Now it was Declan's turn. I was good enough to kiss, but not good enough to accompany him somewhere.

"I don't need to be protected," I said, sharper than I intended.

"You're talking about things you don't understand." Declan's tone was final, dismissive.

"So much for the smart girl, right?" I jerked away from him, irritation flaring. "Maybe you can explain it to me in simpler terms."

"Leigh..." He stepped closer, thinking he was going to toss an arm around my shoulder and magically fix everything. That was what they all did. A condescending 'Leigh...' and the reminder I was the fragile little doll.

It could have been a perfect day. But then there were the men with guns, the dangerous smuggler, and now Declan's reminder that I wasn't qualified. It was like a splash of cold water on my face, a wake-up call.

I barely knew this man.

But I was no damsel in distress, waiting for a fairy tale ending.

"Fine," I snapped. Without another word, I marched past Rav, my chin held high. Time to find my own stupid adventure.

CHAPTER 25

DECLAN

Hours later, I fumed in my hotel room. I yanked open my equipment duffel, the metallic clatter reminding me why I was in Rome. I ran my fingers over the cold steel of my mini-rig drill, its reassuring strength reminding me of what was real and what wasn't. Black and white. Open and closed.

Not *I'll protect you* is good in the vault, but *I'll protect you* at Ferraro's is bad. Not *I want to kiss you now*, then *I don't want to listen to you*.

"Fuck," I muttered, trying to forget Leigh's face as she'd stormed off. I thought keeping her safe was what she wanted. That's what women liked, right? A protective arm? A sturdy presence?

It was easier than expressing the jumbled emotions I wrestled with. I unzipped a side pocket and pulled out one of my lock pick sets. It only reminded me of her skill. The speed she picked the curved keyway faster than I did.

"Women," I huffed out, tossing the picks onto the bed. "Easier cracking an Eisenhart VIII."

God, the vault. It had been all of a day and a half since the world went to shit. Her frightened eyes mirroring the cold steel enclosure. But she'd found comfort in me that night, appreci-ated my hand on her cheek and arm around her in the van.

I'd thought I was giving her that again at Giovanni's. Safety. Stability.

My hands traveled deeper into the bag, pulling out a stetho-scope. The way her heart had beat against mine in the garden. Those deep-brown eyes, her gaze warm like the Italian sun. They always had a distant sadness, but not in the garden. They'd flared with heat and longing—the same longing I'd felt.

"It was just a fucking kiss, Dec." I ran a hand over my face.

But it wasn't just a kiss. It was the catacombs under Rome, the tension and the danger, the metallic taste of fear and excite-ment. The intense hunger behind the kiss. Then Rav's fucking interruption.

And then, just like that, she'd stormed off. I'd thought I was doing right by her. I'd thought our kiss meant something.

I pulled out another piece of equipment, a magnetic case for my phone, and laid it on the table. Sighing, I looked over the array of tools, my own personal chaos mirroring the storm in my head.

"What was so wrong with me saying that?" I asked the empty room, receiving only silence in return.

My fingers brushed against an unexpected object in the duf-fel's bottom, and I pulled out a book—Hartley's *Vaults of the World*. Leigh's book. The worn corners, the soft texture of its well-thumbed pages—a stark contrast to the cold precision of my gear. A rush of memories cascaded through me.

"Women," I whispered, staring at the book.

That was her world, built from paper and ink. A woman who designed vaults from steel, yet harbored a secret love for softer arts. From the day we met, something about her had pulled me closer. She wasn't just another job or another woman. She was Leigh Barton.

It hadn't started that day at Edoardo's.

It had started a month prior. The night I'd snuck into the Barton Safes and Locks building with Scarlett and Rav, searching for some specs. We needed all the details we could find about the case for the Codex of San Marco. The case Leigh had designed was a masterpiece.

Yeah. Some part of me wanted that woman from the moment I laid eyes on her engineering drawings.

Then I got to know her laugh. Her smile.

The way she lit up when we talked shop or she was teasing about filing that chain key faster than me. But how she shut down so completely every time someone said just the wrong thing?

It was only Saturday night. In the pre-dawn hours of Friday morning, we'd hustled to pack up our stuff, trying to stay one step ahead of the Cassaforte fallout. I'd shoved Leigh's books into my bag, not thinking, just moving. And in the confusion and panic, I'd forgotten about them, just as I'd tucked my feelings for her in a corner of my head.

I scanned the room, as if expecting her to materialize, standing there with downcast eyes or fiddling with the hem of her shirt.

Why hadn't she reminded me about the books? Did she forget them too? Or did she just not care as much as I'd thought?

Staring at the book, I muttered, "Guess you're just as confusing as a woman, eh?"

No reply, of course. I returned to my preparations for the catacombs recon, the books a silent reminder of the wrong priorities, which were dominating my brain.

A knock on the door cut through my thoughts. I set the book down, my hand lingering on the cover before I moved to the door. Peering through the peephole, I found Rav's stoic face.

I opened the door, leaning against the frame. "What? Can't let a man wallow in his existential crisis in peace?"

Rav snorted, stepping into the room. "I'm here to check on your prep. We going light tonight?"

I waved toward my duffel, its contents sprawled over the bed and side table. "Just reconnaissance. Brought some extra flashlight batteries. Most of my tools are for metal safes, not thousand-year-old catacombs."

Rav picked up the magnetic case, giving it a once-over before putting it back down. "And the notebook? You've been looking at the photos?"

I rolled my eyes and turned to my gear, stuffing the tools into my mission backpack. "Yes, Mom, I did my homework."

Rav chuckled, the deep sound vibrating through the room. The banter, the camaraderie—it was familiar, comforting. In the face of uncertainty, at least some things never changed. He'd been my friend as long as Scarlett had. He'd been to every birthday party since I was twelve. Double-dates when we were teens. Then he left for special training, and the man I'd known most of my life disappeared. He was close, but his eyes hadn't been the same since before he went off the grid for a year.

Unearthing another book from the chaos of my duffel, I swallowed hard. *The Fortress Within*. A cruel irony, considering my defenses had been anything but fortress-like around Leigh.

"I should've kept my damn walls up," I grumbled, tossing the book onto the table.

Rav slouched down into a chair, frowning deeply for my benefit. "Maybe it's for the best. She's not your type, anyway."

I rounded on him, a long file clutched in my hand. "And what's that supposed to mean?"

He shrugged, unflappable as ever. "You know what I mean. Leigh's not right for you."

"Fuck off, Rav." If I'd gripped the file any harder, I would have snapped the damn thing in half. "This isn't any of your business."

"Of course not." He just smirked at me, the bastard, knowing exactly which buttons to push. "I mean, you're not hurt or anything, right?"

His words were like a punch to the gut.

"I—I just—Shut up, Rav."

"Touched a nerve, did I?" He let out a low chuckle.

He had me. And he knew it. I glared at him, tossing the file onto the bed. For a moment, we were two kids again, one always trying to best the other. Only now, the game was my love life, and I was losing.

Rav leaned back, leveling me with his gaze. "Women's hearts aren't vaults, Dec. You can't just crack them open and think that's the end of it."

"Exactly why I prefer safes," I grumbled. "Thought I'd cracked her, then... boom, angry woman appears."

Rav glanced at the books on the table. "What are you hoping to find in the catacombs?"

His abrupt change of topic caught me off guard, but it was a better conversation than the one we'd been having. "I don't know. It could be anything."

"Exactement." Rav pointed at me. "Just like Leigh. You've cracked her exterior, and now you're overwhelmed by what's inside."

I looked at *The Fortress Within* again, considering his words. "Maybe she's stronger than we all think. Especially Isaac."

Rav snorted. "Isaac's an idiot. Seems like he's been smothering Leigh all her life."

"Maybe..." Something clicked. I nodded slowly, my mind racing. "Maybe she thinks I was trying to treat her like Isaac did—telling her what she can and can't do."

"Now you're thinking. It's one thing to stand by a woman and support her, but it's another to make her feel like she can't do anything without you. It should be her choice, either way."

I sighed, my gaze falling on my tools. "Safes are definitely easier than women."

Rav had a knack for digging straight into the heart of a matter. It pissed me off every time he did it to me. "Plus, if you two spent too much time together, you'd eventually confess about breaking into her family's company."

"You accusing me of being too honest?"

"I'd never." He flipped his hands over in consideration. "Too cocky, more like?"

I pressed a hand to the top book, remembering what we'd found inside Barton Safes. It hadn't seemed important when we were there, but that was the first step on the path to where I stood now. From the Codex job to the Albrecht house to Venice and then to Edoardo's doorstep. "You remember there were two copies of the Codex case?"

"Ben ouais. We could barely pull you away from them."

"Leigh designed it."

Rav sat forward, elbows on knees. "You think she works for Fenix?"

"No." There'd been two versions of the specs. One for Phillip Maguire and one for Fenix. "She's a good person, but it's possible they're using her company."

"Isaac?"

I clenched my jaw. I wanted to say yes. Say the jerk who talked down to Leigh was behind something like that, but I wasn't ready for that yet. "We should get Brie to look into the rest of the Barton employees."

He pushed his shaggy black hair from his forehead. It was a habit he'd picked up over the last few years, after he stopped cutting it military-short. "Is that what you were doing in the garden? Interrogation?"

"Shut up, Rav."

"It's a good lead." He pulled out his phone and typed some notes. "We'll start with looking into Leigh and Isaac again, though, since they're here. I'd rather not let anyone get the jump on us."

"Reasonable." I shook off the discussion and returned to our original goal. "Jayce and I are going underground. Brie and Will will monitor our GPS, keeping us on the right path. We'll all stay in touch via earpieces."

Rav nodded. "I'll be at the wheel, waiting to pick you up. Scarlett, Malcolm, and Emmett are at the catacombs right now, dealing with any potential surveillance."

I mulled over my tools again, selecting the drill and a flexible endoscope. "I'll take these, though I'm not sure how the drill will fare against the vault door without knowing what kind of stone we're dealing with. Sandstone or tufa, sure, but what if it's marble? Granite?"

Rav grunted in agreement, standing and stretching his broad shoulders. "Your portable x-ray may help, but there'll be a lot of playing it by ear."

"A spectrometer would've been handy." I began packing my gear meticulously. I had a job to do, a mystery to unravel. One that wasn't Leigh. One that was a welcome distraction.

"Remember, this is a recon mission. Get the details, snap some photos and videos, then get out. You're not opening that vault tonight." His eyes bore into mine, serious and full of intent. "And watch out for traps."

I frowned at him, holding up my lock pick set. "C'mon, Rav. I've been doing this for a while now. I know all about traps."

My mind flashed back to Leigh's safe, the unexpected trap that had caught me off guard. Stink gas and dye—her trap had bested me because I was too busy trying to impress her. But tonight was different. This was business. She wouldn't be there, and I'd be in game mode.

"All right, all right. I'll be careful. You should probably worry more about Jayce, though. She's the one likely to try and crack the thing open on a whim."

Rav chuckled, shaking his head. "Then make sure you pack a chocolate bar or something. She'll follow you anywhere."

His words were light, but they masked a deeper truth: we were stepping into the unknown, and the stakes were higher than they should have been, because we didn't know what Giovanni would do if we failed. For tonight, the job was clear—gather intel and get out. No heroics, no theatrics. Just pure, professional precision. As much as the thrill of cracking the mystery vault beckoned me, I had to keep my priorities straight.

Another knock rattled the door, pulling my attention away from my gear. Rav stood abruptly, his instincts on high alert as I moved to answer.

Jayce, a lollipop sticking out of her mouth, greeted us as she barged into the room. She shot a quick nod at Rav before turning her attention to me. "You wearing your thermal suit?" she asked, her words garbled around the candy. "Remember how cold it was in the catacombs yesterday?"

"Yeah, I'm wearing it." I pointed to the tight suit on the bed. "Did you bring your respirator mask? It might get dusty down there."

She held up the mask she'd brought, a satisfied grin on her face. "Yep."

"How about elbow pads, knee pads, and a headlamp?"

"Seriously, Declan?" She rolled her eyes. "This isn't my first job, you know."

"I'm just making sure." I nudged her shoulder before pulling out my own mask. "We were told to pack for a fancy wedding job when we left home three weeks ago, not for spelunking in the underbelly of Rome."

"Fair point."

"Did you pack a thermal imaging camera?" I asked.

She shook her head. "That one, I didn't."

"Or a moisture meter?"

"No, but I did bring a crowbar," she announced with a smirk.

It wasn't exactly what I had in mind.

Wait. Did she actually bring one? Or was that a crack about when we met Leigh and Isaac?

"You know..." Jayce pulled the lollipop from her mouth and pointed it at me. "Maybe we should see what Leigh packed. Remember what she did with Edoardo's safe? She said something to me about tar and ball bearings."

I sighed. "Considering recent events, I don't think borrowing anything from Leigh would be the best idea."

"You might be right. She seemed more broody than usual when you guys got back from Giovanni's." Jayce's eyes flicked between Rav and me, suspicion seeping into her gaze. "Wait a second... are you the reason for her mood, Dec?"

Heat was not rising in my cheeks. I did not turn back to Leigh's books. Nor did I contemplate giving them to Jayce to return to their rightful owner.

But as my fingers brushed against the books' covers, a stubborn thought implanted itself in my mind. I didn't want to avoid Leigh; I wanted to see her again, wanted to mend the hole which had formed between us. Tomorrow, after I gathered more information about the vault in the catacombs, I'd ask for her opinion. Leigh, with her insatiable curiosity about history and art, would undoubtedly have insightful thoughts on the matter. That would fix things.

Rav's chuckle interrupted my train of thought. He slapped my shoulder, a knowing grin on his face. "Yes, Dec, you are the reason for her mood." He turned to Jayce. "We should get going. You need to nap before the job."

Jayce, on her way out of the room, threw over her shoulder, "You know, Leigh has a blowtorch. Maybe we could bring her and the blowtorch along?"

"I think she's more likely to use it on me than on the vault." The reminder of Leigh wielding a blowtorch in my direction at Edoardo's made me wince. "Plus, we're going in for reconnaissance, not a demolition job. Remember that."

Jayce winked at me, a mischievous smile dancing on her lips. "Of course we are."

Her tone made it clear her interpretation of reconnaissance was vastly different from mine.

CHAPTER 26

LEIGH

I leaned against the wall outside the room I shared with Jayce. I stared at the scarred wooden floor of the hallway, and took a slow, steadying breath.

"Talk to him," I whispered to myself.

His room was only a few doors away, but my feet remained glued to the floor. I clenched my hands into fists, my nails digging into my palms. His lips on mine. My fists released. His hand trailing down my ass. His moans. The desire he hadn't tried to hide.

Then the sting of his words.

He'd kissed me. God, the sexy safe cracker had kissed the hell out of me, and I yelled at him then ran away. My stomach twisted at the memory of Declan's face when I stormed off.

His words had hurt, not the kiss. The idea that he thought I was some delicate, defenseless damsel needing his protection boiled my blood. Sure, Declan was the Reynolds ace safe cracker, but I wasn't just an engineer; I was an artist. I understood safe construction as well as he did. My place was with that team when Declan and Jayce went to the vault. Scarlett said I was part of the team. I belonged in the depths of Rome with them.

"Dammit," I muttered, pushing myself away from the wall. It was time to set things straight. He needed to see me—really see me—and understand I wouldn't stand on the sidelines. Not while he got to inspect a vault created by Leonardo da Vinci which no one had ever opened.

I took another deep breath, ordered the butterflies in my stomach to calm down, and headed for Declan's door.

My books were a perfectly good excuse to visit him. Innocent enough. Maybe I'd apologize for losing my temper. Maybe I'd look down at my shoes and whisper it out like the good little girl who did what everyone wanted.

Screw that.

Maybe I'd tell him what he could do with his stupid words.

Or maybe he'd sweep me into his arms again. We'd pick up where we'd left off. I'd push him onto the bed and tell him to fuck me. I'd have my Roman fling and be done with it. He was obviously interested, and it wasn't as if Isaac would let me meet anyone else on my own.

The closer I got, the slower I walked, practically jumping at every squeak of the floorboards.

Could I do this?

I tucked my hands into the pockets of my loose jeans and stopped in front of his door. Should I knock or should I retreat? Jayce had come back to the room twenty minutes ago, saying Declan and Rav had ordered naps all around before their venture into the catacombs.

Would I be interrupting him?

I sighed deep inside, the memories of our kiss flushing heat through me. His rough hands, the warmth of his lips. The way he'd said he loved smart women.

You're not weak, Leigh. You're not the woman Finn said you were. You're not the woman your stepmother sees.

And I damn sure wasn't a woman who needed Declan's protection.

I wasn't a little girl who needed to be kept out of harm's way. I was a woman who could stand on her own feet. Who could make her own decisions. I was a damn good safe engineer. I could handle Declan Ramsay.

Squaring my shoulders, I rapped my knuckles against the door. Was I too loud? I didn't want to wake anyone else up. Was I not loud enough? I wanted him to wake up.

The door opened a minute later, revealing a sleepy-eyed, tousled Declan. A somehow-even-sexier Declan. It probably had something to do with the black lounge pants he was wearing, his mouth-watering chiseled chest on full display. Abs for days. A light smattering of hair across his pecs. A trail of it leading lower. "Leigh?"

"Declan." Every word I'd planned fled from my brain. What *was* my plan? What had I rehearsed? "I had a big dream about my trip to Rome."

He blinked slowly, like he was still waking up. It had only been twenty minutes since Jayce came back. How fast did the man get to sleep? "Do you want to come in?"

I hesitated. *You were supposed to ask about the books, Leigh. What a mess.* "Actually, I'm here for my books."

"Of course." Declan stepped aside to let me in. He walked over to a table where my books lay stacked, their familiar covers triggering a surge of longing. As he picked them up, he turned toward me, his lips parting to speak.

"No, listen." I raised a hand before he could say anything, ignoring the books he held. "I had this big dream of coming to Rome, having a grand adventure, meeting a man I'd have a torrid love affair with. We'd ride a Vespa around the city, throw coins into the Trevi Fountain, swearing to return together, knowing we never would."

He stood still, one hand full of my books, the other covering a yawn. The drawn-out sound amplified the pounding of my heart and the ridiculousness of my words. *Keep going, Leigh. You'll get to the point soon enough.*

"Instead, I broke into a vault, fled a hotel in the middle of the night, wore a disguise to see the Catacombs, ran from a crazy security guy, met an antiquities smuggler, and I screwed up my chance at a torrid love affair." The words all tumbled out in a gush. Had I said even half of the things I'd planned? "I messed it all up, Declan."

He returned my books to the table and shook his head slightly. "Leigh, are you okay?"

"My mother died in a car accident when I was ten. I was in the car with her." The words were out before I could stop them. The memory of that night still as vivid as if it had happened yesterday. "She had a ruptured aneurysm that caused it, and they found one in my brain, too. They operated and took care of it, but I spent weeks in the hospital. It took me a long time to recover."

My vision blurred, but I forced myself to keep talking. For once, someone would listen to me. "After that, every man in my family treated me like I was made of glass, like another aneurysm was going to show up any second and they'd lose me, too. Every man I ever dated did exactly the same. My stepmother only made it worse, but I think it was more about jealousy than concern."

Declan scrubbed his hands over his face, the sleepy look finally clearing. "I don't understand."

Tears welled in my eyes, but I blinked them away. I had to say this. I had to let Declan know I wasn't the pathetic, helpless woman they made me out to be. "Everyone's always trying to protect me, Declan. I stayed in a toxic relationship for two years because I didn't know what it was like to make my own decisions. I put my degree on hold for him because he didn't like how much time I was investing in my dissertation, and I didn't think I mattered."

"Dissertation?"

"So you said you wanted to protect me, and it freaked me out." I rubbed my palms against my jeans. "It reminded me of him. And I didn't like that. Especially not when it came from you."

His confused expression softened.

What else was there to say after that ridiculous diatribe? "I know I'm rambling. But after the car ride home, I realized I got the adventure I wanted."

"You've lost me."

"I don't want your protection."

"I'm sorry, Leigh." Declan let out another yawn, running a hand through his messy hair. "I didn't realize that until I got back, too. I said what I thought you wanted to hear."

"What I want—I want the other thing." I stepped closer to him, heat rising in my cheeks. *Say it and to hell with the consequences.* "I want another kiss, Declan."

The corner of his lips twitched, and he closed the distance between us. "Tell me everything you want."

"I want to taste you, to feel your hands on me." I lifted a tentative hand toward him, touching him, running it over the dark hair, down his tanned chest. Hard as a rock. "I want more, no matter how bad an idea it is. I don't care if we'll never see each other again, but I want one night with you." I swallowed hard, steeling myself, trying to prevent my hands from shaking. "What I want to hear is you moaning my name."

That was a first. But the heat creeping up my cheeks was plenty familiar.

Instead of recoiling, Declan's eyes darkened with desire. He grabbed my face, like he had in the garden, and his lips crashed into mine. We picked up where we'd left off, his tongue just as demanding, as urgent.

I surrendered to him, giving in to the need coursing through me. His touch was commanding yet gentle at the same time; possessive yet tender. An eternity later, we finally pulled away from each other, needy and breathless. He kissed me again—softer this time, but no less passionate—as if he couldn't bring himself to let me go.

Heat pooled between my legs as he ran his hands down my body, skating them over curves and angles with purpose. His muscular arms pulled me tight, hoisting me up so my legs wrapped around his hips.

With a groan, he walked us to the bed. His grip was strong but not constricting, his warmth seeping into me. His voice, husky and low, sent shivers down my spine. "I'll moan your name, Leigh Barton," he growled, sex dripping off his words. "But only after you scream mine."

CHAPTER 27

DECLAN

In a rush of desperate craving, I crushed Leigh against me, her legs locked around my waist. Our lips moved in rhythm, exploring, insisting. Every part of her radiated an intoxicating heat that made my blood pound in my veins. The bed's edge grazed the back of my knees, and I sank down so Leigh straddled me. Our kiss deepened, and a moan escaped from somewhere deep within me.

The kiss was an inferno, lighting a spark of desire in me that roared into a wildfire. This wasn't just about physical attraction. This was about Leigh. Clever, talented Leigh with her quiet intensity and her fiery spirit that everyone tamped down. Her curious mind was a labyrinth I wanted to get lost in, a puzzle I longed to decipher.

Simple women weren't what I wanted. Who had I been trying to convince? I wanted a messy, complex, intriguing woman. One that took me longer to figure out than any vault I'd opened.

Leigh was always so agreeable, so soft-spoken, but tonight? Tonight, she'd come to me, demanding, assertive, unyielding.

It was the sexiest, most confident thing I'd ever seen. I loved this side of her, this fire that she hid beneath layers of gentleness.

And a doctoral student? Even fucking sexier.

Rav had ordered me to take a nap, to prepare for the late night in the catacombs. But sleep was not happening. All I wanted was Leigh. The urgency of her against me, the way she moved with an almost desperate eagerness, stirred something primal within me.

My heart hammered against my rib cage, my breaths came in ragged gasps between kisses. Every touch was an electrical charge, every gasp a spark that ignited my senses. It was a dance, a communion, a battle and a surrender all at once.

With every passing moment, the room, the impending re-con, the catacombs—they all faded into insignificance. In this moment, there was only Leigh, only us, only this need that threatened to consume us both.

A knock at the door cut through the heated haze. Leigh stilled, her eyes widening slightly. I cursed under my breath. The knock came again, harder, more insistent, and an unwelcome voice carried through the door, unmistakably Isaac's.

"Ignore it," I murmured against Leigh's lips, but the knock thundered again, louder, more commanding.

Leigh inched back, shaking her head. "I can't."

With a growl, I nipped at her neck. My blood sang with desire, but irritation was attempting to replace it. "I'll get rid of him."

"I'll hide in the bathroom." Leigh slipped off my lap, her eyes full of worry. "I don't want Isaac to know I'm here."

Her confidence deflated. Just like that. It was wrong how easily Isaac's presence robbed her of her assertiveness. I wanted to pull her back, to reignite the flame that was burning just second ago. Open the door and show Isaac my half-naked body and his sister's swollen lips.

Leaning in, I pressed a soft kiss to her temple, my hands brushing her cheeks. "We're picking up right here as soon as he leaves."

Her smile flickered back to life, a hint of mischief glinting in her eyes. "I'd like that."

Once the bathroom door closed behind Leigh, I took a moment to compose myself, let the raging hard-on die a little, then swung open the hotel room door.

Isaac stood there, a plastic smile plastered on his face, oblivious.

"It's late. I'm headed to bed."

Unperturbed, Isaac held up a bottle of red wine and two glasses, barging past me into the room. "I'm here to thank you, Dec."

My gaze flicked back to the bathroom door, my short temper flaring. Leigh was waiting, and this jackass was playing sommelier in my hotel room. "I'm not in the mood for guests or thank yous, Isaac. I need some sleep."

He set the bottle and glasses down on the table beside my gear and uncorked the bottle. As he poured the wine, his gaze roamed over my tools. "No one would give me any info. But you're heading to the catacombs vault, aren't you?"

He'd egged me on earlier, saying how exciting it would be, while I'd maintained the vault was a no-go for safety issues.

"It's the price we have to pay for Edoardo's double-cross," I muttered, my eyes never leaving Isaac.

"Going tonight?" He offered me a glass of wine, his own held high in a toast.

I took it but didn't drink. I didn't like wine and I didn't like intruders. "Isaac, I told you, I am heading to sleep."

"Of course. Before you do, I wanted to offer my official thank you, Declan, for getting my little sister out of that ordeal with the smuggler." His sincerity took me by surprise. "Leigh's not built for excitement like that. She's a quiet, law-abiding girl. Wants to settle down, get married, and have a few kids."

Maybe that was true. Maybe Leigh wanted all those simple, beautiful things. But that wasn't the woman who'd spilled her deepest desires to me moments ago, talking about her longing for a grand adventure and a love affair. Or who wanted me moaning her name. My cock twitched again, practically hauling me to the bathroom door.

Isaac leaned in closer, as though confiding a secret to a confidante. "Normally, I look out for her, but with all these meetings, it's been hard." He raised his glass again. He was stubborn. "Thanks to your team for watching over my little bug."

Enough was enough. I put my untouched glass of wine back on the table, shaking my head. "Have you ever really talked to your sister? Because it doesn't sound like you know her at all."

Isaac handed the glass back to me, but I took it and placed it on the table. "Leigh's capable of a hell of a lot more than you give her credit for."

"You barely know—"

"I know enough. You didn't see her in the Cassaforte vault. The determination in her eyes was inspiring. So were her steady hands when she filed that key for Giovanni's safe deposit box."

I'd seen plenty of contractors crumble under pressure, but not Leigh. She was fucking brilliant.

Isaac frowned. "She was crying when you left Cassaforte."

"So what?" I shot back, not letting him gain the upper hand. "She held it together when it mattered and did exactly what she needed to. She held it in when the pressure was on, then let it out after."

Leigh had too much practice holding everything in, especially around her overbearing brother. Every time she was around Isaac, her vibrant energy dimmed, like she was suppressing who she really was.

Isaac motioned toward Leigh's books on the table beside my tools. "Why do you have her books?"

"Packed them by mistake when we left the other hotel," I snapped. "I forgot about them."

Isaac chuckled. "Bookworm, that one. Bet she could've figured out that catacombs vault."

The words hit me like a punch. He was right. I should've welcomed her help. She was the only one in the meeting with Giovanni who even knew what the lost legion was. I'd been as dismissive as Isaac, treating her like a fragile little thing that needed protecting.

"When are you heading to the catacombs?" Isaac asked. "You taking a nap because you're going tonight?"

That's it. It was none of his damn business. "I'm going to sleep because I'm tired, Isaac. It's been a long couple of days, and I want you to leave."

Isaac offered the wine to me again, insisting on a single toast. I hated wine, but I took the glass.

"To you and your team, Declan. For everything you've done, no matter how insane," Isaac said, lifting his glass in a salute.

We raised our glasses, but I didn't drink. I put mine on the table, my desire to get rid of Isaac outweighing any social courtesies. My mother would have smacked me for being so rude. I didn't care. Handing him the bottle, I ushered him toward the door.

"Let me know when you're heading to the catacombs?" Isaac said, excitement clear in his voice. *Could* he be working with the Fenix kidnappers? If he was, why so insistent about me going? "I'd love to see that vault."

"Sure, I'll let you know," I lied.

"And please, Declan. If Leigh asks, don't tell her when you're going." He stood in the doorway, blocking my opportunity to slam it. "She has health concerns that can flare up if she gets too excited. Anything like that might be dangerous."

"You should have more faith in your sister, Isaac." Part of me knew he was right. The catacombs were no place for Leigh. I needed to keep her safe. No, I *wanted* to keep her safe. I *needed* to let her be herself. "But no, I won't let her go if she asks."

With Isaac finally gone, I turned my attention to my priority. When I opened the bathroom door, a lump lodged in my throat. Tears shimmered in Leigh's eyes. She must've heard everything Isaac said. Our moment had passed. She wouldn't want me now. Not after what Isaac said about her.

"Your brother's an ass," I said, venting my frustration.

To my surprise, she nudged me backward, a determined glint in her eyes.

"Is it true too much excitement is dangerous for you?"

"No." She nudged me again.

"How can you be sure?"

"I get checked regularly by a fantastic medical team. I'm sick and tired of everyone treating me like I'm about to drop dead at any second."

"I won't treat you that way."

"I'm coming with you to the vault tonight," she declared.

My mind screamed at the danger. If the kidnappers were there, it was no place for Leigh. But the look in her eyes told me she would fight me if I disagreed. "Okay."

Leigh nudged me again, this time toward the bed. Maybe we'd have our fun here first. "I know more about historical safe design than you do."

I couldn't deny it. She was right. I gestured toward the untouched glass of red wine on the table. "Do you want that?"

She rolled her eyes. "I hate red wine. I'm tired of telling people I like it just so I don't hurt their feelings."

As she made to nudge me backward once again, I grabbed her wrist, pulling her flush against me. She looked up at me, her eyes wide, her heartbeat vying with mine for which could beat faster.

"I'm done being protected by all the men around me," she breathed. "I want to live my life."

In a swift motion, I picked her up, her surprised yelp ringing in my ears. I spun us around, dropping us onto the bed so I was pinning her underneath me. The look of surprise in her eyes quickly changed into something inviting.

Very inviting.

"I like the sound of that," I said, leaning closer. "And we're going to ignore any further knocks at the door."

CHAPTER 28

LEIGH

Declan hovered above me, his eyes locked with mine, a mischievous smirk playing on his lips. I was still reeling from him agreeing to both my propositions—having sex and joining the Reynolds team for the catacombs vault mission.

Was this really happening? The quiet Leigh Barton had finally spoken up and told someone about her desires. Adrenaline and excitement battled for dominance. It was both terrifying and liberating.

"Leigh," Declan whispered, his breath hot against my neck. He peppered soft kisses along my throat, causing shivers to shoot down my spine. His hands slid under the hem of my loose T-shirt, fingertips grazing my stomach, making me quiver with anticipation.

"Let me give you a blow job." That was always step one.

"No." Declan lifted his head, a hungry grin spreading across his face. "In my world, the woman always comes first."

A bolt of desire shot through me. I wanted this man more than I'd ever wanted anyone else. What was it? Something more than our shared passion, but what? I'd always put my needs last. But Declan wanted to put them first.

"Is that so?" I said, hopefully sounding more confident than I felt. "Show me what you've got, Mr. Ramsay."

Declan's hands moved deliberately, curling around the bottom of my shirt, drawing it up inch by inch, trailing kisses in its wake. Each brush of his tongue was magic, drawing a low moan from deep inside me. With every inch of skin he revealed, his mouth followed, exploring my body as if it were an unknown treasure.

"Declan," I breathed, my heart racing in my chest.

He was attentive, ensuring no part of me went unappreciated. Once my shirt was off and my bra on full display, he paused, his eyes devouring my body. "You are absolutely breathtaking."

His words sent a surge of warmth through me.

Declan abandoned his careful exploration and pulled one bra cup down, latching onto one of my breasts with his lips. He sucked hard, his tongue swirling around the pad of my nipple. I gripped his shoulders and pulled him closer, moaning as the pleasure shot straight to my core.

I needed more. So much more.

When Declan finally released my nipple from his mouth, he continued his torturous journey, kissing his way down my stomach, across my abdomen.

Finn never took the time to make me feel valued or desired in the way Declan did. Instead, he'd insisted on controlling every aspect of our relationship, including our sex life. It was always about what Finn wanted, never about what I needed or desired.

"Don't touch me, I'm tired," or *"Just blow me, angel,"* or *"Stop moving your hips, it's throwing off my rhythm."*

How long had it been since I'd had a partner-induced orgasm? Five years? Maybe seven?

As Declan unbuttoned my jeans, I released my worries and focused on the present moment. Everything else faded away, and Declan was all that mattered. He kept looking up at me, his gaze so intense it felt like he could see right through me.

As soon as my jeans were unzipped, Declan's fingers curled around the waistband of my underwear. He paused for me to bridge so he could slide everything over my hips. My panties were drenched, my clit aching for his touch.

His eyes roamed over my body. "Are you ready, baby?"

"More than ready." My stomach and half my body clenched. Flings guaranteed good orgasms, right?

With a grin, Declan lowered his face between my thighs, his breath hot against my most intimate parts. His fingers found my slick folds, and he explored me with gentle strokes. As his tongue joined in, teasing and flicking at my clit, I gasped, gripping the sheets beneath me. The sensations were exquisite, every touch a new revelation of pleasure.

"That's fantastic." My hips involuntarily lifted to grant his mouth more access.

He didn't respond with words, but his actions spoke volumes. His tongue delved deeper, swirling around my clit before dipping inside me, then returning to that sensitive spot again. It was a dance of pure ecstasy, and the pressure built within me, growing stronger with each skilled stroke.

I neared the edge of climax, and he kept going, thrusting one, then two fingers inside me, hitting that magic spot only my vibrator knew. Finn never listened when I told him how to find—*Stop thinking about him, Leigh.*

Finn didn't care to know.

But Declan? With Declan, there was pleasure. And it was all mine for the taking.

"I've been dreaming about your fingers since we met." My voice barely registered in my ears over the pounding of my heart and my rough breath. "They're so—oh my god! I'm going to—"

He redoubled his efforts, his tongue and fingers moving faster and more insistently.

I reached the peak, and finally the dam broke with a cry. "Declan!"

His fast strokes switched to forceful laps, while my thighs clamped around his head, keeping me strung tight until I crested the wave and every bone in my body turned to jelly.

He pressed one more kiss to my trembling thigh before meeting my eyes. "You liked that?"

"Yes. Very much." I panted, my breath coming in ragged gasps. My body convulsed from an aftershock, but I wanted more of Declan. Not just sex with a random Italian man, I wanted to connect with Declan Ramsay. Wanted to explore our bodies and push our boundaries together.

That was wrong. This was supposed to be a one-time thing. He wanted to protect me, and I didn't want that. He lived in a different country than me, so there was no future. His team flaunted the rules of law. I barely knew him.

But the way he dialed into my body and cracked everything open was more than I could have hoped for.

How could the sex be that good with a man who was so wrong?

My thoughts raced, running on some bizarre autopilot. I flung off my bra and left the bed to find my discarded pants, fishing out a condom from the pocket. Who cared if it was wrong when it felt so good? "Ready for round two?"

He grinned, his eyes filled with a playful hunger that made my stomach flutter. "You came prepared for your grand Roman adventure, didn't you?"

"Guilty," I admitted, heat rising in my cheeks. "Care to help a girl out?"

"More than happy." He slipped out of his lounge pants, and I stopped breathing. He was gorgeous, all tanned skin and toned muscle, standing with the same confidence he always did. His cock stood tall and proud, accentuated by the dips above his pelvic bone. A bead of moisture gleamed on the tip, inviting me to take a taste.

I wanted to do more than just taste; I wanted to devour him whole.

My eyes roved over his body, drinking in every dip and curve like it was the first time I'd seen a naked man. "Lay back. I want on top."

He did as I asked, watching intently as I unwrapped the condom and rolled it over him, the air charged between us.

I straddled him, positioning myself above his thick cock, and paused. I would set the pace. I would dictate the depth and angle of each thrust. And as I lowered myself onto him, the glorious sense of power and freedom screamed through my entire body.

"So fucking wet." Declan groaned, his hands gripping my hips as I moved. "You feel incredible."

"God, Declan, so do you." I ground against him, searching for the perfect friction.

He sat up, his mouth searching for mine. Our connection intensified, the heat threatening to consume me. We moved together, a layer a sweat collecting between us, the sound of slapping flesh and moans filling the room.

I rode him hard, his cock filling me, stretching me, the most excruciating perfection I'd ever felt.

It had never been like this before.

Declan broke from the kiss and his grip tightened, helping me slam faster and harder onto him, the waves of pleasure building rapidly. Through his labored breaths, he whispered, "I'm close."

"Me too," I gasped, my nails digging into his shoulders as the coil within me wound up again.

"Let go," he urged. "Take what you need."

And I did. With a final cry of ecstasy, I surrendered to the waves that washed over me, our bodies continuing to move in perfect harmony.

"Oh, fuck yes, Leigh." His arms shook and he slowed me, his hips bucking into me. "Yes!"

As we came down from the high, I slid my arms around his neck, and his fingers found my hair. Our lips met again, tongues sliding against each other in languid sweeps.

As one, we collapsed on the bed, with him still buried deep inside me.

We lay still together, breathing deep, for long minutes. Could all of this be real?

"Like my fingers, do you?" He combed them through my hair. The touch was sweet, tender.

"Amazing." I snuggled my cheek against his chest, in the hollow of his neck. Everything was going my way. I'd stood up for myself and was finally getting what I wanted. "Are you sure about me going to the catacombs vault with you?"

"Leigh, you shouldn't ask." He pushed me up enough that I could see him clearly. He was going to change his mind. Tell me it was too dangerous. His gaze drilled into me, serious but warm. "You should demand."

"Really?" I bit my lip, suddenly unsure of myself. His cock was still inside of me, and I was suddenly unsure?

"Absolutely. You said it yourself—you're better qualified to study that vault than I am, and far better than anyone else on the team." His fingers brushed against my cheek, and I nuzzled against his palm. "And I loved how assertive you were earlier."

"Then..." How could I ask for more? Two orgasms—from someone other than me!—and encouragement to chase my dreams. I only needed one more thing.

He gripped my chin, pulling my face toward his. "Anything, Leigh."

I blinked slowly. "I want to bring Isaac, too."

Declan stiffened, his support evaporating below me. "No."

"I know he said some things when he was here earlier, but—"

"But nothing." He sat us up.

I lifted off him, the loss of connection jarring. "He's my—"

"He doesn't think you're capable." Declan took me by the shoulders. "If you tell him you're coming with us, he'll want to take your place."

I'd made up my mind. I'd taken what I wanted. I'd demanded I go with them. Almost. "He's just looking out for me."

He squeezed his eyes shut, his mouth opening and closing without any sound.

"You said 'Anything, Leigh.'"

He scrubbed his hands over his face and finally looked at me. "I don't trust him."

"I do."

"He's just riding your coattails."

"That's not true." I slid off the bed, searching for my bra and shirt. This wasn't a conversation to have naked.

Declan followed me off the bed, discarding the condom. "He couldn't have done the job in Cassaforte like you did, and he's nothing more than a liability if he comes with us tonight."

I found the shirt and threw it on. What was I doing? This was a fling. It was a one-off. I was putting too much emotion into it. So what if the orgasms were great? My brother was family. He took care of me. "Isaac taught me everything I know."

"Taught you?" Declan pulled on his pants, while I hauled on my underwear. "What could he possibly teach you? I saw him trying to pick locks and file keys. You're the one who came all this way to repair Edoardo's safe, not him. All he's done is skulk around and keep you cooped up."

"He's protecting—"

"You walked away from me when I said I wanted to do that for you." Declan snatched my wrist and yanked me to him, darkness clouding his features. "Said you were done being protected and that you wanted to live your life. Not his life, Leigh. Yours."

My hand swept across his strong chest, the chiseled muscle hard under my touch. He was right about all of it. My own life was what I wanted.

Wasn't it?

"Why did Edoardo think you were the assistant when you arrived at his villa?"

"Because I'm a woman."

His jaw flexed as he let go of me, pacing toward the desk where my books still lay. "Or because Isaac passes your work off as his?"

Isaac wouldn't do that. "We're a family company. We all work together."

"Stop making excuses for him." Declan clenched his fists and pressed them so hard against the table the muscles flexed all the way up his back. Why was he so upset about this? "It's like talking to my mother about Daphne."

"What?"

"You won't see any of his flaws, will you? Everything's perfect inside your little skull."

I took a half-step back.

Declan sucked in a long breath, his shoulders relaxing. But he didn't turn to look at me. "Who designed the case for the Codex of San Marco?"

"The what?"

"The manuscript Phillip Maguire owned. Who designed it?"

"I—" How did he know about that? "I did."

His head tilted back, like he was staring up at the ceiling. "And who created the copy of those plans for the Fenix Group? I'm assuming it wasn't you, otherwise you would have reacted when Giovanni told us about them."

"I don't know what you're talking about."

"Someone at Barton did, and I'm willing to bet it was Isaac."

I'd designed and built a case for a medieval manuscript for Phillip Maguire, based on work I'd done with a book conservator back home in Boston. It was a beautiful design, but we'd only built one.

That I knew of.

"Declan, there was only one case."

"I was there, Leigh, inside the Barton vault. I saw the plans. I know someone at your office is working for Fenix, whether they're complicit in everything we've been through or not."

"How did you get into..."

He turned around slowly, his face a mask. He didn't have to say the words. Somewhere deep inside, I knew.

"You broke into our office, didn't you?" If the Reynolds team could get past the Cassaforte defenses, why wouldn't they be able to get past ours?

"The Codex belonged to the British Museum, not Phillip Maguire."

I stumbled backward, nearly tripping over my discarded pants. Bright lights flashed in front of my eyes, and it was all I could do not to rub at my temples. "I need to go."

Declan neared me, but I dodged and swept up my pants.

"Don't touch me." We'd had our fun and now it was time to—*to what, Leigh?* I pulled the pants on awkwardly, dancing from one foot to the other as I neared the door. He'd broken into my family's company. Walked through the building without anyone else there and taken things.

It was an invasion.

Those were my plans.

"Be careful." Declan reached out, steadying me before I fell over.

I jerked out of his grip and did up my button. "I've been dressing myself since—"

"With Isaac, I mean." His mask faltered, the skin around his eyes and mouth growing taut. "If I'm right, if he's involved with—"

"Shut up, Declan." I was done. How many times did I have to make that choice? How many times would the universe bring me this close to what I wanted and yank it away again? Why couldn't I have anything I wanted?

I wanted to go with Declan to the catacombs. But I wanted to bring Isaac there. I wanted Isaac to see what I could do. I wanted to make him proud.

Declan walked backward to the table where my books sat, not taking his eyes off mine. "You're still welcome to—"

"I said, 'Shut up.'" I marched across the room and snatched the books.

He just stood there, half naked, doing exactly what I'd told him to. Nothing. Part of me wanted him to grab me and kiss me again. Convince me it was a lame joke. Apologize. Something.

I spun away from him before I could say anything stupid or change my mind. I didn't need men telling me what I could or couldn't do. Telling me what I should or shouldn't think.

And I really didn't need a thief telling me who to trust.

CHAPTER 29

LEIGH

The door practically crashed closed behind me, the sound far too loud for this close to midnight. I clutched my books to my chest, like a foolish schoolgirl just leaving her crush's house. How could I have fallen so hard, so fast? From the peak of physical bliss to this crushing... Tears pricked at the backs of my eyes.

How much more did my life have to suck before it got any better?

Numb legs, I took a few steps down the hall toward my room. I couldn't go there. Jayce would be there. What would she say? I had my books back from Declan, so she'd know I'd visited him. His smell would be all over me. She'd guess at how long I'd been gone and what we'd done.

Jayce wasn't the kind of woman to hold back, and she'd make one too many cracks or ask questions I wasn't ready to answer.

Where was I going to go?

I sagged against the wall where Declan wouldn't be able to see me through his peephole anymore, just in case he was watching.

Don't cry, Leigh. Not over another stupid man. All you wanted was a fling and that's what you got.

I could still feel him between my thighs. The scrape of his stubble, his thickness filling me, the earth-shattering orgasms. Orgasms I'd never felt with a man before. How could that be so wrong?

When would I ever fall for the right man?

A door opened down the hall, and I practically jumped. I had to go somewhere, hide myself before I started to cry, hide my—

But it was Isaac. His brows rose, no doubt wondering why I was out of my room alone in the middle of the night. "Where are you off to?"

I couldn't tell him I was just coming from having mind-blowing sex with a thief who'd broken into our company office. I swallowed, my mind fumbling for a lie. "Just... um, hungry. Thought I'd grab something from the café next door."

Isaac's gaze lingered on me for a moment too long, then he nodded. "You should have someone with you if you're going out at this hour."

Declan wasn't right about Isaac. He wasn't keeping me down to build himself up. He wasn't riding my coattails. And he definitely wasn't working with Fenix.

"You're right." I forced a smile. "I'll get Jayce."

"Good idea. Jayce could eat a horse." Isaac laughed, but his smile didn't reach his eyes before he stopped. He put a hand on my upper arm. "Are you okay?"

Yes. My throat grew tighter the more that words formed in my brain, which grew progressively more truthful. *No. Not even close. Miserable.*

"You've been crying."

"I'm fine." With those words, the tears spilled free with full force, tumbling down my cheeks. "It's just been a really intense trip."

Before I could respond, Isaac pulled me into a hug, his grip stronger than usual. Isaac wasn't one for hugs, but I leaned into it, letting my big brother absorb all the unspoken shit I was dealing with.

Stop crying. Declan's going to hear you. Why did I care? What was he going to do, even if he did hear me?

I sniffled and inched back. "Sorry about that."

Isaac kept hold of my upper arms. "Do you want to talk?"

I spluttered a laugh and sniffled away the rest of the tears. That wasn't the type of relationship we had. But the offer had been nice. "Not really."

"This isn't about Declan, is it? You have your books back, so you must have seen him tonight. Did he..." Isaac leaned in to look at me directly. "I noticed how he looks at you. Did he try something?"

Something? Declan had done so much more to me than that.

He frowned. "We should have brought Finn with us."

I rolled my head forward so he couldn't see my eyes bugging out of my head. "We broke up, Isaac. Two weeks ago."

"How about this..." He let go of me and pulled out his phone, once again ignoring my news about Finn. "I was supposed to be heading out for drinks with one of our prospects."

"At this hour?"

Isaac had already been to countless meetings in the past few days. The shadows under his eyes had deepened, telling the tale of sleepless nights. He shrugged. "Says the woman who was going out for food."

"Fair." I dragged the back of my hand across my eyes.

"It's not even midnight yet." He held up his phone. "Let me call them and cancel. I'll take you for something to eat and you can talk if you want to, or we can just hang out."

Declan was wrong about Isaac. He didn't know the whole story. All he had was a glimpse into our lives, without our other brothers, my dad, or my stepmother. Declan was nothing more than a liar and a manipulator. A safe cracker. He was the type of person I devoted my life to stopping.

"Can I drop my books off in your room?"

Isaac nodded and took the books, slipping into his room to make the phone call, then joining me in the hallway. "Everything's arranged."

"Thanks. I really appreciate it." I walked with him down the hall, his presence a comfort. "This won't screw up the plans with them, will it?"

"No need to worry. I'll touch base with them in the morning." He ushered me down the stairs and out into the warm evening. "They recommended a better place than the one next door, though."

I wasn't actually hungry. The churning inside my stomach would have spit anything back out, but maybe the fresh air would help. Or sitting to chat with Isaac. Even if he wanted to talk about everything I didn't care about, at least it would keep my mind off Declan.

Isaac and I passed the café next door, with people filling its outdoor tables, passed closed-up shops, and wove our way between a throng of late-night partygoers.

We turned down a small side street, into one of the many mazes that made up Rome.

"How's your head feeling?" asked Isaac.

Slight headache from the fight with Declan, but I wasn't about to tell Isaac that, either. "All good."

He nodded and put out his hand to stop me before we crossed another narrow street. A scooter zipped past us, followed by a white van, which slowed.

I looked around for a traffic sign or to see which building they were approaching.

It stopped directly in front of us, and the side door rolled open. A huge man bolted forward and threw a hood over my head.

I screa— He clamped a hand over my mouth.

Lifted me.

"No!" yelled Isaac.

Followed by the sound of fist meeting flesh. A pained groan.

I crashed against a floor. Grooved. Rubbery. Cold against my hands and through my shirt.

"Go!" ordered a deep voice.

Something thudded into the van next to me, and the door rolled closed. The van rumbled over cobblestones, too fast.

A pair of hands grabbed me by the shoulders and sat me up.

Ripped the hood off.

"Hello, Leigh Barton." Oh god. It was the man from the photo Scarlett showed Giovanni. The one with the scar. The one behind Edoardo's wife's kidnapping.

And now my kidnapping and—I couldn't tear my eyes away from him, but from the sound of the groaning next to me—Isaac's kidnapping, too.

"My name is Enzo." He smiled, sending a layer of dread through my soul. "And I have a vault I need you to open."

Chapter 30

Declan

The Mercedes sped its way along the Via Appia Antica, toward our target. Rav sat at the wheel, our lookout and getaway driver for the evening. Next to him, Jayce munched away on a bag of chips. The woman never stopped.

Alone in the back, my hand curled into a fist. My mind raced with memories of what I'd been doing just two hours ago with Leigh. A primal surge claimed me, almost as strong as the one I'd claimed her with.

I'd thought she was mine after I'd sank myself inside her, made her scream my name, but no. Her brother stole her away again. Every time she separated from him, another side of her emerged. A strong and confident side. Just my luck she'd stand up for once and defend him, even after we'd had sex.

And then there were my stupid words. Why did I tell her about the Codex's case? I'd been so frustrated, I couldn't keep my suspicions inside anymore. But she wouldn't even listen to that.

What had I accomplished? I'd pushed away a good woman. For the second time.

Get a grip, Dec. There's a job to do. You chose to tell her the truth and she did exactly what you knew she would.

Jayce's chip munching snapped me back to the moment.

It had irritated the shit out of me for the first two years she'd worked with us. At some point, it became comfortable background noise, but tonight? It was pissing me off again. "Are you almost done with that bag?"

Laughter bubbled in my earpiece. Brie's giggles were one of our most effective mic checks. "You sound like you're on edge tonight, Dec."

"I told you," said Jayce, around a mouthful of food, "we should have brought Leigh."

As if that would have improved my mood. Although it would have given me a chance to fix things. She would have seen us all in action and been impressed. Would have seen that sometimes we had to live in the *ends justify the means* world.

It wasn't as if we'd stolen anything from Barton, other than information.

Fuck Fenix.

And fuck whoever at Barton was working with them.

Or maybe for them. It could have been a simple job for a paying client. Not every company researched their clients as thoroughly as Reynolds did. Once we were back home, I'd go through everything the analysts had collected on the Barton staff. And if I didn't find the guilty party, I'd demand they do the research again.

Rav, all business in the driver's seat, flicked his gaze to me in the rear-view mirror. "Brie's right. Do we need to reschedule?"

"No." The word came out more forcefully than I'd intended.

"You know..." Jayce swiveled in her seat to look directly at me. "Leigh wasn't in our room when I got up from my nap. Don't suppose you and she made up after whatever boneheaded thing you said to her at Ferraro's?"

I did not huff out a breath and stare out the window.

Jayce squealed. "She's back in your room right now, isn't she?"

Someone gasped over the earpiece. It was female, which meant it was either Scarlett or Brie. Considering Scarlett didn't react with any emotions when we were on a job, it had to be her sister. "Do you have a new girlfriend?"

Girlfriend? Bah.

It was one night of sex. That was it. Good sex, though.

Really good.

And then a fight.

"There's nothing going on between Leigh and me. We aren't even on speaking terms, so you can both calm down."

Scarlett cut in before the women could probe any further. "Focus, you three."

"Relax, boss." Jayce twisted in her seat and tossed another chip into her mouth. "It's just recon. Low-risk trip in. Eyeballs only. Yadda, yadda."

"Stop eating in my ear, Jayce," said Scarlett.

"Don't get cocky." Rav didn't need the reminder to focus. Our safety was always top of his mind, no matter what else was going on around us. "Remember Noah's thug and the kidnappers? They wanted info on the vault. It's possible they've already gone down and looted the place."

Jayce scoffed, turning in her seat to face him. "Rav, you see ghosts everywhere."

A glimmer of a memory flitted across my mind. Rav, years ago, his face shadowed by secrets and memories of some far-off country where he served with JTF. The man I'd known most of my life had changed after that last mission. But that transformation made him perfect for our team. He'd go to the ends of the earth to protect us.

I studied his reflection in the mirror. The same determination was there, mirroring my own resolve. We were about to infiltrate a centuries-old catacomb in search of a mystery vault. This was no time for distractions.

"Rav's right. We need to be careful." I flexed my hand before it locked in place in the fist. "We stick together. We stay alert and get the job done, like always."

"Status update?" said Scarlett.

Brie's bright voice filled my ear. "Got all your GPS locations up on my screen. Will's almost done with the map imaging from the notebook."

A wave of anticipation rolled over me as the car pulled off to the side at a transit stop. The road into the Callixtus Catacombs, where we'd done our tour, was a small, private one that could bring too much attention if we went in after hours. Instead, Rav was dropping us off a two-minute jog away and would wait nearby.

Jayce swiveled in her seat again, giving me an intentionally narrowed-eyed stare. "You should fix whatever stupid thing you said to her that put you two on the outs. She likes you and she's had more than enough men making her feel like shit."

Scarlett cut Jayce off. "Back on task, team. I've got Brie and Will feeding me data. Plus, Emmett and Malcolm are on stand-by if we need extra hands."

Jayce rolled her eyes. "And if we find something at the vault?"

Recon only. No opening it, Dec. "We look. We don't open. But if we do find something and have to open it, it belongs to the Roman authorities."

Rav's glower found mine in the rear-view mirror, as though he knew how desperately I wanted to crack her open. "What about Ferraro? What'll he think of that?"

"Any finds get turned over to Ferraro," Scarlett said. "He decides what goes to the Carabinieri or to a museum. That was part of our agreement."

Rav put the car into park. "I'll be close by. Let me know if you need backup, but you're on your own in there."

I slipped on my tactical gloves, each finger covered in a re-active fabric so they'd work with the phone strapped to my forearm. Jayce followed my lead, and we both hauled on our backpacks, ready for whatever the night had in store.

Rav scanned the road. "You've got a break in traffic coming."

Jayce and I hopped out of the car. We sprinted across the well-lit road and vaulted over the low stone wall separating us from the green space surrounding the catacomb's entrance. Skirting the edge of the property, we stayed in the shadows by the wall, then cut toward the building complex along a treed walkway. The tall, narrow cypress pines provided little cover, but the area was silent and void of people.

"I've got eyes on you." Brie had tapped into the security feed outside of the building complex. Easy job, she'd said, although the coverage was sparse. "You're clear."

We passed between the squat buildings of pale brick and stucco, the gardens Leigh had fawned over, and the historical displays she'd lingered at. Avoided the long, curved souvenir shop where she'd picked up items for her stepmother, and headed straight for the main building.

Jayce made quick work of the lock, using the picks stored in a pouch at her thigh. "We're in."

We bypassed more displays, where Leigh had told me about various symbols used in the catacombs, including the alpha and omega, the fish, the monogram of Christ, and the phoenix—a strange coincidence, in the end.

Jayce and I headed through the hallway, down the fifty or so uneven steps into the depths. The lights were still on, but we'd be going deeper into the labyrinth than the public were allowed and would no doubt need our own headlamps before long.

The air chilled with each step, the sounds of Rome swallowed by the stone's embrace. Jayce led the way, and I trailed behind, the narrow walls of the passage we were in brushing my shoulders at random intervals.

Will said, "How's the temperature? Need the suits on?"

"Couple degrees, please," said Jayce.

My memory strayed to Leigh, who'd waved off Jayce's complaints about the chill, insisting she was fine when we did our tour. She'd been so excited, the adrenaline must have kept her warm. Or, like usual, she didn't want to burden anyone with her discomfort. *Stop thinking about her, Dec.* "Brie, can you feed us the map displays?"

A soft glow emanated from the phone on my arm, displaying the most direct path ahead.

"It's ironic, isn't it?" The eerie quiet of the catacombs amplified my words. "Using cutting-edge technology to break into an ancient vault."

Jayce chuckled softly. "Our gear might be overkill. Who knows if it'll be of any use?"

As we navigated through the narrow tunnels, a gentle sprinkling of dust floated from the ceiling. I hadn't seen that on our first tour. An unsettling churn of my stomach prompted me to ask, "Has there been any seismic activity lately?"

"Not that I know of, but I'll check." Will's tone was infused with curiosity. "You know, Rome experiences thousands of minor quakes each year. Most of them are less than two on the Richter scale, so they're barely noticeable."

Barely noticeable, but causing dust to fall?

Will sounded more serious the longer he talked. "There was, however, a three-point-four magnitude quake earlier today."

My shoulders tensed. I didn't suffer from claustrophobia, but the thought of being buried alive wasn't an appealing one. "Tell me events like that are rare in Rome, Will?"

"Indeed." Will was oblivious to my heart skipping a few beats. Good thing the thermal suits only had temperature gauges and not heart rate monitors. "Earthquakes are much more common inland, along the mountains."

"I should have eaten the rest of those chips." Jayce turned on her headlamp, pointing it into crevasses and down side tunnels which lacked their own lights. "How far in do you think the vault is, Will?"

"Based on the maps, I'd say somewhere between thirty to forty minutes to get all the way there."

Jayce groaned.

I nudged her from behind. "I brought you a couple of chocolate bars for while I'm checking out the vault."

Her pace quickened. "Then try to keep up. I'm going to make it in twenty."

CHAPTER 31

LEIGH

The damp chill of the catacombs snaked through my clothes, crawling under my skin. Jeans and a loose T-shirt weren't enough down here. The smell of earth and decay consumed my senses. Terror ran through my veins, turning my blood cold. When the corridor had widened just enough that we could walk side-by-side, Isaac had wrapped his hand around mine. Just as unlike him as the hugs he'd offered in the hotel hallway.

"Leigh, stay with me," he whispered. His eyes, swollen from the blow he'd taken in the van, were still determined. I'd seen him play the tough guy before, but never when it counted. Never when it was me on the line.

I squeezed Isaac's hand, forcing a smile onto my lips.

Ahead of us, Dr. Daniel Weber's shoulders slouched and he walked with a noticeable limp. He'd been slumped in the back of the van next to me. No surprise, our kidnappers hadn't introduced us, but I recognized him from the photo in the notebook.

Daniel carried the lead flashlight, walking fast despite his condition, obviously aware of the direction he was going. He'd worked for Giovanni Ferraro, researching the vault; how many times had he been down with the thugs? And had they caused the limp?

The ancient Roman frescoes came alive in the shifting shadows from his flashlight and the two carried behind us. Enzo was the mouthpiece, the boss with the barest hint of an Italian accent. His eyes glinted with a cruel satisfaction. Pavel was the muscle, a snarling guard dog on a short leash, Russian or some other Slavic accent tinging his words.

They'd made their intentions clear in the van: we were going to the vault and it was to be opened tonight.

Enzo's words rolled around in my brain, piling on top of my fear. "No more stalling, Daniel. You have your experts. No more delays." His impatience was palpable, a thick fog in the already stifling air. The Fenix Group, the mysterious masters they served, were finally going to get what they wanted.

Fenix. Was it true what Declan had said? Had someone at Barton created a copy of the manuscript case for them? Had it really been Isaac?

As we continued to wind through the narrow passages, the sensation of being trapped magnified with each step.

Isaac leaned in closer, keeping his volume down. "We just need to get to the vault, open it, and then we're out. We pretend none of this ever happened."

I fought against the urge to look over my shoulder to Enzo and Pavel. The metallic glint from their waistbands earlier hadn't gone unnoticed. Guns. Even if we opened the vault, the odds of us walking out unscathed seemed bleak.

When were Declan and Jayce leaving the hotel? Would they be inside already? Ahead of us? Behind us? Would their map be right?

They'd notice something amiss. They'd save us.

They had to.

My mouth was dry, but I leaned toward Isaac. "Declan and—"

Before I could finish, a sharp finger prodded my back.

Pavel said, "No whispering."

Enzo's laugh cut through the space. "Come now, Leigh. We're all friends here. You've got nothing to hide from us, right?" He laughed again, and the weight in the air grew heavier.

Isaac tightened his grip on my hand, giving me a look that pleaded for discretion. But inside, my mind was racing. If Declan was here, he'd figure something out. He took care of me in the Cassaforte vault and again in the city when Leonardo came after us.

Unless I'd screwed up so royally, he'd just leave without me.

Isaac craned his neck, shooting a venomous look at Enzo and Pavel. His voice had a rare edge to it. "Let my sister go. You don't need her."

Enzo shifted into playful taunts. "Maybe. Let's see how she does with the vault first."

Daniel, his flashlight sweeping in front of us, said, "We were supposed to have the Reynolds' safe cracker down here. Where is he?"

Confusion knotted inside my chest. Declan was supposed to be with them? Was that the plan Scarlett had worked out with Giovanni Ferraro?

"Fucking Reynolds Recoveries." Enzo spat in disgust. "We brought him to Rome for the Cassaforte job because you couldn't get your notebook from Ferraro. He's not the one we wanted for the eagle's vault."

"We've got the real expert with us." Pavel snickered, and my breath hitched at the level of disdain filling his words. "Isaac here created the case for the San Marco Codex manuscript. Did you know that, Daniel? Surely, the catacombs vault is child's play for him."

A jolt of anger surged through me. *I designed that case, not Isaac.* The intricate mechanisms, the artistic flair, every bit was mine. Declan's warning came back to me: Isaac duplicating my designs. A hint of betrayal slithered through my insides.

Shouldn't I have looked through our full inventory of schematics at some point? Instead of simply designing and building in my little office?

"I doubt that very much," muttered Daniel, as he took a turn into a wider tunnel. Bricks lined an archway at the turn, and we passed walls where it appeared some tombs were still intact.

"You may be right, Daniel. It's a complicated beast." Enzo nudged Isaac. "What do you think, Isaac? Is your sister's expertise what we've been missing? Between her and Dr. Weber, we're going to see the eagle tonight, aren't we?"

"I told you in the van," hissed Isaac. "I can do this. You don't need her."

Enzo hummed aloud. "Honestly, I would've preferred Declan here. His team's become a thorn in our side. It would have given me a great deal of pleasure to leave his corpse inside the vault."

Oh, shit. Panic burst inside me.

We weren't getting out of here alive tonight.

Delay. The longer I could delay, the higher the chance Declan and Jayce would find us. Declan would come for me. No matter what I said to him, he'd rescue me. That connection I'd felt when our lips met wasn't mere attraction; it was trust. The team would rescue all of us. We just had to stay alive long enough.

Please don't have postponed. Please come soon, Declan.

"What's the big fuss about her?" Pavel's words broke into my thoughts. "The safe she made for Edoardo didn't seem like anything special."

I felt a prick of defensiveness, but before I could retort, Enzo smacked Pavel and laughed. "She had to simplify her design. You know, something her dear brother could install."

"I could have opened it, if that's what we were really doing," said Pavel.

The hell he could have.

"This whole ruse," he continued, "was a waste of my skills."

What was the ruse? Not actually trying to break into my safe? I slowed my breathing, so it wouldn't interfere with the conversation behind me.

"You should have let me get the notebook."

"It would have been a stupid risk," said Enzo. "And you still couldn't open this vault."

"And you think the game with Edoardo was smarter?"

One of them smacked the other.

"What?" Pavel must have been the one hit. "Taking his wife and pretending to break into the safes? We should have brought explosives down—"

Another smack.

No wonder the drilled holes in my safe looked like little more than vandalism. They wanted Isaac or Ben—the installers—here. But why?

Unless I really was the target?

It didn't make any sense. I added history-inspired ideas to my designs, but my research was into metal foams, not stone doors. Surely, there were dozens, if not hundreds, of safe technicians who were better suited to this than me.

And Declan. They'd staged two break-ins. One to bring Isaac, Ben, or me here. Another to bring Declan here.

Reynolds *was* in Fenix's crosshairs. That much was clear.

But why Isaac and me?

Fenix. Of course. Declan had said someone at Barton had made a copy of the manuscript case for them. Whoever was behind that must have been behind Enzo and Pavel messing with my safe, so Isaac and I would come.

Who was it? The contracts went through Dad. It wouldn't have been him.

Unless it was Ann? Was she trying to get rid of us? Was she really an evil stepmother?

A burst of air flew out of me. What irony. Isaac warned me not to go out alone. But he was in just as much danger as I was.

Pavel shoved me again. "What's the matter with you?"

What wasn't the matter with me? I was cold. I'd been betrayed. And I wanted Declan. "Nothing. How much longer?"

"Daniel," Enzo said, "tell her about the Ninth Legion."

"I don't need him to tell me that," I said. "The Legio IX Hispana is a mystery to historians. They were one of the greatest units in the Roman Empire, until Boudicca defeated them. More than half survived and then they continued serving."

Daniel nodded and took another sharp turn, so the corridor narrowed again. "You know your history."

Isaac glanced at me, lips a thin line. Keep your mouth shut, that look said.

Why bother, Isaac? Don't want me to outshine you down here, too?

I'd done additional research after visiting Ferraro. "No one knows what happened in the end, but they vanished sometime around 108 AD. The most common theory is that they went north of Hadrian's Wall and were decimated there. A few years ago, some artifacts were found in the Netherlands, which suggests they survived and moved, though it's still hotly debated."

I paused, looking at the walls around us, the weight of history pressing in. These catacombs were in use that long ago. The dead couldn't be buried within the city walls, and the Christians didn't believe in cremation. So, they built huge underground spaces which were cheaper than graveyards.

Daniel said, "There was a listing of all legions written in 197, and they weren't on it."

"They just vanished. Like ghosts." A shiver ran up my spine. Would Isaac and I vanish forever down here? If we did, it was likely no one would ever find us. I swallowed hard.

We weren't going to die down here. I just started standing up for myself. There was a whole new life for me to live.

"You still haven't explained," said Daniel, "what that has to do with a vault crafted by da Vinci?"

The sound of Pavel's disdain bounced off the cool stone walls. What was the dynamic at play there? How long had they had Daniel? Ferraro said he'd gone missing a month ago. Had he been with Fenix that long? Was he a willing participant like

Ferraro's head of security suspected? Or was he a prisoner like us?

Either way, if Daniel didn't understand the connection between the two legends, what use was I? I kept my composure and turned my attention to the more pressing matter at hand, trying to piece the puzzle together. When Giovanni had mentioned a Pope's involvement, it had struck a chord in me.

My mind raced back to the stolen notebook from Cassaforte. It was a well of knowledge, a window into the research Daniel had done. Did Enzo and Pavel know I'd reviewed the notebook in detail? How much could I say without giving them too much? "We were on a tour here yesterday, and our guide said they found a door with markings that resembled da Vinci's sketches. He didn't really build a vault down here, did he?"

Daniel rubbed his forehead, his flashlight wavering. "From what I've seen, and the design intricacies of the vault itself, it's possible. But the timeline doesn't make sense."

I'd said the same thing to Ferraro.

"Whether it was da Vinci himself or a student of his school of thought..." Daniel let out a sigh, rolling his shoulder and holding it close to his body. "Whatever's inside isn't just a treasure. It could be dangerous."

Not more dangerous than the men walking behind me.

You just have to survive until Declan arrives. Be valuable.

"I think I can help." If we ever got there. "Are there specifics you can share about this vault? Something that might help us figure it out?"

Daniel hesitated for a beat, then offered, "There are twelve symbols which evoke the zodiac carved into its front. Each has a slot, but my suspicion is only one of them serves as the true keyhole."

That detail hadn't been in the notebook. Too bad, since I could have done some research if I had the internet. "What do the symbols look like?"

"You're a curious little one." Enzo chuckled. "I like that."

Isaac halted, and Enzo nearly ran into him. He didn't even glance at me, though, his glower trained on Enzo. "Shut up."

Daniel and I stopped, with Isaac between us and the thugs.

"Maybe we should hire her to help rebuild the phoenix." Enzo said to Pavel, as he walked straight up to Isaac, easily four inches taller, stopping just before their chests touched.

"Isaac, stop." I grabbed his arm. This was foolish. I had a plan—get to the vault and kill time. Not get killed before we even arrived.

But Isaac's reaction wasn't fear. It was confidence. He lifted an accusatory finger at Enzo. "She doesn't belong down here!"

Enzo swatted the finger away, the scar on his cheek puckering as the corner of his lip curled into a snarl. "And yet here she is, ready to do whatever we need."

My heart raced. We needed a way out of this.

Before I could find any other words, Enzo's viselike grip closed around my arm, yanking me closer.

"Don't be naïve, Leigh. We only wanted Declan to get Daniel's notebook back. You're the one we wanted for the vault." He paused, looking me dead in the eyes. "We've had our eye on you for some time now."

Bright lights danced in front of my eyes and pain ripped through my head. *Calm down. You have a plan.*

Enzo released me abruptly, and the room spun.

I stumbled, but Isaac was there to catch me, steadying me with an arm around my waist.

My brother held me for a moment, his face pinched with pain and regret. "I'm so sorry I couldn't protect you from this, Leigh."

"Keep going." Enzo waved to Daniel, who did as he was told.

Isaac began moving, and I clenched my eyes shut, accepting his lead.

What did Enzo mean about them watching me? And would I live long enough to find out?

Chapter 32

Declan

Jayce pointed around a corner in the cryptic maze. "Here's the turn from the public area."

"That's the halfway mark." I flicked on my headlamp and checked my watch. "You're losing your touch, Jayce. It's going to take us the full thirty minutes if you keep this pace."

"I was afraid you'd roll your ankle if I went at my full speed."

With a chuckle to myself, I turned the corner behind her. A simple metal gate barred the path deeper into the catacombs. "This wasn't on the map."

"Guess we need to scale it." Jayce tilted her head, the light reflecting off a dented silver padlock on the gate.

Scarlett cleared her throat, authoritative tone breaking through. "If it's simple, open it. No need to risk life and limb unnecessarily."

I stared at the gate a beat longer. Once upon a time, things like locked gates held me back. It was an obvious sign we weren't supposed to head down that path, but the days of obeying every rule were well behind me. We had a job to do, were already breaking the trespassing law, so a little gate was nothing more than a polite request to turn around, not an all-out order.

"Lock's open, anyway," said Jayce.

I nudged her. "No scaling required."

"Too bad." Once she removed the lock, the gate creaked open, revealing a steep set of rough-hewn stairs descending into a deeper darkness. Above, an open space loomed. Like a vaulted third story in the confining catacomb. My headlamp's light bounced off the uneven stone, casting surreal shadows that danced with every movement.

Before I took my first step down, a faint noise broke through the silence.

Instinct kicked in. I turned off my headlamp and tapped my earpiece three times.

Trouble.

"What's wrong?" Scarlett asked.

Jayce shielded her lamp and turned to face me, the faint glow barely enough to see her. The signal had her pausing, her normally easy-going demeanor replaced by a focused seriousness. Eyes closed, she listened. Then nodded.

I pulled close to whisper. "Voices. I can't tell which direction."

Rav cut through the earpiece, a concerned undertone beneath his gruff exterior. "Do I need to come in?"

"No," I whispered back, signaling to Jayce.

She extinguished her headlamp and we both switched to compact flashlights with a dim, red glow. The red light seeped into the darkness, illuminating our way forward—or back—without announcing our presence to anyone who'd see the brilliant glow from a second ago.

"It could be tour guides," I said. "Maybe kids sneaking in for fun? Even engineers surveying passageways during non-tourist hours?"

Will said, "Or maybe after the earthquake, checking for structural damage?"

"No one entered from the main building," said Brie.

Will added, "There are at least two entrances to this section of the catacombs. Could be more."

"I think they're coming from down there." Jayce hooked a thumb over her shoulder, indicating the stairs beyond the gate. "I'm going to check it out. If we can avoid them, we keep going."

"Be safe and stay on the map," I said.

Her response was a smirk barely visible in the red light. "I'm always safe, Declan."

"Don't take any risks," said Scarlett.

Jayce just shrugged, that cocky grin never leaving her face. "No promises on that one, boss."

She took the steps slowly, the glow of her flashlight dimming the farther away she got. After thirty seconds, her GPS signal on the map gained speed. The floor was uneven in many of the tourist areas, and no doubt would be far rougher below. Running was a risk but was probably the safest one she could make.

"I'm going down, too. There's at least twenty kilometers of tunnels down here, so the voices could be coming from any-where."

"Or we reschedule," said Scarlett. "Giovanni didn't give us a time frame, so we can try again tomorrow."

"Noted." The red light from my flashlight illuminated the carved stairwell, barely penetrating the inky blackness that swirled around me. Half of me wanted to turn around and head back to the hotel. It was the middle of the night, but Leigh would wake up when Jayce got back and maybe I could talk to her. Patch things up. Agree to take her slimy brother with us tomorrow night.

Why bother? The sex had been fantastic, but once we each left Rome, that would be the end of it. No use in prolonging the inevitable for a few extra orgasms.

At the bottom of the stairs, the tunnel branched out ahead, a shadowy divergence offering two paths into the unknown. The digital map on my phone suggested no choice, only one straight course. "Which direction did you go, Jayce?"

"She went right," said Brie. "The GPS is spotty that deep. Will, we need to fix that in the next phone update."

Scarlett said, "Malcolm and Emmett are en route in a secondary vehicle. The notebook said there's a hidden entrance further down the Via Appia Antica. Will's going to work out how to get you there from inside."

Their backup, although unseen and not yet present, was a relief. Even in these shadowy depths, I was never entirely alone. I always had the team around me.

I continued after Jayce. No sign of her red flashlight, but once I'd walked another minute, the GPS cleared up again. She was at least ten minutes ahead of me if I continued at this pace. The path must have been clear. I paused again, twisting my head to listen. The voices were still there, louder. "Jayce, have you spotted anyone yet?"

Two taps on the earpiece. It was the sign for going forward, but the GPS on my map showed me she'd slowed.

The earpiece sounded with three quick taps. A message vibrated against my forearm, and I quickly checked my phone.

It was a text from Jayce to the group. *I've got eyes. And you won't like this.*

I hurried my steps forward. "What is it?"

Another text pinged on my arm, and I nearly dropped my flashlight. *It's Leigh.*

CHAPTER 33

LEIGH

After what felt like hours of trudging through the chill, the narrow corridor finally opened into a grand chamber. Daniel's flashlight landed on a huge stone door, covered in shapes and symbols. It towered twelve feet high, its surface a sentry in the dark for centuries. He approached it, running a hand over the etchings, muttering to himself.

I might have done the same if my hands weren't wrapped up in the hem of my shirt. It was far from freezing, but between the damp air and the low temperatures, my fingers had grown stiff.

"Pavel, get the generator going." Enzo grabbed my upper arm and hauled me closer to the door. "You play coy, but I know you had time to look at Daniel's notebook. We were watching you and know you and Isaac spoke about wanting to open the vault. The three of you need to work this out. If you do, we let you go. If you don't, Pavel gets to have his fun."

Fear pricked at the back of my eyes, and bile rose in my throat. I didn't want to know what *fun* meant to Pavel.

The generator roared to life and brilliant work lights flooded the room, so bright I had to shield my eyes. Noise bounced off the ancient walls, muffled by the earth surrounding us.

I blinked my eyes open slowly, adjusting to the near daylight. What was my next play? I was being held by two armed men, and I didn't know if Daniel Weber was on my side, theirs, or somewhere in between. "It's going to take time."

"I know." Enzo let go of me and crossed to the other side of the chamber where two folding chairs sat. "We have all night."

"I don't even have my tools."

Pavel sat next to Enzo and pulled out his gun. He used it to gesture at a tool chest by the generator. "Good thing we brought some."

Daniel walked up to me and handed me his notebook. He spoke loud enough I could hear him over the generator, but quiet enough the thugs likely didn't. "I'm sorry, Leigh. I tried figuring it out so they wouldn't bring anyone else down here."

"It's not your fault." I gave him a tight smile and opened the notebook, flipping through pages and sketches. I plucked some photographs out of a pocket at the back of the book.

Declan had been right. It was too dangerous for me down here. I tried not to think of the pained look in his eyes when I left. When I told him not to talk to me anymore. He hadn't wanted to tell me the truth, had he? He thought he was protecting me yet again.

"Isaac..." I closed the notebook, not needing to read it. Between storming off at Giovanni's and storming into Declan's bed, Jayce had given me her phone with the images of the notebook, telling me to study it. I'd suspected she wanted to bring me along tonight and wanted me prepared. "Why do they think you built the case for that manuscript?"

"I don't know." He stared down at the photographs in my hand, of a fresco somewhere in the catacombs. "I don't even know how they know about it."

"Because someone at Barton created a set of specs for it, with Fenix as the client."

He stepped in front of me, dipping down so he could meet my eyes. "Seriously? Who?"

"Stop whispering," snapped Pavel. Not a man I wanted to piss off. "Get to work at a louder volume."

Keeping my lips as still as possible, I said, "I don't think they're going to let us go."

"They will." Isaac gripped my shoulders and gave a quick squeeze. "They said they would, so they will. As soon as we open the vault."

Daniel tapped the stack of photographs. "We need to get to work, if that's going to happen."

"You're right." Slow work. Lots of thinking. *Please, Declan, please come for me.* "I noticed patterns that repeated in the notebook—a dodecahedron, stuff about a study of fluid dynamics, and mirror writing, like da Vinci did."

"I copied some of those from the frescoes and etchings in proximity to this chamber. The study was from one of his works." Daniel gestured to the top of the wall, where tubes had been carved, like terracotta gutters. Carved? Attached? "The fluid dynamics study was because of those."

"What are they for?"

"I'm not certain, but there's one on either side of the door, so I suspect—"

"It has something to do with how to open the vault?"

Daniel nodded.

"I also noticed a few illustrations of cogs and thunderbolts?"

Isaac strolled to the left side of the vault door. "There's no evidence of hinges, so it might slide open? It would need cogs for that. Maybe the lightning represents a power source?"

Power source? I frowned inwardly. That was a modern convention. "Thunderbolts were used in…"

Goose bumps shot up my arms, and not from the cold. On the Roman standard, an eagle sat atop Jupiter's thunderbolts. Could that really be what was inside?

Isaac, oblivious to my words, said, "The vault's door mechanism must be more complex than anything I've worked with, despite its age."

Internally, I was at war. My heart pounded a hectic rhythm against my ribcage, as if it were desperate to leap out and escape. But I wanted to dig in, ask all the questions, pop the vault open.

Was this a test of my newfound resolution? Or was it the universe's cruel way of showing me I'd made the wrong choice when I'd gone to Declan's room? The quiet, agreeable Leigh would've been safe at the hotel, not threading through catacombs with danger pressing closer.

I couldn't open the vault for these men. Whatever was inside, whether or not it was a genuine Roman standard, anything which someone had hidden away centuries ago didn't belong with treasure hunters. Or whatever Fenix was. Giovanni had said they were collecting specific artifacts. But for what?

Time to be smart, Leigh. Delay just the right amount. Ask questions. Ponder.

Enzo had said we had hours.

I focused on the photos again, a whole series of them which hadn't been there when we retrieved it from Cassaforte. One of them snagged my attention.

Something.

Something off.

A rough image of the apostles, all crowded together, but in the corner... "A dodecahedron. That doesn't belong. Wrong time period."

Daniel nodded. "I found that fresco this week."

"That's not pre-third-century artwork." I looked at him, noticing the darkness around his eyes, likely a healing bruise. "And you think it's related to the vault?"

"It must be. Why would someone other than the vault's builder inscribe that down here?"

The three-dimensional shapes weren't it. They weren't what had caught my attention. I held the photo up and pointed to a faint scrawl under the feet of the apostles. I said to Enzo, "Do either of you have a phone I can use?"

"For what?" he asked.

"I just need to take a picture."

Pavel's eyebrow rose in Enzo's direction. It didn't matter what he thought. It only mattered if he gave me the phone.

Enzo stood and handed me a smartphone. "Pavel's trigger finger is faster than any call or email will connect."

"I know." I snapped a picture of the photograph as he sat back down, flipped the image horizontally, and zoomed in. "There. See that?"

Daniel leaned closer. "Mirror writing."

"A code from da Vinci?" asked Isaac.

"Some people think he wrote in reverse as a secret code, but I subscribe to the theory it was simply because he was left-handed." It made sense. That way, he wouldn't smudge ink as he wrote. But these words were etched into the fresco, then painted over so they stood out. Was I wrong about that theory? Was it really a code? "Either way, I still can't read it."

"It's in Italian." Daniel's gaze rose to meet mine, his gaunt face growing paler. "It says, 'Turn Back.'"

CHAPTER 34
DECLAN

I hurried through the darkness, my tiny red light only enough to keep me heading straight. My toes and shoulders pinged off rocks and walls as I ran. Why was Leigh down there? What was she doing?

"Jayce," I hissed. "I need more intel."

My phone buzzed with another message from her, and I slowed enough to read it. *Isaac, Daniel, and two burly guys who don't look happy.*

"What the hell is she doing?" Did she get so angry with me she went straight to her brother? Or did she... no, she wasn't working with Fenix all along. Isaac hadn't played us all to ensure she was in Cassaforte with me.

But the way she'd interacted with Giovanni Ferraro. She didn't flinch when we talked to him. Had everything else been an act?

I stumbled and took a turn too sharp, careening into the wall. All the air flew out of me.

"Declan, slow down." Scarlett's command held a hard edge. "I can see on the display you're moving too fast."

"Tell me what she's doing, dammit." It was just doubts, nothing more. Leigh had been hurt and confused when I told her about the duplicate plans for the Codex case. If she'd known about it, if she'd been behind it, she wouldn't have reacted like that.

"Jayce, are you hidden?" Scarlett was far calmer than me. Then again, that was her superpower.

A text alert flashed on my forearm. *Like a chameleon.*

"Show us." I started moving again, more carefully, eyes on my phone.

The instant the video notification came through, I switched to watch Jayce's feed. It started dark, then gradually lit up as she moved it past the edge of a wall. She must have been around a corner from them. A large chamber opened up, two brilliant work lights pointing at something off-screen.

The vault.

There stood Leigh, arms tight to her body, holding something. The notebook? She was still wearing the light T-shirt she'd worn to my hotel room—she must have been so cold down here—and her hair was a mess.

Brie said, "Who's who?"

"Leigh's in the middle," I said, unable to say more. Her shoulders were down again, like every time she got near Isaac. I picked up my pace. I needed to get to her.

"Tabarnak," Rav growled over the line. "I'm parking the car and coming in."

"Shit," said Malcolm. Everyone was watching Jayce's video. "That's Noah's thug, isn't it?"

Scarlett's affirmative sent a wave of dread coiling around my stomach. "And the injured man, it's Daniel Weber. Giovanni's man."

Giovanni had accused Weber of betraying him—revealing the notebook's location to the kidnappers. And the kidnappers were there.

Oh, god. "They took Leigh."

Emmett added, "Daniel Weber. That's the name of the guy the clowns had with me in Venice. They called him their historian."

"Did they beat him, too?" Scarlett's voice was thick. Emmett's ordeal had taken its toll on her.

"Yeah," came his simple reply.

"Doesn't sound like he betrayed Giovanni." Did my words matter at this moment?

"Brie? Will?" snapped Scarlett. "Can you get more info on the map? Find them a way to the other exit. I don't like this. I want egress points now."

I drew closer to Jayce's hiding spot, enough that the work lights shone around the next corner. I took the opportunity to riffle through my pack, a slim sack filled with the tools of my trade. Rav was on his way in, but it would take him too long to reach us if something happened.

We needed traps or ways to slow them down if we had to run.

I wasn't leaving Leigh down here with Fenix. She wasn't working with them. They'd kidnapped her. They must have. And she was scared. *I'm coming, baby. Just hold on.*

My fingers skimmed over spools of wire, and I eyed the walls of the catacombs. Damn it, there wasn't anything to tie it off on. Carabiners were an option, but hammering them into the stone would travel through the catacombs like a dinner bell. "I should've brought some smoke bombs or something."

Scarlett said, "What are you talking about?"

"I could have thrown them in there, grabbed her and ran," I grumbled, still mentally kicking myself for my lack of foresight. Screw the vault. Protecting Leigh was my job, and here I was, failing at that, too.

"Keep your head on straight." Scarlett knew me too damn well. "Wait for Rav."

"What you got in that pack of yours?" Will asked.

I zipped up my pack and straightened, speaking just above a whisper since I was so close. Although there was obviously a generator running in the chamber. "Drill and bits. Wire, carabiners, rope, my endoscope, and extra gloves."

Another message from Jayce popped up on my phone. *Thugs have guns.*

Fuck.

Will's silence was not a good sign.

"Do you have night vision goggles?" Brie said through the earpiece.

"I packed for a black-tie wedding, not for underground." My tone was too sharp, but I couldn't control myself. My woman was being held by men with guns.

I flicked off my flashlight and stowed it in a pouch at my thigh before turning the last corner where I could see Jayce. "I see you."

Her tiny form was curled up on the floor, peeking around the edge to watch the men. She'd donned her black head covering, so it was unlikely anyone would spot her, even if they looked directly at her. Her fingers wiggled in my direction as a hello.

My heart pounded with increasing anxiety as I neared Jayce, the voices beyond becoming clear. I knelt behind her, leaning to her ear to keep as quiet as possible. "She's not working with them."

Jayce tucked back against the wall to look—glower—at me. "Of course she isn't. No one thinks she is."

"What do we do?" I cupped my hands around my mouth to ensure I was silent to everyone but the team.

"Get out," said Scarlett. "They're armed."

"I'm not leaving her. Come up with something better."

"Just passing the gate." Rav wasn't on my GPS display, but his steady breaths told me he was moving through the corridor faster than I had. "But I'm not armed."

"Crap." Brie wasn't the bravest of the Reynolds siblings, but her tone had me plastering myself against the wall that blocked Jayce and me from the armed men in the chamber. "You've got company. I can see police cars pulling in along the private road. No lights, but there's two of them, so it's not likely a random patrol."

Leigh's words carried down the hall. "There's more of the mirror writing on that plaque by the vault door. Let me flip that one, too."

One of the men—not Isaac—said, "It's also Italian, but different from the last one. It says to turn back. And that the contents of the vault are cursed."

I peeked around the corner, my eyes finally landing on Leigh for real. What was I going to do? How was I going to fix this?

We had to separate Leigh—and Isaac and Daniel, if possible—from the two thugs. Distract the big men. Take them out separately.

I ducked behind the corner again and slipped my pack around, opening the top. There had to be something. I rummaged, more to get my brain running than anything. I knew exactly what was in this pack. I just had to change how I was thinking about things. Then my hand landed on a small container tucked neatly in a pouch near the top. "Will, I have the drone. Can you pilot it if it's connected to my phone?"

Will hummed aloud. "It worked in Venice."

"Good." I withdrew the tiny drone's case and pulled out the technical marvel—it would be Leigh's savior—which spanned less than two inches. "Glad you built it so small."

"Finally! Someone's appreciating it," said Will. "Brie, I'll need you to take over the map and figuring out the other exit."

"Got it," she said.

"What are you planning?" Scarlett would give me some latitude to improvise, but only if the plan made sense to her.

"Step one, we separate the two thugs. Step two, we get everyone to safety."

"Step three?" she asked.

I pressed the back of my head against the cool brick behind me, a war battling in there. *Step three, I'm going to open that beautiful safe and see what's inside.*

Rav's rhythmic breaths sounded again. He must have muted himself, which was rule number one at Reynolds—never turn off your earpiece. Somehow, most of our rules didn't apply to our head of security. "You missed the step where you wait for me to take care of whichever man stays behind."

I could take one of them. Rav had given me plenty of hand-to-hand lessons, and I'd have help from Isaac and Daniel. "Jayce, you up for a little distraction?"

She smacked my shoulder, hauling off her hood so I could see her familiar grin. "Let me guess. Make noise and stay ten steps ahead of whoever chases me and the drone?"

"You read my mind."

She hopped up from her spot on the ground. "Those assholes aren't going to hurt my best student."

"Student?"

She shrugged. "Friend?"

I stood with her. "I'll give you as much chocolate as you want if you don't get caught."

She pointed down the hallway, the way we'd come. "In case you didn't see it, there's an alcove about twenty feet back. You hide in there until we pass you."

"You're the best." I squeezed her arm. "Will, get their attention with the drone, then stick with Jayce. Brie, you may have to guide her. Keep her on the known path."

"We're good to proceed, Scar?" asked Brie.

"I told Leigh she was on our team," said Scarlett. "And we never leave anyone behind."

The drone's blades began spinning and it lifted from my hand, whirring quietly, the barest puff of wind blowing against my cheek. A pinprick of light cast out from one end.

"Give me until the count of twenty to get into position." I flicked my red flashlight back on and hurried to the alcove Jayce had pointed out, where I'd wait in the blackness for my chance.

We're coming, Leigh. Be ready.

CHAPTER 35

LEIGH

"Cursed?" As if things couldn't get any worse. I stared at the little plaque beside the vault door. What did cursed mean to a sixteenth century pope?

"Keep working," snarled Pavel. "A curse is the least of your worries. Ferraro knows we have the notebook, and he won't sit on his hands much longer. We need to get this done."

So much for having all night.

I closed my eyes, remembering Declan's room. When he'd picked me up and tossed me on the bed. The laughter and smiles. His thoughtfulness and care. His warm breath on my cheek as I lay naked on top of him.

Same screaming heart rate. Very different cause.

I reopened my eyes, scanning the notebook and photos, the frescoes and terracotta tubes that held the key to unlocking the vault. Something didn't add up. Flat pentagons I could have understood, but these three-dimensional figures were an anachronism. I cast my mind back, skimming through memories of dusty textbooks and intricate blueprints.

Talk it out, Leigh. Show them you're working. I knelt by the tool chest and rummaged through the contents. They had everything I could have used for Edoardo's vault or switching out a lock on a standard home safe, but a stone door?

Isaac joined me. "What do you—"

"Che cazzo!" Enzo shot out of his seat, gun in hand. "Chi è?"

I spun to find out what he was looking at. A flash of light shone in the corridor we'd entered from. A flashlight?

My heart leaped. Was it Declan?

It bobbed four feet from the ground and vanished down the hallway. Would Declan run if he found us? If it wasn't him, who?

"Andiamo!" Enzo kicked Pavel's chair. "No witnesses."

A wicked grin spread across Pavel's face as he stood. "I'll find whoever it is. A body or two won't be hard to dispose of down here."

Pavel turned on his industrial flashlight and took off at a jog. How well did he know the maze surrounding us? Surely, he wouldn't have gone so fast if he didn't have his bearings.

"Stay here and do what you've been told." Enzo's gaze swept across the rest of us, finally landing on Isaac. He jabbed a threatening finger at my brother. "Get that vault open, or we all pay the price."

As Enzo left to join Pavel on the hunt, icy tendrils of fear crept down my spine. *I* was a witness. I looked at Isaac. So was he. I whispered, "I'm not dying down here. We need to get out."

Daniel ran a hand over his head. "I know a way out they don't."

"No," hissed Isaac. "You heard him. We need to open the vault. They know these catacombs too well. They'll find us if we run."

Daniel ambled backward until he leaned against the massive door. "And then they'll kill us, too."

I stared after the spot where Pavel and Enzo had left. "Do you still have your flashlight, Daniel?"

"Enzo took it."

We didn't even have our own lights to get out with. It was too far back to the public areas and the light. We could wander the tunnels for hours, if not days, lost. My throat tightened. Where was—

A red light appeared down the hall. The Fenix men didn't have red lights. It was moving fast.

The tightness fell to my chest. *Please. Please.*

A dark form appeared. A thermal suit. A rugged jaw. Down-turned hazel eyes.

I launched from my spot by the tool chest and ran to Declan, throwing my arms around his neck. "I'm sorry. I'm so sorry. They threw a hood over me and forced me into—"

"I've got you, baby." He kissed the top of my head. "No apologies. Not until we're out of here."

"What the—" Isaac blurted, his volume far too loud over the generator. "You said you weren't coming down—"

"Quiet." One strong arm latched around me, holding me close, Declan's warm scent enveloping me. Oranges. And spice. Cloves? "We need to move fast while my team distracts them."

I pulled back to look at Declan, searching for the anger from our last meeting. "I should have stayed with you."

He forced a smile, the best I could hope for in the moment. "We can talk about that later. Right now, I'm getting you out of here."

"We can't." Isaac planted a hand on the door. "They threatened to kill us if we didn't get this open. Leaving won't change that. They'll just grab us again."

I released my grip on Declan's neck and turned around in his arm to face my brother. "Reynolds can protect you."

"The hell they can." Isaac stalked toward us. "They said that after Cassaforte and look what happened? The first time you leave the hotel, you're thrown into a van!"

"The first time I left without them," I shot back. Why was I arguing? We had to get out. Leave. Not waste time yelling at each other. "We have to trust Declan."

"Isaac's right," said Daniel. "These men took me out of my home. I'm only alive now because I've cooperated."

"Scar, you hear that?" Declan held me against his chest, like I was something special. Something he treasured and wouldn't let go. He made noises of affirmation, no doubt having a discussion with Scarlett and his team over an earpiece.

I stared at the vault door, thinking over Daniel's notes, the photos, and the symbols on its front. It wasn't fair that men like Enzo and Pavel would discover its secrets, let alone what was behind it.

But our lives were more important. Declan—I wrapped my arms over the one he'd threaded around my waist, nestling into the warmth of his frame and his suit—was more important.

"Okay," Declan finally said. "One of them's chasing a drone, the other's after Jayce."

My stomach couldn't sink any lower. Jayce was out there, alone, and one of those two monsters was hunting her. I turned inside his grip. "Enzo's the one with the cheek scar who took

Martina. Pavel's his partner. Jayce needs to stay out of their way."

"Don't worry about her. She's leading him toward Rav." Declan glanced at the door, nearly masked wonder shining in his gorgeous eyes. "We have time, but I don't know how much. Brie's monitoring everything."

"Can she help? I have some theories she or Will may be able to speed up."

Declan kissed my forehead and finally let go of me. Keeping his eyes on mine, he stowed his flashlight in a pouch and slid his pack around to the front. He handed me a pair of gloves. "I can't give you my suit, but these might help."

"Thanks." They weren't heated and they were too long for my fingers, but they'd cut some of the chill.

He removed his phone from his forearm and unlocked it before handing it over. "Leigh needs a hand, Brie. I've got you on speaker."

"I'll do my best," came a female voice from the phone. "Scar, can you manage Jayce and the GPS? I've got another algorithm working on the map."

"I can, but take everyone else off that channel. No one in the room—" Scarlett's sentence cut off.

"Leigh, I've isolated this line," said Brie. "What do you need?"

"Before you start—" Declan grabbed my chin in his hand. "I'm going to watch your back. You need to accept me being a little protective right now."

His words, primal in their intensity, reassured me. Not like Finn, whose control strangled me. Declan let me breathe. Let me be me. He was watching out for me, not watching to be sure I didn't step out of line.

"I'm sorry about..." I whispered, trying to find some level of control, so I could say what I needed to. "Earlier, I... Every minute with you was the adventure I hoped for when I came to Rome."

"When we get out of this, I'm taking you on a proper date." His lips grazed mine. "And I promise, it's going to have a lot less adventure."

I pressed my hand to his chest, feeling the steady rhythm of his heart beating against my palm through his tight-fitting thermal suit. "I'm looking forward to it."

He leaned in, pressing a soft kiss on my cheek, his lips lingering. "You can do this."

"You're a bad influence, Declan."

With our faces still inches apart, he said in a low rumble that reverberated through me, "I'm exactly the influence you need."

A smile formed deep inside of me. Declan wasn't just the flirtatious safe cracker or the charming rogue. He was brave, determined, willing to risk everything for others.

He was so unlike the men I had dated, men who were confident, even charismatic, like my brothers. But their confidence, their charm, their charisma—it was always about them. Always about what they wanted, their needs, their desires.

But Declan was different. He'd come to rescue us and would risk himself to ensure we survived.

An overwhelming realization hit me. Declan Ramsay was exactly the kind of man I'd been looking for. A protector, not a controller. *That* was what I wanted.

I gripped his neck, pulling him closer. How lucky was I to have met this amazing man? "You're right."

"You said you needed help?" said Brie, from the phone still in my hand.

"Yeah, sorry." I let go of Declan's neck and got back to work.

"Come on." A hand landed on my arm. Isaac. "Let's do this. Then we get out."

CHAPTER 36
DECLAN

The part none of the people in the room had heard? We were now little more than bait.

If the plan unfolding over my earpiece went down the way Scarlett expected, one kidnapper would end up on the short end of Rav's fist. Rav would cinch him up with zip ties, then Jayce or the drone would bring the other guy to him with the same result. He was looking forward to meeting the men who'd set Scarlett up.

But odds were, Rav would only get one. The other would hear the fight and come back for the vault. A man like that would only chase a drone so long before he got wise to the distraction.

And when he did, he'd come for us. That's what I had to prepare for.

I stepped back from Leigh before I did something ridiculous, like kiss her again. She was my distraction, and we had a job to do.

Twelve feet of etched stone stared back at us. From the photos, I'd expected a flat door, covered in the zodiac symbols. Instead, dips and waves marred its surface.

My heart thrummed with excitement, my fingers itching to trace the lines and curves of the carvings. The vault door wasn't just a barrier to be overcome, but a reluctant lover, begging to be coaxed open. Now, I had the door and my actual lover by my side.

This vault wasn't my job. My priority was listening to the communication coming over my earpiece and being ready. Leigh had my phone, so I couldn't monitor the GPS map, but the team would give me a heads-up if we were in danger.

Isaac walked Leigh to the vault. He was braver in the face of danger than I'd expected, despite the flicker in his eyes, a shadow I couldn't shake off. Jealousy that his sister put her faith in someone else? Anger that I'd lied to him to shoo him off earlier?

Scarlett said over my earpiece, "He's almost to you, Rav."

Leigh walked to the center of the room. "I think I've figured it out."

Isaac's hand brushed against Leigh's arm, a soft, brotherly gesture. "I knew you could do it."

A grunt came over the line, then the sound of a struggle. My heart pounded in my chest.

Jayce, more winded than I'd heard her in some time, said, "I'm circling around, Rav."

Combat sounded over the line, punctuated by the occasional swear, mostly in French. I'd seen Rav in a few fights over the years. He was more likely to diffuse a situation than escalate it, but when he did, no one ever took him down.

Scarlett provided another update. "The other man's in pursuit of the drone and Will's guided him away from the original path. If you are going to leave, now's the perfect time."

My gaze shifted back to Leigh. She was talking to Brie and Daniel about fluid dynamics. She was confident, strong. How much time did she need?

I cupped a hand over my mouth, so no one in the room would hear. "What about the police?"

Isaac spun to look at me. So much for secrecy. "Police? Where?"

I held up a finger to hold him off. "If they're at the main building, we still can't leave that way."

"You can," said Scarlett. "Considering your gear, we can construct a cover story easily."

"How's it coming, Leigh?" I asked.

She raised my phone toward the door. "Do you see it, Brie?"

"I do."

Leigh was in her own world. Focused. Brilliant. Working seamlessly with my team and too engrossed in her examination of the vault door to hear anything Isaac and I were talking about.

I couldn't help but smile at that. This was what she needed to forget about the chaos, about being kidnapped. It was a similar feeling to the one I'd found with my first lock.

Memories of my teenage years flashed back, to the collection of salvaged and purchased locks hidden away in my closet. Whenever I was upset, I'd retreat there, pulling out the set of lockpicks Scarlett had gifted me, passed down from her mother. In a world of unpredictable variables, the locks were a constant, a binary equation of locked or unlocked. It wasn't like the swim meets I lost, which my parents nitpicked and criticized. It wasn't the math tests where I fell short of perfection by a measly five percent.

The locks, they were a sanctuary, a place where I found tranquility in the midst of reality's messiness. Even now, I couldn't imagine doing anything that didn't involve their mystery, their truth, their clarity.

Leigh was the same. Her focus. Nothing but the puzzle existing. We both found our peace in the challenges, in the riddles. I used to think it made me lesser, that I wasn't as good as whoever my parents were comparing me to. Scarlett and Rav had always reassured me growing up. Anyone who judged me for being less than perfect, they said, wasn't worth stressing over. It was a lesson that had stayed with me, and now, under the harsh work lights, watching my woman—she *was* my woman, and this proved it—I truly understood it.

"Isaac." I gestured for him to join me. "We've almost got one man down. When the other gets back, I'll retreat into the hallway, so he doesn't suspect anything. Then you and I can take him down. Can you help with that?"

A vein throbbed in his forehead. "That's your plan? Beat up one of the massive men with the gun?"

"Can you do that?"

"Yeah." He straightened, like it could convince me.

Inside, I crossed my fingers. Hopefully, Rav would show before I had to face off against anyone.

Leigh said, "A dodecahedron has twelve sides, right? And each side is a pentagon."

Jayce whooped in my ear. "The champion and still undefeated—Rav LaPierre!"

Relief washed over me at the familiar sound of zip ties and Rav threatening the thug to stay down.

"It's not the one with the scar," said Rav. "But he also has a phoenix tattoo."

"We've taken out Pavel," I said to the room. "Scar, how are we doing with the other guy?"

"He's lagging," Scarlett said. "Jayce, I'll need you to do your thing again. Be careful—I think he's the smarter of the two."

"I'm always careful."

"No, you're not," said at least Scarlett, Rav, and Will at the same time.

Leigh was unphased, continuing her discussion with Brie. "There are twelve carved images on the door. I believe five of them are potential keyholes."

There were three corridors leading into the chamber. The one I'd come through, its extension leading into the depths beyond, and a third which faced the door. Enzo had left through the first, but would he return that way? How well did he know the tunnels?

"Daniel." I pointed to the tunnel beyond him. "Help her, but watch the exit for Enzo coming back."

Isaac gestured to the corridor opposite the door. "I've got that one."

Brie said, "The trick is figuring out which five are the keyholes."

"The pipes." Daniel gestured to the terracotta forms at the top of the wall, which were vaguely cylindrical. "If we had something pouring down the front, I think it would cover some of the symbols?"

"Do we have water?" Leigh asked.

Daniel shook his head. "Not enough."

Brie said, "Leigh, hold the camera up to the door. Maybe I can get a reading and make some guesses."

"The drone would be better for that," I said. It had a special camera that could map distances and feed into a program of Will's to construct 3D images. We'd used it for the London heist a couple of weeks ago.

"Yes," Scarlett interjected. "But that drone's doing something more important than satisfying your need to open vaults, Dec. This is non-negotiable."

There were many rules at Reynolds Recoveries, and one of them was to never argue with Scarlett's command voice. We were running out of time and options. We had to trust each other, and right now, that meant trusting Leigh's brain and the technology she had available.

Emmett joined the conversation. "We're at the alternate exit. Any luck mapping a way for us to—"

"Fuck," Scarlett muttered. Not good. She was always in control of everything on an op, including her language. This was bad. "Will, find the bastard."

"I'm tracking backward to where I last had him." Will's drone must have lost track of Enzo.

Rav said, "Jayce and I are en route to the vault."

"Get back to the alcove, Dec," said Scarlett. "He won't suspect anything's up if they're working on the vault."

I glanced at Leigh, who was holding up my phone, complying with Brie's instruction. None of the emergency on the earpieces filtered through from Brie. She normally reacted to everything with nervous giggles, but she was controlling herself even better than Scarlett for once.

Scarlett was right. I should hide. But I wasn't leaving Leigh.

The only questions were: Which entrance would Enzo come through, and how could I get the jump on him?

"If you knew the pipes connected to water, why didn't you tell them to bring gallons of it, Daniel?" Isaac snapped.

"I thought they were a security feature at first, meant to flood the vault if anyone tried to break in." Daniel's gaze flitted from the corridor he was watching and back to Isaac. "I didn't realize—"

A faint light appeared behind Daniel, rapidly brightening.

"Daniel," I hissed, pointing to the door.

He didn't take his eyes off Isaac. "—they might be part of the—"

Enzo burst into the room at a run, barreling into Daniel and knocking him forward. "Cazzo madre!"

Instead of hiding, I lunged for Leigh, pulling her away from the center of the room. We fell to the ground, rolling to avoid the commotion. With her safely out of harm's way, I sprang back to my feet and charged at Enzo, who'd fallen when he collided with Daniel. "Isaac! Help me!"

No help came. Isaac grabbed Leigh instead. Close enough. If he protected her, I could do my job.

Enzo only had enough time to pull his gun before I tackled him, sending us both tumbling across the ground. And sending the gun skittering away. Something tore through my thigh, the warmth of the thermal suit faltering.

We grappled and wrestled, trading punches and dodging out of each other's way. I managed a few good jabs to his ribs before he retaliated with a well-aimed knee to my gut.

The pain was sharp and sudden. I gasped for air, but none came.

"Declan!" screamed Leigh. "Let me go, Isaac!"

Enzo tried to pin me. I twisted away from his grip, rolling across the floor in an attempt to escape him. But he was too quick and too strong, the sickening agony screaming through my body slowing me.

He landed on top of me again and pinned me face-down.

Grunting in frustration, I tried to buck up against him, but it was no use—he wrenched my arm up so high he must have been trying to tear it from its socket.

He leaned in and snarled, "How many of your team members do I get to kill tonight?"

His gloating would give me time for— Enzo launched off me.

I craned my neck to see a massive arm circling his neck from behind.

Rav.

Fucking hell, Rav had arrived.

I scrambled out from underneath Enzo and grabbed the gun while he and Rav rocked back and forth. Rav's arm didn't budge, and the thug's resistance gradually slowed, until Rav eased the—thank god—unconscious man to the ground.

Jayce appeared from the shadows, zip ties in hand.

"You're going to jail, you prick." Daniel—who'd gotten up and out of the way during the fight—spat at the now-listless Enzo.

Leigh freed herself from Isaac's protective grip and ran to me. "Are you okay?"

"Not really." I held her tighter and gritted my teeth against the stabbing in my chest. "But I will be. Pretty sure at least one rib's broken."

She pulled back, looking me up and down. "And your leg's bleeding."

"Is it?" I looked down, the crimson gash marring the beautiful thermal suit. "Well, shit."

"I told you to wait for me," growled Rav. "Sit down so I can check you over."

"That was fun," said Brie over my earpiece and through the phone Leigh still held. "Leigh, let the boys do their thing. We've got work to do."

CHAPTER 37

LEIGH

Isaac wrapped his arm around my shoulder. "How's your head?"

Declan had fought to protect me, and Isaac had shielded me with his body. How had I decided I didn't want a man's protection anymore and then ended up needing it like never before?

"I'm fine, Isaac." I gave him a thin smile. "Thanks for everything."

Declan went to the far wall with Rav, his dark thermal suit slashed and glistening with moisture. Blood. My heartbeat should have escalated in panic at that sight, but it didn't. Instead, I admired the way the suit clung to his lean frame, tracing the lines of muscles I'd recently discovered.

Isaac broke into my moment, dropping his voice. "Easy to forget you've got a boyfriend when he's bleeding for you, huh?"

So much for the amazing brother routine.

"Finn and I broke up, Isaac. You might've missed that memo the first five times I told you."

Before Isaac could retort about how unfairly I'd treated his buddy, Jayce slipped in next to me, her arms folded.

"What'd Brie come up with?" she asked, pointedly changing the topic.

"While Declan was busy playing hero," Brie said, "I created a model of how water would flow across the vault door's surface. The door isn't as vertical as it looks. There's a gentle grade to it, with textures you can barely see. Think of it like a game of Plinko. The water would divert around high spots and flow across low spots."

I held up Declan's phone to display the model as augmented reality.

Brie's overlay splashed the live view of the vault door in hues of green, tracing the paths water would take from the terracotta pipes above, down the curves and glyphs on the stone. The digital waterfall avoided five of the twelve symbols.

Jayce's brow furrowed. "So, water doesn't cover five of the symbols—"

"Which means there's either a keyhole," I said, "or something we need to manipulate in at least one of them."

A ragged groan slipped from Daniel, looking as if he'd just survived a marathon. "Not very good at playing lookout, but I make a mean pylon."

I angled the phone so he could see it. "We've got our next clue."

"Declan will be fine. Nothing's actually broken, but I've covered up the wound." Rav strode over to us, lethal precision in his every move. His gaze flicked pointedly to Isaac. "Scarlett says the police are checking the entrance, so I'm going to collect the other man first and deliver him. If sleeping beauty so much as twitches, try to be useful."

Isaac's jaw clenched, but he kept his mouth shut.

Rav inclined his head toward Declan. "He's got the gun, so all you need to do is alert him."

Daniel said, "I know another way out if you want to avoid the police."

"Good plan," said Rav. "You have exactly as long as it takes me to deliver these two to the police. Depending on how fast they can convince the authorities to search for trespassers, you may not have much more than an hour."

Declan handed Rav a headlamp, and the big man was off at a jog.

Daniel limped toward the work lights, adjusting one of them to illuminate the pipes better. "I didn't put all of my research into the notebook. I suspected da Vinci's sketches of Platonic solids could be crucial."

Jayce stifled a laugh. "What, like solids who are just friends?"

Daniel blinked, and I couldn't hold my own laugh in.

"Three-dimensional shapes," I said. "There are five core ones through history, like a cube or a tetrahedron. No one's sure who first came up with the concept, but Plato hypothesized they made up the Earth and universe."

"I need a snack after that." Jayce dropped her pack to the floor and began rummaging. "Declan, where's that chocolate you promised?"

Declan waved her to the spot where Rav had stationed him. "In my bag."

I turned back to Daniel. "Do you think the solids play a role in this? It might explain why they're on the frescoes."

Daniel nodded, standing taller the longer he spoke, as though he gained strength from the intellectual discussion. "Da Vinci put substantial weight on symmetry and balance, even in the Platonic solids. The dodecahedron is special. It has twelve faces, corresponding to the twelve zodiac signs"—he gestured to the carvings on the door—"and is often associated with the aether or spirit, while the other four are linked to the elements."

I hummed in assent. "Fire, water, earth, and air."

"Exactly. And the surface area and volume of a dodecahedron are related to the golden ratio, which da Vinci also studied extensively."

I nodded. It was a detail I knew. "He used it in many of his paintings and sketches."

Jayce rolled her eyes, unwrapping a bar of dark chocolate Declan had handed her. "History lessons later, people. Rav's only going to take so long."

"Sorry, I didn't..." I winced, the apology slipping out before I could stop it.

Jayce waved a hand dismissively. "Save it. Every sorry is another second wasted."

Declan groaned, pushing himself up. "If one of those five carvings that aren't under water is the keyhole, maybe there's a way to overlay the golden rectangle?"

"Or the golden spiral?" I ventured, the idea taking hold.

"Brilliant." Declan's tone was low and urgent, excitement threading underneath his pained groans. "Brie, can we overlay the golden spiral on the image of the door?"

"Try every direction," I said, stepping back and trying to visualize the spiral on the door. I recalled the proportions from the Mona Lisa, my mind's eye tracing the unseen spiral's path from the lady's hand, over her shoulder, above her head, curling finally to her nose.

The thug on the ground let out a low moan, stirring.

Jayce said around a mouthful of chocolate, "Rav, we've got movement here."

"Should we tie him to a chair or something?" I asked.

Declan approached the vault door. "Rav wants Jayce topside to help him lure the police close enough to find Pavel."

Jayce squeezed my arm, her gaze heavy. "You good if I leave you here with the guys?"

I smiled back, grateful for her support. I had Declan. What else did I need? "I'm good."

"Stay safe." Jayce winked as she threw her pack over her shoulders and popped the last bite of chocolate into her mouth. She disappeared into the maze, a path lit by her headlamp.

Declan kept one arm tight to his chest, pointing with the gun at a carving about six feet off the ground. "That one's the odd one out."

Brie blew a raspberry, her voice a mix of annoyance and respect. "Of course Declan would get it first."

"How did you figure that out?" I asked.

"Adrenaline." He puffed up as a taunt, grimacing through it. "I had to beat you to something."

"I just found the right angle," Brie said. "If Declan picked the scorpion, then he's right."

Declan tucked the gun into his tool belt. "What's next?"

Our group fell into discussion. Daniel brought up theories about the Vitruvian Man, Brie questioned the possibility of the door shifting position over the centuries, while Isaac debated whether the water model was accurate. Declan closed in on the scorpion carving, dictating every bump and edge.

The conversation swirled around me, their chatter melding into a distant hum as my mind spun.

Suddenly, a thought pierced the din, crystal clear. It was as if a veil had been lifted, revealing a truth that was right in front of us.

"Turn back!" I blurted out.

The room fell silent, and all eyes fell on me.

"Rav and Jayce have just dropped off Pavel." Declan swiveled to look at me. "Scarlett says someone met the police at the entrance, possibly an owner or manager. Looks like they're coming in."

"Turn back," I repeated, excitement coiling in my gut, ready to spring free. "The mirror writing on the panel next to the door—it doesn't mean go away because the contents are cursed. It means we should literally turn it back."

"We have twenty minutes." Declan paused, nodding. "Rav says be ready to go in fifteen."

We had enough time. We had to. I could do this. "It's an invitation, not a warning. The plaque says turn back. We literally need to turn the plaque back."

Daniel straightened fully for the first time since we'd entered the catacombs. "You're right. Look at the fresco opposite the vault door. It's a man holding a key where the plaque is. I thought it symbolized the existence of a key, but maybe it's telling us where it's hidden."

Declan waved me to the side of the door and hoisted me up so I could reach the plaque. He grunted, no doubt from the pain in his arm, his ribs, and his leg, but he insisted. Isaac handed me a small crowbar from the tool chest, which I used to pop the plaque off.

It didn't fall. It swiveled.

"There's a hole." *Don't be a trap that's going to cut off my arm.* I reached in slowly, inch by inch. Nothing slammed shut and no creepy crawlies skittered over me. My hand landed on something metallic. A key! Massive, nearly a foot long.

Enzo groaned again and everyone paused, but he didn't move.

Daniel edged closer to the rest of us. "Declan, you should put her down and get the gun out."

Isaac stood so close to Declan, there was barely room to put me down. "Hurry up, Leigh! Open the vault."

Declan intervened. "I'll do it. Everyone else, get back. It's safer in the corridor."

Isaac shook his head. "I'm not leaving all the glory to you. I want to see what's inside."

Declan held his ground. "This isn't about glory, Isaac. It's about safety."

Isaac's stubbornness was ridiculous. His need to prove he was as clever or talented as anyone else in the room. How had I never seen it before? Except I had seen it. I'd just chosen to ignore it most of my life. Once we were out of the catacombs, he and I were having a serious discussion about the plans Declan found inside the Barton vault. "Declan's right. But we need to pull Enzo back with us."

"He gets what he deserves if something happens," hissed Daniel.

"Leigh, please. Get around the corner," Declan pleaded. "We don't have time for this."

Time was precious, and we couldn't afford to argue. Scarlett couldn't have been happy about us delaying for so long. I reached for Isaac, hoping my request would change his mind. "Come with me, Isaac."

He didn't budge. "No, I want to see what's inside."

"Then protect Enzo. Get a chair over him or something." I helped Daniel into the corridor. Why did I care about the guy who'd kidnapped us and threatened to kill us? Because I was a good person? Or because I was still trying to keep everyone—even my kidnapper—happy. *Get a grip, Leigh.* Once we were around the corner, I called out, "We're safe."

"Last chance, Isaac," Declan said.

"Just open it."

"I'm inserting the key." Declan sighed, followed by the sound of metal scraping against stone carrying around the corner. "Turning it now."

Isaac gasped, a sound of pure awe and wonder.

Declan called, "Something's happening..."

Chapter 38

Declan

When the key turned inside the scorpion carving, the door shifted. Not enough to peer inside, but enough to force her open. I shoved the crowbar into the gap so Isaac and I could work together. After a good couple of minute's effort, she budged again, and a rush of chilly air escaped, followed by a loud crash like a landslide.

"Shit," Isaac coughed, as dust billowed into the room.

My own cough echoed his, wracking pain through my injured ribs, where Enzo had kneed me. We kept pushing on the crowbar, forcing the stubborn vault door. Stone scraped against stone, the vault cracking open by inches, then a foot.

Rubble and small rocks clattered down from the top of the door, narrowly missing Isaac and me as we darted back. We shielded our faces with our arms, struggling to remain steady under the onslaught.

"What is it? Did it open?" Brie's voice buzzed in my earpiece and from somewhere in the room—she was still on speaker on the phone Leigh was carrying.

When I uncovered my head, Leigh was already in the room, moving to Enzo's unconscious body.

She grimaced as she squinted through the dust, her mouth and nose covered with her arm. "They're dusty and a bit scraped up, but don't look injured."

"Good," came Rav's reply, his tone softer but still filled with urgency. "Police have taken Pavel away. He was ranting about thieves in the catacombs, so I guarantee they'll be down soon."

"You need to hurry and get out," Scarlett said, impatience clear in her tone.

Leigh assessed Enzo's condition while Isaac continued to work on the door, coughing violently as he tried to clear his lungs.

"The carvings... they moved... when you turned the key," Isaac rasped, his hand braced against the ancient door. "Did you see that?"

A wave of energy coursed through me. We were doing it—breaching a vault built by Leonardo da Vinci. It was a mad thrill and an unsettling nightmare at the same time.

"I'm thinking we should wait, come back with gear," Leigh said, leaving Enzo's side.

I straightened, our gazes meeting. "No, Leigh. We open it now."

"Do you want us all to get buried, Declan?" she snapped back, gesturing at the rockfall around the door. "Would that make you happy?"

"It was just rubble that settled on top." I was trying to convince myself as much as I was convincing her. "Everything else will hold up. The ceiling's been fine in the rest of these catacombs."

Isaac continued wrestling with the door, a mix of dread and anticipation mingling in my stomach.

"I've dreamed of this moment," said Daniel, a wild gleam in his eyes.

Leigh grabbed Isaac's arm. "Slow down! What if there are traps? The mirror writing revealed the key, but it also said there was a curse. What if there's an ancient strain of bacteria or something?"

Daniel hovered near them, craning his neck to see inside. "It has to be the Legion's eagle standard."

Leigh's brow furrowed. "Do you really believe that?"

"Let me check for obvious signs of traps." I nudged in between Daniel and the opening, running my fingers over the edge of the door. No visible locks. How had it stayed closed? What had the key triggered to open it?

"Just open it." Daniel practically vibrated next to me. "Da Vinci wouldn't have trapped the vault. At least, not if someone opened it correctly. He wouldn't want to risk harm to his apprentices."

His words did little to ease my concerns, but I was too close. I had to get inside her. I switched from inspecting to wedging myself in the opening to get the most leverage. With a final pained effort, Isaac and I pulled the door open wide enough to reveal the vault's interior, illuminated by the work lights.

I went in first, taking in the small space. Shelves lined the left wall, filled with ancient tools. At the back sat a simple wooden desk. On top of it, a lump of fabric and a thick block of something I couldn't make out, both covered in a layer of dust.

Isaac gravitated toward the desk while Daniel remained near the entrance, seeming unable to move.

"Don't touch anything," Daniel warned us. "These items could be fragile. We can't risk losing this piece of history. We need to inform the authorities about what's down here."

Leigh approached the desk with Isaac, leaning closer to blow gently on the block. Her efforts revealed a leather-bound folio. She reached for the folio, pausing before she touched it. She seemed torn, as though debating between the knowledge that she shouldn't disturb anything but wanting to uncover its secrets.

Moving to stand behind her, I placed my hands on her hips, lending her my support. "What's that?"

"I told myself I'd stand my ground and seize what I wanted." Leigh's breath quickened. "A treasure like this, lost to the centuries... I want to know what it is."

Isaac, who'd been rifling through the fabric on the desk, turned to us, his face pale. "It's eternity."

"What?" The hint of dread which had been circling inside my gut expanded. Eternity?

Without warning, Isaac lifted the fabric, causing Daniel to squawk a protest. But it was too late. The sudden movement knocked the folio from the desk, spilling its loose contents across the floor.

Leigh crouched to gather the scattered sheets.

I knelt with her, catching flashes of sketches as she hurriedly collected the papers—an eagle in its glory and next to it, an exploded view of a feather, a beak, and a talon.

"I need you here, Rav." I needed to get everyone out, including Enzo. My leg hurt from my fight with him, and there was no way I was carrying his unconscious ass all the way upstairs. A beat of silence passed. No one answered. "Rav?"

Leigh pulled my phone out of a pocket and lifted it to her mouth. "Brie?"

Nothing.

"Why can't they hear us?" As Leigh stood, pages of the folio carefully gathered in her arms, the room quaked. Dirt trickled from the ceiling, dust clouding the air once again.

Panic knotted in my gut, and I grabbed Leigh to me, as though I could shield her with my height alone.

"This isn't right. We need to leave. Now." Leigh's worry matched my own, but it seemed Isaac had lost all sense of caution.

He buried his arm deep within the fabric, cradling something precious within its folds. As he unwrapped the object, a golden eagle statuette emerged, glinting in the harsh work light filtering through the dust.

When the fabric fell away completely, he tossed it onto the desk, patches of faded red standing stark against the brown, aged exterior. My mind whirred. Could this really be the lost legion's battle standard?

Isaac was muttering to himself, a triumphant gleam in his eyes as he cradled the eagle. "I knew she'd figure it out. Now it's just a matter of choosing the right talon."

"What are you talking about?" Leigh asked.

"They were so stupid." Isaac's attention lay solely on the golden bird, mumbling to himself. "I told them the safe cracker wouldn't drink the wine, and now look who's holding the talon!"

"Isaac, snap out of it," I said.

Leigh placed a hand on Isaac's arm, concerned. "Are you okay?"

"Bringing you to Rome was the right decision." He blinked, his wild gaze settling on her, a disturbing certainty in his words. "I told them you were the key."

Leigh took a half-step back. "What do you—"

Daniel began barking orders, cutting her off. "Leigh, put that folio back. Isaac, you too with that eagle. We can't risk disturbing this place further."

More dust rained down from the ceiling, a few rocks breaking away from the massive vault door. The room shook, an ominous growl reverberating through the underground chamber.

I channeled every ounce of Scarlett's command voice. "We're getting out of here. Now. This room isn't stable, and neither is that door. If it collapses, we'll be trapped in here."

Isaac's eyes snapped to me, his mania replaced with sudden clarity. "You're right. We need to save the talon."

Before I could appreciate him finally listening for once, Isaac lifted the golden eagle above his head and brought it crashing down onto the stone floor with a horrifying crack.

My head spun as Daniel lashed out at Isaac. "You goddamn fool! That was an irreplaceable artifact!"

Isaac just crouched there, clenching a shard of the broken eagle. Sure, I'd thought Isaac was a bit of a prick, but this was a whole new level.

As if he'd lost part of his mind.

Was it the curse the plaque outside had warned us about? Something in the stagnant air in here turning us all into fucking lunatics?

Frantic footfalls broke my thoughts, and my body relaxed. Rav and Jayce were back, and just in time. The sound of shattering pottery tore my attention from Isaac and the eagle.

I spun around in time for Enzo to plow into me, the two of us careening into the desk, smashing it. Daniel slumped against the shelves on the side, pottery shards surrounding him.

Goddamn it, how the hell had he gotten out of the zip ties?

Chunks of stone fell from the ceiling, dust filling the air.

"Isaac!" Enzo roared, his knuckles finding my jaw a second later. "Get the talon to safety."

CHAPTER 39

LEIGH

Isaac gripped my arm, his wild eyes flashing in the hazy, rock-dusted light. "We need to go, Leigh. Declan's right." He gestured frantically toward the door. "The exit Daniel mentioned. There's a car there. We can use it once we're out."

My heart thumped against my ribs, threatening to burst through my chest. Declan, grimacing with effort, rolled on the floor with Enzo. His shouted curse filled the dusty cavern. Isaac wanted to run, to abandon them.

Dust choked the air, making it thick and hard to breathe. A wave of fear washed over me as more rocks tumbled from the ceiling. The crack of colliding stone mingled with the violence behind me.

I coughed, the taste of ancient dirt sticking to the back of my throat.

"The talon's part of something bigger." Isaac's speech grew faster, his grip on my arm stronger than I'd expected he was capable of. "We could have saved Mom."

A hollow pain unfurled in my stomach, like a silent scream. The raw, leftover ache of her absence bit into my chest.

Declan, my brilliant, puzzle-loving, safe-cracking Declan, was getting the shit kicked out of him.

Was I just going to run?

"No." I tried to pull away from him, but he held tighter. "We help Declan, then we all get out."

Isaac gawked at me, as if seeing his little sister for the first time. But I was no longer just his little sister. I was Leigh Barton. Engineer. Survivor. And I wasn't about to leave anyone behind.

"I brought you here, Leigh," Isaac said, a strange calm falling over him. "Because I knew. I knew you'd figure out the vault and find the talon. You have to come with me and see what we're building."

His words ricocheted in my head, souring my tongue.

I'd been his tool, his means to an end.

Declan was right about someone at Barton working with Fenix. It wasn't Ann. It was Isaac.

Rage bubbled inside me, and I hauled my arm away from Isaac. "You were working with them, weren't you?"

Declan grunted, the sound raw and pained. I glanced back, my resolve hardening. I reached for the broken eagle statuette, its weight comforting in my hand.

But before I could make a move, Isaac seized my arm again, his grip cold and hard, eyes even colder. "Leave them, Leigh."

Anger and fear waged a battle in my heart. Was he serious? Abandon Declan, the man who'd believed in me, who'd made me believe in myself, while Isaac had done nothing but erode my confidence for years?

"I'm not leaving without him."

Isaac looked at me, a mix of frustration and incredulity etched on his face. But I stood my ground. I was no longer the scared little sister, but a woman with a will of her own. And I'd be damned if I'd leave Declan behind.

Isaac's nails dug into my skin. "You're a bookworm, Leigh. A good girl. Declan's just a criminal. And you have a good man at home."

Suddenly, the room rumbled again, a loud groan of stone and earth so deep it jostled inside my chest. The door shifted, seeming to close in on itself, cutting off part of the light. The movement caught Isaac off guard, his grip slackening just enough for me to yank my arm free.

Panic surged through me, icy and swift. I was done with Isaac, done with his condescending tone, his constant attempts to belittle me. He'd never listened to me, always dismissing me. And he was working with these men!

"Isaac, piss off," I shot back, spinning around to find my opportunity.

Enzo was on top of Declan now, his fists flying. I swallowed hard, dread sitting heavy in my stomach. I was not about to let Isaac, or anyone else, dictate what I should or shouldn't do. I was going to help Declan, no matter what.

Lifting the statuette high above me, I brought it down on Enzo's head with all the strength I could muster. He faltered, a curse escaping him, but he remained on top of Declan.

It was just the opening Declan needed. With a surge of energy, he landed a solid punch to Enzo's jaw and, with a heave, threw him off.

I rushed over, extending a hand to help Declan up.

The room shook once more, and a chunk of rock fell, hitting me squarely on the head. I collapsed onto the dusty ground, brilliant white lights exploding in my vision. More rocks rained down on Enzo, trapping him.

"That'll keep him occupied," Declan gasped, pulling my arm over his shoulder and helping me to my feet. "Can you walk?"

I nodded, fighting the wave of dizziness that washed over me.

"I'm fine," I lied, my vision swimming. My head throbbed with the intensity of a beating drum, but I pushed it aside. The doctors said I was fine. Head injuries and concussions weren't aneurysms.

Daniel lay a few feet away, blood staining his pants and the collar of his shirt.

"Help Daniel," I said.

Declan paused as I wavered, but I shooed him toward the injured man.

I scanned the room. Isaac was gone. Without a word, without a glance. He'd vanished, abandoning us as if we meant nothing. The betrayal stung, but I pushed it aside.

We hadn't gone through all this for nothing. I gathered the folio, the broken eagle statuette, and the battered banner, stumbling out of the vault. Declan and Daniel were close behind me, as another shower of rocks thundered down behind us.

Once outside the vault, Brie's voice came through the phone again. "—a relay down there, maybe? Jayce, where—"

"We're out of the vault," I practically shouted.

"Dec? Do you hear me?" Brie asked.

"I do," he grunted.

Out here, the devastation was less severe. A work light had tipped over, its glass casing shattered into a thousand pieces. That must have been how Enzo had cut his zip ties.

"Maybe we didn't open the door properly?" Could we have triggered a trap when we opened the vault? The thought sent a shiver down my spine. If we'd done something wrong, what else could happen?

CHAPTER 40
DECLAN

The second I was out of the vault, my earpiece had exploded with voices. Will was angry the earpieces had cut out, Rav said he was close, and Emmett and Malcolm were looking for the other exit.

"Is everyone all right?" Scarlett broke through the cacophony, an unfamiliar level of worry underlying the question.

"We're fine, but Isaac got out ahead of us." I turned to Daniel, who was leaning heavily against the wall beside the door. "Where's the other exit?"

"It's to the south of the public entrance, in the Tenuta di Tormarancia," Daniel rasped, his face pale.

"On it," Emmett said. "Malcolm and I are heading there now."

Relief washed over me. "Our team is heading there now to pick us up."

We weren't out of the woods yet, but with the team on their way, everything would be fine. As if on cue, Jayce and Rav appeared, rounding a corner at a sprint.

Rav's eyes were hard and focused. "Where's the thug?"

"In the vault." I put a hand on Rav's chest before he dove in to the rescue. "I say we leave him."

Scarlett's command voice was a welcome sound. "Another police car just arrived, and a few other vehicles. They're heading into the catacombs. You need to get out. Now."

The air staled in my lungs, cloying as old wine. Looking at the unconscious Enzo sprawled inside the vault, I swore. "The cops are on their way down and they'll pick him up."

"Too much fallen rock in there. He'll be crushed if more falls." Rav shook his head, always playing the hero. He gestured around the vault door, where the ground was clear. "Out here, he's safe."

"Rav, be careful!" Leigh was pale, a tiny rivulet of blood trickling down her forehead. "There's a lot of rock falling in there."

Ignoring her protest, Rav ducked inside the crumbling vault. Panic, cold and sharp, needled me. I wedged my body in the diminishing entrance, bracing against the slow, groaning descent of the ancient stone door. A wave of nausea flowed through me from the pain, but I wasn't about to risk Rav.

He was fast, dodging another cascade of stone, and picked Enzo up in a fireman's carry. He had the asshole out in less than ten seconds. Goddamn hero mode.

Jayce whispered to Leigh, whose fingers were brushing the eagle's broken wing. "Let me take those, Leigh."

She wavered, her gaze wandering aimlessly. "That might be best. The room's spinning a little."

I darted to her side and slung her arm around my shoulder. "Hang on, Leigh. We're getting out of here."

Was she truly okay? Had she really talked to her doctors recently? Could a blow to the head trigger something in her brain? *Push it down, man. Don't be like her brother.*

"Daniel needs to lead us out." Glancing back, I caught Rav's eye. "Give him a hand."

Rav and Daniel moved ahead, leaving Leigh and me trailing behind, Jayce forming our rear guard. I needed answers, and fast.

"What the hell happened with Isaac?" I asked Leigh.

She looked up at me, her face pale. "I think you were right about him. I think he was working with Fenix."

My world turned red. I should have insisted. Should have had Brie doing a deeper dive into his background.

"Enzo and Pavel said they staged the break-ins at Edoardo's. One to bring you here for the Cassaforte job and the other..." Leigh's gaze went distant. "I think it was a ploy for Isaac to bring me here for this vault."

He had been the one conspiring with them.

"They said you were supposed to be down here." Leigh tightened her grip on my hand at her waist, brows raising as if in hope. "I think Isaac was trying to protect me by making you the expert."

"Explains why he kept egging me on about it, trying to pique my curiosity."

"Part of me thinks he didn't want to do any of it, but—" Leigh closed her eyes and slowed her steps. "Daniel, why did you act like you didn't know Isaac? Hadn't you two been working on the vault?"

"I met him in the van," said Daniel over his shoulder. "Pavel said they were working during the daytime with an expert he didn't think could do the job. They only brought me down at night, to ensure I didn't tip anyone off about being kidnapped."

Leigh's breath hitched. "Did he attend any meetings or was he just down in the catacombs every day?"

Asshole prick. My team was going to find him and make him pay for everything he'd done to her.

Leigh trembled as she continued. "Isaac said something... about being able to save my mom. Said the talon was part of something greater."

Scarlett's sharp gasp over the earpiece sent a fresh wave of goose bumps up my arms. She needed to get control of that. "What?"

"He was off, looked like he was losing it," Leigh continued, unable to hear Scarlett. "He was muttering about eternity."

"Fuck," Scarlett breathed. "Noah said almost the same thing about the feather in Venice."

My stomach dropped. "If we had any doubt Isaac was involved with Fenix, this pretty much seals it."

Leigh looked at me, brows drawing down in confusion. "How do you mean?"

I wanted to explain everything, but I knew the right answer: It was Reynolds business.

Daniel spoke before I had to answer her. "I need to take everything we found in the catacombs to my boss."

"Who's your boss?" I asked.

Daniel hesitated, glancing nervously over his shoulder at us.

Rav glowered at Daniel while continuing to help him walk. "You can either tell us, or we leave you in these catacombs to find your own way out."

"His—his name is Giovanni," Daniel said. "He's an—um—art dealer."

I couldn't help but chuckle at the way he stumbled over the words. "Giovanni Ferraro?"

"Yeah, that's him," Daniel said.

"Good," Scarlett said. "We'll return the items to Giovanni directly. Let Daniel know he can accompany you, but he's not taking anything. I don't want to risk those artifacts falling into the wrong hands."

"We found a leather folio in there," I said to both the team and the people in the room. "It's full of notes and sketches. I think we need to keep that, at least long enough to digitize the whole thing."

"But the papers. You can't continue mishandling them." Daniel sounded on the brink of desperation, more concerned about the artifacts than his own life.

"Relax," Rav said. "We have a book conservator on our team. She'll take care of it."

I bit back a chuckle at Rav calling Kiera a book conservator. She was a forger by trade, but I had to admit, she knew her way around paper and fabric. It was part of what made her so good at her job, even though we didn't call on her often.

After what felt like an eternity of twists and turns, we made it out of the catacombs. The exit, hidden by an overgrowth of brush and trees, led us to a grassy knoll under the night sky. Malcolm and Emmett were there, a getaway car parked nearby.

Glancing over at the vehicle, I muttered, "That car won't fit everyone."

"No worries," Malcolm said. "We'll take Rav and Jayce to pick up the car he left earlier. We'll circle back for you."

Everyone signed off from the earpieces as Malcolm, Emmett, Rav, and Jayce took off. Daniel, Leigh, and I sat on the grass, catching our breath, clearing our lungs of the dust. The entrance to the catacombs sat quietly, hiding in the shadows behind us.

Leigh pulled out the phone I'd loaned her and stared at it.

"What are you thinking?" I asked.

"I want to call Isaac." She turned the phone over once, twice, three times. "But I don't know what I'd say to him even if I did."

"You could check if he got out of the catacombs all right."

She sighed and made the call. After a few beats of silence, she ended it and handed the phone back to me. "No answer."

"Are you okay?" I wrapped an arm around her filthy, dusty shoulders.

"He's involved with kidnappers, thieves, and men who threatened to kill us, Declan." She leaned her head on my shoulder, still shivering slightly. "I'm worried about him."

I held Leigh closer, kissing her temple gently. "The Reynolds team can track him down if you want."

She nodded slowly, a faraway look in her eyes. "I don't understand why he'd do this."

As I held her, I remembered Isaac's frenzied look as he unwrapped the eagle statuette. Even if Leigh didn't want us to track Isaac, he was clearly involved with Fenix. They'd targeted my friends twice now. We needed to find out if they'd come for us a third time.

I had a sinking feeling this game wasn't over yet.

CHAPTER 41
DECLAN

I gripped the cool silk sheets, hovering over Leigh, my cock buried deep inside her. Our bodies were a tangled mess of limbs and desire, moving in perfect harmony. The sensation of her nails digging into my flesh fueled the carnal need within me.

"God, I love this side of you," I whispered into her ear. It was our third day since the chaos in the catacombs, and I'd had lots of time to get to know the new Leigh Barton.

"My god, Declan," she panted, her voice thick with lust. "I've never been fucked so completely before."

The words tumbled out of her mouth like a secret confession. The thrill of being the one who'd unlocked this hidden passion within her consumed my soul. She was no longer the people-pleasing Leigh Barton I'd first met, but a wild, untamed goddess, claiming her needs without restraint.

"Tell me what you want, Leigh," I commanded, nipping at her neck as I continued thrusting into her.

"More, Declan. Harder!" she cried out, wrapping her legs around my waist, urging me deeper.

I obliged, plunging into her with an intensity that bordered on ferocious. Her moans grew louder, more urgent, filling my ears with the sweetest symphony. I couldn't get enough of her—her taste, her scent, the feel of her body wrapped around mine. It was an addiction I never wanted to break free from.

"Leigh," I growled in her ear. "I want you on your knees for me."

"Oh, yes," she replied breathlessly, a sexy smile playing on her lips.

I pulled out and guided her onto her hands and knees, the sight of her perfectly curved ass sending a jolt of desire through me. Without hesitation, I positioned myself behind her and drove back inside, our bodies colliding in a violent, reckless force.

"Mmm," Leigh groaned, gripping the sheets as I continued pounding into her.

"Tell me how much you love it," I demanded, reaching around to grasp her breast, my fingers teasing her hardened nipple.

"I love it so much," she gasped, arching her back to meet my thrusts. "Fuck me harder!"

Her words spurred me on, my movements becoming more aggressive, more primal. I reveled in the sound of her cries, each one bringing me closer to the precipice. As if sensing my impending climax, Leigh moved her hips in time with mine, grinding against me as I sank myself deeper within her.

"Declan, I'm so close," she whimpered, barely audible over the sound of our bodies slamming together.

"Me too, Leigh," I choked out, feeling the pressure building at the base of my spine.

"Come with me, Declan," she begged, her body trembling with need.

"Fuck, yes, baby," I groaned, unable to resist her plea.

Our rhythm intensified, our bodies desperate to reach that peak together. And then, just as we were teetering on the edge, Leigh's inner walls clenched around me, sending us both spiraling into the abyss of pleasure.

"Declan!" she cried out, her body shuddering beneath mine as the orgasm tore through her.

"Yes, Leigh!" I exploded inside of her, filling her with everything I was.

Together, we rode the waves of ecstasy, our bodies entwined, our breaths coming wildly in unison. As the aftershocks of our climax subsided, I collapsed onto the bed next to her, my chest heaving as I struggled to catch my breath. The sweat that coated our bodies cooled on my skin.

"God, Declan," she sighed, her words a soft, sultry whisper against my ear. "This has been the most amazing couple of weeks of my life."

"Really?" I would have used a lot of words other than amazing. But considering the thoroughly sated naked woman next to me, maybe amazing should be on the list. "Has it lived up to the fantasy of your trip to Rome?"

She shifted her body to face me, her eyes sparkling with mischief and desire. "I got to have my adventure." She drew lazy patterns across my chest. "I got to have a wild fling with a man I just met, and—"

I cut her off, crushing my lips against hers, my tongue eagerly seeking entrance into her mouth. Her surprised gasp was all the invitation I needed, and for a moment, we were lost in another kiss.

She was going to say she hadn't made it to the Trevi Fountain yet.

Instead, I threw her a curveball. I broke our embrace, my body protesting the entire time. "We only have four hours before the jet leaves for home. We need to get going."

"Wait, what?" Leigh blinked at me, clearly not expecting this sudden change of direction. "What do you mean? Where are we going?"

"Ah!" I grinned at her, drawing out the syllable as I sat up and swung my legs over the side of the bed. "That's a surprise."

My cock, still semi-hard from our exploits, bobbed slightly as I stood, drawing Leigh's gaze. She bit her lip and looked up at me, curiosity and anticipation warring in her face.

"Declan," she purred, her voice taking on that seductive quality that never failed to get a reaction. "You can't just drop a bomb like that and expect me not to press for details."

"It's going to be worth it." I offered her a hand to help her up from the bed. "Trust me?"

• • • • ● • ● • • • •

Under Tuesday's midday sun, I navigated through Rome's labyrinth of narrow streets, my free hand loosely gripping a cup of creamy pistachio gelato. Leigh walked beside me, a small spoon balanced delicately between her fingers as she took in the ancient buildings that hugged the passageway, her dark eyes sparkling with unspoken admiration.

"You sure about Boston?" she asked, just loud enough for me to hear above the hum of chatter and laughter that filled the air.

I nodded. "With Isaac missing in action, I want to make sure you're settled. Plus, Barton Safes could use an extra hand."

We'd discussed the plan on Sunday, when she still couldn't get hold of Isaac. She'd asked me to confirm at least a half dozen times. "You'd do that? You hardly know me."

"Reynolds can spare me, and Boston's close to Halifax. If they need me for a job, they can have me quick enough." I kept my eyes on the throng of locals and tourists alike, dodging between them.

Leigh trailed behind me for a few steps, when there wasn't enough space between the café tables on either side of the narrow street. The scents of pizza and tomatoes and basil filled the air as we passed a small table being served.

I paused when the crowd thinned enough for us to walk side-by-side again.

"How often do you do jobs like this one in Rome?"

"Every few months, maybe?" My mind flicked back to the Cassaforte job, the sting of betrayal still fresh. "And most of the time, it's pretty mundane stuff. Complex jobs like Cassaforte are usually a couple a year."

"And have you ever been double-crossed like that before?" She raised a slender brow, her focus returning to her raspberry gelato.

I pushed away the lingering taste of pistachio, rolling my eyes upward as I replayed the circus of the past couple of weeks in my head. "It's a first for me. Betrayed by an old friend, hounded by Ferraro's goon, and almost buried alive in the Roman catacombs. It's been one hell of a fortnight."

"But?" Leigh prodded at her gelato, not eating any of it.

"But," I echoed, wrapping an arm around her shoulders to pull her close. Her dark hair fell in soft waves around her face, the sun highlighting the red undertones. The sight stirred an uncomfortable desire within me, a warmth that spread to my chest. I forced the thought away. "It's the first time I've been betrayed and ended up... Well, this isn't so bad."

"Not so bad?"

What did I mean? What were the right words? I wasn't ready to admit I might be falling for her, that she'd occupied every crevice of my brain over the last two weeks.

It was just a bit of fun. A way to pass the time.

I could almost hear Jayce and Scarlett's laughter when they'd called me a goner. Scarlett liked her—that was a first. She hadn't liked any of my girlfriends. She'd always been polite about it, but she had a way of being polite while still making her distaste clear to anyone who knew her well enough.

I let go of Leigh, dragging a hand through my hair. *I am not falling in love. We haven't known each other long enough.*

And yet, I'd made plans to go to Boston. Not out of worry for Isaac and Fenix, but because I didn't want to stop being with her.

Leigh looked up at me as we walked. "What do you mean, Declan?"

For a fleeting moment, I contemplated telling her, laying it all bare. How she'd unlocked something in me I hadn't known existed, how peeling back her layers had been more satisfying than any vault or safe I'd ever cracked. I'd always preferred the simplicity of steel boxes to the complexities of women.

But Leigh? Leigh was worth the risk.

"Nothing," I finally said, forcing a smile. "I'm just happy we met, that's all."

A soft blush crept up her cheeks. She nudged me with her hip, a shy smile tugging at the corners of her lips. "I feel the same."

I chuckled, leaning in to kiss her temple. "After everything we've done, you shouldn't be blushing at something as mundane as that."

She grinned up at me, the blush still coloring her makeup-free cheeks. "I'll work on it."

As we turned a corner, the narrow cobblestone street opened into a bustling square. The momentary silence between us was shattered by Leigh's gasp, her hand reaching out to grip my arm.

Before us, the Trevi Fountain reared majestically, a dazzling display of baroque artistry. Intricate figures of Neptune, god of the sea, and his tritons carved out of travertine stone. Above them, a grand arch framed the scene, crested by the papal coat of arms. Cascades of water drove beneath it all, the scene a testament to the power and grandeur of the sea.

Surrounding the monument, spectators jostled for space. People of all ages, some clad in loose summer attire, others with phones up capturing every inch, milled around the fountain's periphery.

"It's beautiful," Leigh whispered, barely audible over the sounds of the crowd. "That was the only thing missing from my trip to Rome."

Yesterday, we'd toured the city on foot and by Vespa, just like she'd wanted. She'd seen every highlight she wanted to, although we hadn't had time to linger.

I waggled my eyebrows. "Oh really? I had no idea."

Her face softened into a smile as she led me down steps, between people, and to the edge of the fountain. Placing our half-empty gelato cups on the lip of the fountain, she dug into her bag and handed me a coin. "You throw your coins one at a time, right hand over your left shoulder. It's very specific."

"Isn't it supposed to be three coins?"

"One coin to return to Rome." She forced me to turn my back to the fountain. Standing side by side at the edge of the busy fountain, we both tossed a coin into the shimmering pool.

Leigh smiled as she continued, "The next coin is to fall in love with a beautiful Italian." She put a coin in my hand and readied another for herself.

I held up a hand to pause her. "Does it have to be an Italian?"

"That's how the legend goes." She shrugged. "Not sure if you can argue with legends."

"Fair. What about the third coin?"

"The third coin is to marry the one you fell in love with."

I nodded, rolling her words around in my head. As I flung the second coin into the fountain, an unexpected thought passed through my mind. *This one's for you, Nonna.*

Leigh chuckled, her laughter music to my ears, as we tossed our third coins into the water. Without another thought, I pulled her close, my arms enveloping her as I kissed her. The crowd, the noise, the entire world, faded away.

As our lips separated, I held her close, reluctant to let her go. Boston was a good city—home to a lot of craft breweries, after all.

"I'm happy you're coming home with me, Declan," Leigh whispered into my chest.

"I am, too."

As she placed her delicate hand in mine, I couldn't help but marvel at how perfectly we fit together—both in body and soul. The past weeks had been a whirlwind of passion, adventure, and self-discovery for both of us, and I'd never be the same.

CHAPTER 42

JAYCE

The sleek body of the Gulfstream G650ER was a welcome sight. I stepped onto the jet, the familiar smell of leather and ambition filling my nose. The team trailed close behind, exhaustion coloring their faces in the afternoon sunshine.

"Patricia," I called, making a beeline for our flight attendant. "Please tell me you restocked the nut mix like you promised."

She opened a galley drawer with an over-dramatic flourish. "But of course."

Satisfied, I snatched a bag of nuts and a water bottle from the fridge. A few steps past, I slid into a plush leather seat near the front, popping the cap and taking a sip from the water.

Leigh came through the cabin next, her arm looped through Declan's. The girl was glowing. It was almost infectious. *Love can do that, I suppose.* A lot had changed for her over the past two weeks, and she was different now. Her confidence shone. No more hunched shoulders or downcast eyes.

I'd only met two of the women Declan's mother had convinced him to date. Daphne and... I couldn't even remember the other's name. He'd been miserable with both of them.

But the ease between him and Leigh was a wonderful thing. He was better with her. Happier. They made their way to the mid cabin, sinking onto the divan, their body language telegraphing an intimacy that made me want to avert my eyes.

"Hey, you two," I called, pointing my bottle at them. "No canoodling on the flight, you hear me?"

Leigh's blush could've outshone the sun. I took another gulp of my water. No way would they listen to me.

My attention shifted as Scarlett and Malcolm entered the cabin, their bodies brushing against each other in whispers. I watched as Malcolm leaned in, murmuring something that sparked a smile on Scarlett's face, a sight that was more myth than reality a month ago. Now they were inseparable.

Malcolm's hand ghosted down Scarlett's arm, tracing a path that seemed all too familiar to them. The tactile connection was as constant as it was conspicuous. I mean, literally, all the time. His fingers trailed up her arm, brushing a loose curl off her face, his touch lingering for a moment. I caught Scarlett's eyes flickering closed, a soft smile playing on her lips.

That smile, it was brighter, more frequent. It was a sight I hadn't seen on Scarlett's face in years. Something had shifted, settled between them, and it brought out a version of Scarlett that had been buried deep within for far too long.

They chose her usual spot in the rear cabin.

Downing the rest of my water, I turned my attention away, praying that the remnants of the nut mix would be enough to distract me from my lovey-dovey co-workers.

My gaze bounced between the two couples, their intimate whispers and lingering smiles awkward but welcome at the same time. Seeing Scarlett and Declan genuinely happy was a sight to behold. Not that I'd ever admit it out loud.

Still, a warmth filled me as I watched them, a sense of satisfaction that my friends found a happiness that was all too rare in our line of work.

Yet, a sharp contrast stabbed at me—a tinge of loneliness. A faded memory of a past where happiness was a routine away, a gold medal within reach. A time when I was on the brink of Olympic stardom, a path violently interrupted by an unfortunate accident.

The man I'd lost. The mother who'd moved on.

My throat tightened. *Stop thinking about it, Jayce.*

A life that could have been. A dream which had shattered and reshaped itself into something unexpected. I swallowed down the pang of regret. Despite everything, I was happier now. I was more than an athlete, more than a gymnast. I was Jayce. The snack-happy thief. The greaseman.

With the Reynolds team, I'd found a family that would never leave me behind. They accepted me for who I was—quirks, snark, and all. They saw me, not the former athlete or the skilled thief, but Jayce. And that was worth more than any gold medal.

As Emmett and Rav took their places opposite me, Patricia breezed through with her usual pre-flight instructions. She pointed this way and that, the regular routine of reminding us to buckle up and where the exits were.

Proving how amazing she was, she also handed me a fresh bottle of water.

The jet began to move, the cabin vibrating as we taxied onto the runway. I stared out the window as we climbed, the city dropping away. I stole a glance at Leigh, her eyes locked with Declan's. Her brother was with Fenix. A knot of worry clenched in my stomach for my new friend, but she seemed oblivious, wrapped in her quiet conversation.

I let out a low hum, catching Rav's eye as I shifted the conversation to the subject none of us could ignore—the Fenix Group and those sketches from the folio.

"So..." I popped a pecan into my mouth, the sugar and cinnamon coating dancing over my tastebuds. "We have any ideas where these Fenix folks might be hiding?"

Rav stared out the window. "Brie's team is already on it."

"And?"

"She's tracking a connection with Gideon Tremaine."

"The tech billionaire?" If I had my billionaires right, he'd made his money in security. Started with virus protection and gradually moved up to government contracts and chip manufacturing.

Rav nodded. "Apparently, he owns a data storage company that Brie suspects is hosting servers for some heavy-duty criminals. Fenix included."

Emmett leaned forward, the remnants of his cuts and bruises still etched on his face. "If there's a chance to take them down, I want in."

The fierceness in his voice was unlike him. He was another friend who'd been changed by the events of the last month. He used to be the easy-going one. Now there was a darkness underlying it.

"And what about the photos of Scarlett at the Albrecht house?" I'd been in the shadows for that event, covered from head to toe, so it wouldn't matter if someone snapped pictures of me scaling the side of the house. "I can't imagine Enzo was the only one with copies."

Rav's face hardened, his intense protectiveness of Scarlett on full display. "Brie's team is also working on her cover story, in case they surface."

Good. The last thing we needed was legal attention. A month ago, Scarlett had suggested we stick to fully above-board work for a while. But Fenix had drawn us into their web.

As we lifted into the sky, my mind churned with questions. A billionaire, a data storage facility, and whispers of eternity. Scarlett said Noah had mentioned resurrection.

Like the literal phoenix.

Who were they? And why did we keep running into them?

Epilogue
Leigh

I steered my car into the Barton Safes and Locks parking lot Wednesday morning. Glancing over at Declan, his hazel eyes focused on the building's facade, my insides twisted a bit more. A sense of dread grew in my chest. One part of it was Isaac's mysterious disappearance, the other was the prospect of introducing Declan to my father. I put the car into park and tugged at a loose thread on my jeans, thoughts looping in my mind.

We'd discussed his team's break-in, when he found the Codex case specifications. I'd built something to house a stolen manuscript. And the Reynolds team had gotten it back. I was still coming to terms with it, and he hadn't been able to tell me everything, but some part of me understood.

At least, I understood enough to bring him here. Enough to understand Isaac had copied my specs for the Fenix Group.

How was I going to introduce him? Boyfriend? Was that what Declan was? We agreed he'd stick around Boston for a couple of weeks, but the whole 'what happens next' question remained unanswered. The corner of his mouth twitched upward, as if he'd read my mind.

"Think you can handle this?" A hint of concern tinged his question.

I forced a smile, my gaze sliding back to the shop. It was familiar territory, a place I'd grown up around. But the events of the past few days cast a new, harsh light on it.

"I told Dad I'm bringing in a consultant I met in Rome to help streamline things." The piece of thread pulled out like it hadn't belonged. "He doesn't know about us."

Declan put his fingers under my chin and tilted my face up. "You don't have to shrink yourself to make others happy, Leigh. That includes me. If you want to keep this professional, I can do that."

I sucked in a quick breath. "I don't want it strictly professional."

His lips twitched into a grin. "Thank god, because I wasn't sure I could manage that."

I let out a laugh, more from relief than amusement.

He leaned over, pressing a soft kiss to my cheek.

My heart fluttered. "I don't want to tell them just yet about us…"

"Dating?" Declan suggested, his eyebrows raised in mock challenge. "Spending every possible minute together?"

That sounded about right. I lifted my shoulders, squaring them. This was the new me. The Leigh who said what she wanted. "I'm not sure I want to tell them that my consultant is my boyfriend."

"Boyfriend?" His smile deepened, a spark of satisfaction in his eyes. "I like that. But I get if you don't want to break the news yet. I can come back tomorrow, if you'd rather?"

"It's time. I also have to tell them about Isaac." My voice faltered at the thought of my brother. "I'm even less sure what to do about that."

"Tell them the truth."

"The truth? I don't even know what that is. Is Isaac coming back? What happened? I still haven't heard from him since he took off with the talon. Hell, I don't even know if he's alive."

"Brie's going to find him," Declan said. "If the Fenix Group really are collecting special items, like Giovanni said, and Isaac returned with one of those items, then odds are good they're taking care of him."

I bit my lip, the taste of impending doom bitter on my tongue. No matter how it played out, revealing Isaac's involvement with those criminals would shatter Dad. His heart would break, just like mine had.

We stepped out of the car, the thick Boston air wrapping around us. My gaze drifted to Declan, taking in his ensemble. Black slacks and a white button-up with the top couple of buttons undone. It accentuated his tall, lean physique in a way that took my breath away.

We'd debated what he should wear this morning. Declan had first opted for a tie, but I'd promptly relieved him of it. My family was more the casual type.

"Are they expecting an actual Roman or just someone you met in Rome?" Declan asked, a playful glint in his eye.

A memory flashed through my mind—throwing our coins into the Trevi Fountain yesterday. The second coin, as the legend goes, was to fall in love with an Italian. 'Ramsay' wasn't Italian, that much was obvious. But there was something about

Declan, maybe in the dark hair or the five o'clock shadow that was present by noon, that made me think maybe there was some Italian in his lineage.

Or maybe it was just me, well on my way to falling in love with him.

The thought made my heart pound. Love? Was that even possible? Was it realistic to hope he'd stick around after his consulting stint was over? That he'd want more than just a temporary fling?

"Leigh?" Declan jolted me to the moment.

"Sorry." I shook my head, chasing away the thoughts. "Let's go."

I was getting ahead of myself. It was time to focus. I had to deal with Isaac and Dad first. Whatever was brewing between Declan and me would have to wait. Or at least, that's what I had to keep telling myself as we walked toward the office, otherwise I would have turned around.

The door swung open at Declan's touch, revealing the glass display counters. The chime over the door chirped, and I pulled in the familiar scent of home. Metallic, but citrusy from the cleaning fluids. Before Ann, it had been metal and cinnamon from the air freshener Mom used and Dad continued using after her death.

Dad appeared through a door from the back, his face splitting into a beaming smile. He rounded the counter to wrap me up in a tremendous hug. The familiar comfort of his arms, the smell of his cologne—these were things that would always bring me peace.

I introduced Declan as the consultant from Rome.

Declan offered his hand, referring to Dad as "Mr. Barton."

Dad looked quite pleased with himself. "I just got off the phone with Isaac."

My stomach sank. How much had Isaac told him? Would there be anything new to help Brie track him down?

Dad continued, "You don't need to worry. Isaac told me everything."

I glanced at Declan, surprise surging through me. Surely, Isaac hadn't actually told him everything.

Dad kept talking, oblivious to my shock. "He sent me an itinerary for his European tour this summer, to visit other companies like Cassaforte and see how they operate. I think it's a wonderful idea."

I bit my lip, holding back a million things I wanted to say. There was no way Isaac was touring Europe. He was working with criminals. Smugglers. Kidnappers.

"It leaves us short-staffed, but Ann came up with a perfect solution." Dad called over his shoulder, "Ann, can you come here?"

And then, like some sort of twisted nightmare, she came into the room. But she wasn't alone. Following her like a shadow was a face I hadn't wanted to see ever again.

Finn.

Goose bumps crawled up my arms, but I held my ground. I wouldn't let him intimidate me. Not anymore.

Memories of raised hands that never landed started on a loop in my mind. *"You don't need a PhD"* and *"All that makeup makes you look cheap."*

Declan's hand was on my back, a silent reminder that I was going inward. Be strong, that touch said. I was the new Leigh now. I didn't need protection. I could do this on my own.

Declan extended a hand to Ann. "Leigh told me all about you, Mrs. Barton."

She gave him an appreciative once-over. "We're always happy to have an Italian consultant on staff."

Declan gave her a casual smile. "Only a quarter Italian, I'm afraid. From my paternal grandmother."

The conversation barely registered. I couldn't tear my eyes from Finn. The lopsided grin. The cocky swagger. Memories I couldn't forget. *That dress is too tight—it shows off your lumpy hips.*

Declan held out a hand to Finn, introducing himself.

Finn met his gaze with a challenging one of his own. "Finn," he said, and then added with extra emphasis, "Leigh's boyfriend."

I barely stopped myself from choking. Boyfriend? Finn was definitely not my boyfriend anymore. I took a quick breath. "Ex."

Declan's response was even and measured. "I've heard plenty about you, as well, Finn. Didn't know you worked here, though."

Dad smiled at my slimy ex. "It's temporary, until Isaac gets home."

"But Finn doesn't know anything about the business." Was I the only one who saw how ridiculous this was? "Plus, he already has a job."

"It's perfect." Ann dismissed me with a wave of her hand. "Leigh, you can teach Finn all about the business, then he can travel to client sites and conferences, be the public face of your designs, just like Isaac was."

What?

"That way, you won't have to overtax yourself; you can just settle down and get back to work." She smiled at Declan. "I'm sure you can help speed that up."

Finn approached me, a calculated grin on his face.

I tried to step back, but Declan's sturdy presence stopped me.

"Leigh," said Finn, his tone too serious. "I've spent a lot of time thinking about the direction things were headed before you left for Rome. I realize now what I did wrong."

Doubtful.

Finn reached into his pocket and pulled out a small jewelry box. He sank onto one knee, opening the box to reveal a diamond solitaire.

What the hell?

"I talked to Isaac, and he made it clear. He said, 'Finn, you fool, Leigh wanted to get married.' I was an idiot for not jumping at the opportunity to put a ring on your finger." He held the box toward me, the display lights exploding inside the diamond. "What about it, angel?"

Panic, cold and icy in my spine, ran through me. Memories of how he dictated what I wore, how he never let me choose where we went for dinner, and when he made fun of my passions. My mind was spinning, struggling to piece my thoughts together.

I looked at my father. "What did Ann mean by Isaac being the 'public face' of my designs?"

My father exchanged a glance with Ann before returning his gaze to me. "Isaac was just better suited to the attention than you, Leigh. He has a more charismatic personality, while you? You're more reserved, shy. I was concerned you might be too stressed to manage it."

A fire lit inside me. Stoked by Declan's steady presence beside me. Declan never failed to highlight my talent. He consistently encouraged me to stand up for myself.

Ann gestured toward me, an air of superiority about her. "Just look at you, Leigh. After two weeks in Rome, you have bags under your eyes and too much of a tan. You need to be more careful with your health."

"Why on earth did you think I couldn't handle those things?" A wave of anger surged through me. "No, wait. Because Isaac is a selfish, arrogant jerk, and I let him muscle his way into the lead designer position."

Another memory hit me, sharp and bitter. Isaac's angry reaction when I was chosen for the Cassaforte job. My success, my potential—it threatened him. That's why he taunted me about the job at Edoardo's. He knew I was better than him, so he did everything he could to make me feel small.

A sickening realization washed over me. I'd been making myself small for years, all to inflate Isaac's ego. He'd overshadowed me because I let him. I let him take credit for my work. I played the role as the supportive little sister, all while he stole my spotlight.

So, of course, I let Finn do exactly the same thing. It's what I'd been taught most of my life.

Not anymore.

"That's enough." I stood taller, feeling myself grow by inches. "I can't be who I really am if I stay here. I can't be around a father who would let that happen, or Ann, who thinks I just need to get married, or Finn who…"

I couldn't even finish the sentence. He was still on his stupid knee.

"I love you, Dad," I told him, meeting his stunned eyes. "But I quit."

The words rang out in the silent room. My father, Ann, and Finn stared at me, shock etched on their faces.

But I was past caring.

Turning on my heel, I plucked at Declan's shirt, unable to say another word.

Finn sputtered in protest, rising from his knee to grab my arm, the grip painful. "I'm proposing to you!"

I cringed, pulling away before I could stop myself.

Declan took one step forward and punched Finn hard in the face.

Finn stumbled back against the displays, clutching at his now bleeding nose.

Declan pointed an angry finger at him. "You touch her again, and I'll do more than break your nose."

Before Finn regained his footing, I said, "I'm in love with Declan. And I still quit."

With that, Declan and I walked out of Barton Safes and Locks, leaving my old life behind.

My new, amazing boyfriend walked with a confident strut, a smirk tugging at his lips. "In love with me, eh?"

I tried to brush off the comment, tried pretending it was a ruse, but deep down, there was truth in it.

Instead of pushing it, Declan opened my door for me, then rounded the car to slide into the passenger seat. He pulled his phone from his pocket and dialed a number. "Scarlett, looks like I'm not on loan to Barton Safes anymore. Can you send the jet back or do Leigh and I need to fly commercial?"

My mouth fell open. The jet? He could order it on a whim?

"Thanks, Scar." He hung up, glancing over at me with raised eyebrows. "If you want to? At least until you sort things out?"

A wave of relief flooded through me.

"Yes." I bit on my bottom lip to hold back a smile that could have broken my face. I wanted nothing more in the world than to spend time with Declan. It didn't matter where. It just mattered that I was with him. "I'd like that. I'd like that a lot."

"Good. And for the record?" He leaned close and pressed a slow kiss to my lips. As he pulled away, he cupped my cheek, a soft smile spreading across his handsome face. "I love you, too, Leigh Barton."

THE END OF BOOK 2

BOOK 3: Jayce and the team pursue information on Gideon Tremaine's data storage center, but wind up hired to protect one of his experimental data chips. And the worst (best?) part? She's forced undercover with a sinfully tempting former spy she's clashed with before.

Find *The Twilight Theft* at
https://janetoppedisano.com/product/the-twilight-theft

BONUS SCENE: We got to see what happened when Leigh took Declan to meet her parents... but what happens when he takes her home? How will his mother's *interview* of Leigh go?

Sign up for this and all the other bonuses at
https://janetoppedisano.com/newsletter_reynolds

ACKNOWLEDGEMENTS

This book was a tough one to write. I had an absolute blast with the characters, their escape from Cassaforte, re-introducing some old friends (for more on Giovanni Ferraro and his crew, see the Caine & Ferraro series – they're in books 2+, at least as references), and their trek into the underbelly of Rome. But this book was a departure for me—Leigh was the first heroine I've written who didn't start out already confident. Yes, she's incredibly smart and talented, but the way she lets the men in her life weigh her down was hard for me to write. I found myself doubting the book soooo many times! But in the end, she found the courage she needed, which made my heart happy.

I hope her journey (and the amazingly supportive man at her side by the end) was as gratifying for you as it was for me.

As always, I want to send my appreciation to my husband and son. This book took a bit of a toll on me, including skipping half of my summer vacation, so their patience and support means the world!

To my continued beta readers, Paula and Pat, who helped me feel more comfortable with Leigh's character and the heart of adventure. They're always there to give helpful critique but also to bolster my spirits.

Many thanks to my editors: To Miranda Darrow for helping me rip apart half the book (ugh, that hurt!); and to Brandi Aquino for ensuring the words were polished.

And finally, I'd like to thank you, my dear reader, for sticking by my side through this adventure. May you find strength and joy in my words.

About Janet

Janet Oppedisano hails from Canada's East Coast and has lived in five provinces, from the Maritimes to the Prairies. Growing up with a Mountie for a father and marrying a Navy diver, it's no surprise she writes romance with a hint of danger and mystery in it. Not to mention strong heroes and equally strong heroines.

When not writing, you can find her... thinking about writing. And indulging in her favorite pastimes, like baking, traveling, hiking, playing with her dog, and watching her hockey goalie son on the ice.

Oh, and it's pronounced oh-ped-ih-SAH-no. Exactly the way it's spelled. Honest!

You can find Janet and all her social media profiles at: https://janetoppedisano.com